The Internet Murders

by

Michael Davies

The Internet Murders

For information address
michaelxdavies@gmail.com

First Printing 2023

ISBN: 978-0-6454434-6-2

Other Works by Michael Davies

The Nightmares of God
The Janus Conspiracy
Accounts of a Killing
A Friendly Killing
Dreamkill
Ready, Steady, KILL!
Helix Dreams
Helix – The Second Renaissance
Helix-Ascension
The Ninth of the Month Murders
The Death Gambit

For the Young Adults (12-18)
The Many Worlds of Mickie Dalton
The Many Galaxies of Mickie Dalton
The Many Universes of Mickie Dalton
The Strange World of Mark and Anna

For the 8-12 age group
The Julie Malloy Gang and the Smugglers
The Quest for the Locket
The Secret of Yuri Kirilenko
The United Nations and the Extra-Terrestrial
The Secret of Charlotte's Cello
The Star of the Yshan Kings
The War of the Yshan Empire
The Star of the New Yshan Empire
The Red Fog of Time
The Mysterious Recorder and The Door to Elsewhere
Prisoners of the Picture
A Step Back in Time
What Can't be Seen Can Exist
How I Spent My Evening

For the Little Ones (3-5)
Mary's World

And in non-fiction
The Business School Approach to Writing Your Novel

Acknowledgements

This is the fifth book written in collaboration with Greg Dickson in our standard approach of a series of three-day, intensive brainstorming sessions at my home over several months. Each session involved a great deal of discussion, photographing the notes wrote on the white boards and closing each day with significant quantities of fine single-malt scotch.

After each three days, Greg returned home and I got down to the task of writing the book. Yet again, it seems to have worked.

My thanks to Greg.

Many thanks also to MJ Spelliscy who gave up a lot of time to review and edit the final draft. Her eagle eye spotted a number of errors and logical inconsistencies and her input was invaluable.

$Prologue$

Open Warfare

Chapter 1. First Warning, Australia, October, 2023

Gloucester, NSW, Australia

Gerald Bryce sat comfortably in his armchair, the wood stove emitting a pleasing warmth. He was binge-watching the television series, "The West Wing" on his tv, having ordered it from his streaming service.

The telephone rang. Irritated, he stopped the program and checked the phone. It informed him that the call was "Out of Area." Unsure of what to do, as he received so many calls from charities asking for money, but at the same time, this was the indicator shown when the call came from the hospital where he had his pacemaker installed just a few weeks ago, he picked up the phone.

"Yes," he snapped.

"Good evening, Gerald," said a strange voice. It was not human, it was a robotic, electronically distorted sound. "I trust you are enjoying your pleasant evening."

"Who the hell is this?" Gerald felt a mixture of anger and a fear that this call heralded something unpleasant.

"I'm the man you are going to pay a thousand dollars to keep you alive."

"What are you talking about? Why the hell should I pay you anything? Get off my phone."

"Ah, Gerald, you need to learn something about the pacemaker you had installed recently. Remember those nasty heart attacks you used to get? That little device sure has helped stop those, hasn't it?"

"How do you know about that?" Gerald's anger was declining as the fear increased. Something terrible was happening.

"I know everything, Gerald. I have your entire medical history in front of me. I know the make and model of the pacemaker, the date it was installed, the surgeon who did it and the hospital where it was done. And you know something else? I can stop that little device at the touch of a button."

"Don't be daft," retorted Gerald, some confidence returning. "Nobody can do that. Now fuck off and go and bother somebody else."

"I hope you are sitting down," said the ugly voice.

Gerald felt a jolt in his chest, and he blacked out. He had no idea how long he was out, but he had fallen back against his armchair and the telephone had fallen down by his thigh. The same ugly voice was calling his name. Gerald picked it up.

"Now, Gerald, do you believe me?"

The fear he had been feeling was now overwhelmed by terror. "I believe you," croaked.

"Good. Now here is what you do. You have fifteen hundred dollars in your chequing account and a savings account of eighteen thousand dollars. You get two thousand dollars a month in pensions. You are going to draw five thousand dollars from your savings into your chequing account and leave it there. I'll take in when it's there. Do you understand?"

Gerald had no doubts at all that this terrifying caller could do just that. The numbers he had been quoted were accurate.

"I understand," he said, his voice hoarse from shock.

"Good. Now, you will not go to the police with this, you will not get your doctor to check your heart or the pacemaker, because they will find nothing, no record of that little jolt I gave you. If you do any of this, I'll kill you. I'm sure you believe that I can do that."

"Yes," replied Gerald.

"Excellent," said the alien voice. "Good night, Gerald."

The call was disconnected.

Coffs Harbour, NSW, Australia, October, 2022

Pauline Rush felt she was a fortunate woman. She had always experienced good health until the shock of her heart troubles of last year, but the quick, uncomplicated installation of the pacemaker eight months ago had solved that problem and now she felt like a new woman, able to ride her bike daily, spend twenty minutes exercising with a five-kilo barbell in each hand every morning and she had stuck faithfully to a healthy diet since being asked to lose weight some months before the surgery.

As she sat at her computer that morning, the words of the novel she had always wanted to write seemed to flow smoothly and she was enjoying translating the scene she saw in her head into words on the computer monitor.

The shock when the words were replaced by a white mask with an evil, wide, smile with a thin, black beard and moustache was severe. She drew in her breath sharply and her hands froze on the keyboard.

"Good morning, Pauline," said a frightening voice. It was harsh, distorted, impossible to identify as a man or a woman and caused a shiver of panic to run through her. She had heard such voices before, occasionally they appeared on the detective shows she enjoyed so much and represented somebody using electronic systems to hide their voice.

"Not going to reply, eh, Pauline?" said the distorted voice. "And here I am, trying to be friendly. So, how are you, young lady?"

Pauline swallowed, her throat dry. "Who the hell are you?" she croaked.

"No need for you to know that, Pauline. What you *do* need to know is that you are going to have a thousand dollars sitting in your chequing account by Friday."

"Why?" she managed to say.

"Because on Friday, I'm going to take it out of your account and transfer it to mine."

"You're nuts," she said, confidence returning. "Nobody can break into bank accounts and even if you could, the bank could see where it was sent."

"Oh Pauline, such innocence." Even under the distortion, Pauline could hear the amusement in the nightmare voice. "Not only can I do that, I can do much worse. You had a pacemaker fitted a few months ago, right?"

Pauline sat rigid, refusing to acknowledge the question.

"Well, never mind, Pauline, because I know you did. And I can break into those little devices, also. Shall I show you?"

Pauline felt a jolt in her chest and she fell forward on the keyboard. She had no idea of how long she had been unconscious, but when she was able to sit up again, the ugly mask was still on her monitor.

"So now do you believe me, Pauline?"

Trembling with the shock of the blackout, Pauline nodded.

"Great. So let me tell you what I tell all my clients. There's no point in going to the hospital to be checked, there'll be no record in your pacemaker or the hospital computer of that little jolt I just gave you. And there's no point in going to the police, either. But believe me, if you do, I'll know about it and I'll kill you. Do you believe me?"

Again, she managed to nod.

"Great. Have the money in your account by Friday. If it's not there, I think you know what I'll do, don't you?"

Pauline felt frozen in fear. She didn't move. But she knew she would obey all the orders she had received.

"Lovely talking to you, dear Pauline," said the horrible voice. "We'll be in touch."

The face disappeared and her manuscript returned to the screen. Pauline found she was quite unable to resume her creative work.

Phase One

Early Discoveries

Chapter 2

Manchester, England, 3rd May, 2019

"Hey, Phil, I think I've done it." Peter Chang clasped his hands above his head in a champion's gesture. "Come and look at this."

His words broke the silence of the school library. The hour was late, only one other person was working at a desk across the room, well out of earshot.

Next to Chang, Murray looked across and stared at the computer screen filled with lines of code. "What, you've broken into the system?" He moved his chair over and stared at the screen. "Show me," he demanded.

Chang pressed a set of keys. "Look," he said.

On the screen were the words, "Final Grades, History Examination," followed by a date. As Chang pressed a button, up came a screen full of data.

"Those are the results for last week's exam," said Chang, a wide smile of pride on his face.

"Holy shit," said Murray. "Damn, you're right. Can you alter them?"

"Yes, I can. But that would be silly to upgrade our marks, they'll see that very quickly when the lecturers review them for their reports. We'd be found immediately."

"Hey, what if you change the grades for that bastard Nowell? Never could stand that prick, always smirking at how clever he is. I'd love to see him accused of trying to cheat the system."

Chang laughed. "Great idea! Let's fail the bastard." He moved the cursor to the line of data opposite the name of James Nowell and entered different figures. "They'll spot the change, but they'll have to assume it's an error, because nobody could deliberately get in and change the grades to a fail."

"Well, fuck a duck, Peter, we've been working on this for a year and finally you've found a way to do it. What are the key points?"

"Watch," said Chang and entered a few characters. Back to the screen came the lines of code.

"That's the protection code for access to the university system. I finally saw where the main protection was, but I couldn't work out what to change. I wrote a simple program that tested every instruction, running through every possible alternative and one by one, it identified where the change would permit entry. It took about an hour, but then Bingo! I got through."

"Bloody amazing, Peter. Will that work on my project?"

"Should. What have you been working on?"

"Just something simple for an exercise, the pharmaceuticals firm in Stretford."

"Let's have a look. Bring up their website."

Murray moved back to his computer and brought up the website of the company. Chang moved alongside him, plugged a USB drive into a port.

"That's my program," he said. "Let it run and see if it comes up with anything."

"If this works, we've got it made," said Murray.

"Not yet. First, I have to develop a way of hiding the source of the program and where the computer is that initiates it. But I think I know how to do that. Anyway, this may take a while."

"You always were the brightest spark in the class," said Murray. "Assuming you get the grades, where do you plan on going to university?"

"My dad wants me to go to Manchester, like he did. That's why he sent me to this school, he said it would really set me up for the university here."

"What does you dad do?

"He's a surgeon, a heart surgeon."

"Wow, that's impressive! And your mother?"

"Speech pathologist. She got her degree in Manchester, also, so they're both keen on me staying in this area."

"You don't want to go back to live in Hong Kong?"

"Correct." Chang pulled a face. "I'm happy to be in England all these years since I was fifteen when my parents sent me here. Hong Kong is not the fun place they said it was before China took over. Mind you, my dad did say he'd buy me an apartment when I graduated, so at least I'll be able to live my own life."

"Yeah, my dad says the same thing. He used to go to Hong Kong a lot before that happened, just a fabulous place, he said."

"So are you going to university, Phil?"

"Probably not. I can't afford it and my parents can't either. It's been hard enough on them sending me here for three years, but they said having an English education would be a great help. I reckon I'll head home to Australia when we're finished, maybe get a job with one of the computer companies. What we've learnt here should help."

"I'll do the same in Hong Kong after I graduate from university, but I'd say when we get this finalised, we can make a decent living outside of our day jobs."

"Holy cow, mate, do you really think we could do that? We could get really rich very quickly."

"Or land in prison, just as quickly. Before we try that, I need to work out how to set up false bank accounts elsewhere and then transfer money to those, with blocks in place to stop anyone seeing them. I think that I could get most of that code from the dark web."

"I think we should keep in touch and help each other. If we're careful, we should do okay."

Chang suddenly gripped Murray's arm. "Look," he said. "The first weak point discovered."

The two men stared at the screen. The code was complex, but they could follow it.

"There," said Chang. "Modify that equation, change that instruction and the first door is open. Let's see what else happens."

They sat back again. They didn't speak for a while, but twenty minutes later, they sat up.

"The second access point," said Chang, pointing at the screen. "Dammit, Phil, this is working."

In the next fifteen minutes, the remainder of the screen was gradually filled with the final points of access to the computer systems of the company in Stretford.

"Let's see," said Murray and pressed a few keys, laughing as the payroll lists appeared on the screen. "Jeez, Peter, this bloody works."

"With this routine you should be able to break into corporate systems fairly quickly," said Chang. "But don't get too greedy. When I've worked it out, I suggest we set up bank accounts in the Caymans and if we take money from somebody, pay it into those with the blocks I've shown you how to create. That way, nobody will be able to identify where the money came from or went to. And the Cayman banks aren't too worried about big sums being transferred there, it's happening all the time."

"Meanwhile," said Murray, "now that we're into this company, what can we do without transferring money to some secret account?"

"I tell you what we can do," replied Chang. A small smile sat on his lips. "Look, they have a system of rewarding staff with dinner vouchers at a few restaurants. Look, the biggest one is for a hundred pounds! We could get a decent oink-out for that!"

"Can you direct one to us? We could ask a couple of the girls from the other school, you never know what could happen after that!"

"Let's have a look," said Chang and studied the files. "Yes," he said after a few minutes. "I can have one posted to me, then I can immediately delete the transaction so there's no record of my address. That'll have the accountants in a real spin! They'll never solve the question of what happened."

"Do it," said Murray. He watched as Chang pressed a series of keys then sat back.

"Done," said Chang. "A hundred quid to spend at Taylor's restaurant in the city."

"I'll call that girl I know," said Murray and took out his mobile phone.

Manchester, England, 7th May, 2019

"Damn, that was a good dinner," said Murray as they sat at the computer terminal.

"I liked the second half of the evening," said Chang. "Shirley and I had a nice snog in the park after."

"Yeah, I had the same with Jennifer. All in all, a successful evening." Murray had a wide smile on his face.

"Hey, who's that over there?" asked Chang. He pointed at a man seated at a computer terminal at the other side of the computer room.

"That's Lloyd. He's a history teacher," said Murray.

"He was there the other afternoon when we got our breakthrough," said Chang. "I think he's been watching us both times we've been here."

"Nothing to worry about," said Murray. "He can't hear us from there."

"No, probably not. Okay, let's think about the next steps. We'll need to keep in touch after school ends and we go home."

"What are you going to do?" Murray was still watching the history teacher. Lloyd had been casting numerous glances in their direction, but he was far too far away to have overheard the conversations.

"I'll go home to Hong Kong for the summer break," said Chang. "My dad says he's arranged a place at the university here, so I'll come back in September and do a degree in computer science."

"Sounds good. I'll head back to Australia and see what happens. I'll try and get a job with one of the computer companies. It shouldn't be difficult with my grades from here and I know that computer people are in demand there."

"Don't worry about money," said Chang. "I reckon I can get this business fully operational and I'll show you then how to do it as well as I do."

The conversation was interrupted by a tall man moving to the desks they were working on. They looked up in irritation and were surprised to see Lloyd.

"Can I join this conversation?" said Lloyd. He was dressed on casual manner, grey slacks, a blue shirt with a yellow tie and his shirt sleeves rolled up above his elbow.

"Who the hell are you?" demanded Murray, though he did know the identity of the intruder.

"William Lloyd, lecturer in History and I'm the bloke that can provide you a lot of protection for the stuff you're planning."

"And just how do you know what we're planning?" said Chang in contempt. "You've been sitting well across the room from us, there's no way you could hear what we've been saying."

"Ah well now, that's a story in itself," said the newcomer. "When I was seven, my sister was born, and she was soon diagnosed as being completely deaf. So my parents started learning sign language and lip reading and they made me learn the same. I got pretty good at it. I've been following your conversation since you sat down."

"Bullshit," said Murray. "Bugger off, we've got things to talk about."

"Now that's no way to talk to a teacher," said Lloyd. "I could put you both in detention for that. But to answer your question, what about Peter's parents buying him an apartment in Hong Kong? Or the plan to open bank accounts in the Caymans for the money you plan to steal by breaking into corporate computer systems? How about your obtaining a hundred pound dinner voucher from that company and using it to wine and dine a couple of local girls? Did you enjoy your after-dinner experiences in the park?"

The two young men looked at each other, eyes wide with astonishment.

"You'd better sit down," said Chang. "Tell us what you think you can do for us."

Hong Kong, July, 2019

"So you're firm about doing computer science?" Doctor Chang was a tall, thin man with rimless spectacles over an unlined face that made him look in his twenties. "I'd always hoped you'd do medicine like me."

"Dad, you saw my marks for biology and chemistry. I was never going to qualify for med school."

"No, I realised that. But I suppose computer technology is the big thing for a long time to come. You'll do well at it."

"Actually, I was thinking that it could be useful in medical equipment. I was reading the other day that more and more devices are computer controlled. I think I'd find that fascinating."

"You're probably right. A lot of my work is with pacemakers and they are certainly computer-based. Let me show you how they work. I've got an open one here and all the diagrams, you should find it interesting."

"I'm sure you're right, Dad."

* * *

Manchester, England, October, 2019

Peter Chang looked up from his coffee as a shadow fell over his table in the student refectory.

"Mr Lloyd," he said in mixed irritation and surprise. "What are you doing here? I haven't seen you since school."

"It's time we talked business," said Lloyd and pulled out a seat to sit opposite Chang.

"What sort of business?" Chang was feeling overloaded with the pressures of studies in his first year. "How could I fit any business in with all the stuff I have on my plate?"

"You won't need to do much for quite a while," said Lloyd. "But I want to talk about setting you up in the way we talked when you and Phil Murray were still at school."

"We didn't think you were serious."

"Oh, I was serious, alright. I'm quite sure you could make a lot of money with the talents you displayed."

"And how could you help us? And what's in it for you?" Despite some reluctance, Chang found himself interested in the possibilities that Lloyd seemed to be opening up.

"Here's what I propose. I'll buy the equipment you need at home to keep developing the skills. I'll do the same for Phil in Australia. In return, you promise to keep working at it. What have you achieved so far?"

"Quite a bit, actually. I've been able to set up a bank account in the Caymans. I was able to break into one small bank in Leeds and transfer five hundred pounds to that account, but I haven't taken it further. I tried a couple of bigger banks, couldn't break in yet."

"Okay, keep trying. I'm damned sure you'll eventually be able to break down any barriers."

"You didn't tell me what you get out of it."

Lloyd hesitated. "Nothing initially. But here's the deal. I work for a very large organisation. They'll be interested in your work, and they could help you a lot, particularly in identifying people of great wealth with big bank balances that could be tapped."

"A very large organisation?" Chang laughed. "That sounds like organised crime. What is it, the Mafia?"

Lloyd said nothing.

"Holy shit, man, you do mean the Mafia. I don't think I want to be involved with the Mafia." Chang sat back, his arms crossed over his chest in classic defensive mode.

"In practice, you wouldn't be," replied Lloyd. "You'd deal only with me. But the one thing they would want is a slice of the action."

"How big a slice?" Chang's arms returned to his side and he leaned forward.

"Twenty percent of what you take would be transferred to another bank in Europe."

"Twenty...? Why would I want to pay somebody a fifth of what Phil and I make to somebody else?"

"Like I said, they could identify useful marks for you and they could provide considerable cover for your work."

"You said you could provide us with the equipment we need."

"I can. Where do you live? Are you alone there?"

"I've got a flat in Rusholme, my dad insisted I have my privacy."

"That's good. Give me the address, list the items you need and I'll arrange it all. What about Phil?"

"He's working for a computer company in Sydney, he got a studio apartment to get away from his parents."

"Contact him, tell him what we talked about and then we'll do the same for him."

"Okay, I'll do that, but I don't know if he'll be all that interested.."

"Excellent, Peter. I'll be back in touch later."

Sydney, Australia, October, 2019

"Phillip, we spent all that money sending you to school in England and you couldn't get the grades for university. Your mother and I are very disappointed."

Murray stared down at his lap. Critical lectures from his father were a feature of his life for as long as he could remember.

"So, what are you going to do now?" his father demanded, giving Murray the angry glare that had always terrified him.

"Look for a job in the computer industry. That's one area where I got excellent grades at school."

"That's something, I suppose." His father took a step backward, no longer threatening. But Murray felt the anger rising in him. This was a scene played out so often since his childhood, usually culminating in a beating.

"So, isn't this where you start slapping me around?" he said, the rage of so many years of fear growing stronger by the moment.

His father looked startled. "I will if you talk to me like that," he said.

Murray stood up. He was the same height as his father and built on heavier lines. He knew he was far fitter than the older man. "Come on then, show me what a big brave man you are. You always liked hitting me before, let's see if you still can."

His father's face was white. He stood silently, deeply shocked.

"Jennifer," he called out to his wife in the kitchen.

The petite woman came in, wiping her hands on a towel.

"Your son is threatening me," said the older man.

"What?" The mother's voice was almost a shriek.

Murray began to feel good. "Yeah, I invited him to come and start hitting me like he used to when he needed to feel like a big brave man beating up a little boy," he said. "Look how frightened he is now. He needs his tiny little wife to protect him. Like all bullies, he's just a bloody coward."

She stared at him, her hands to her mouth. Murray pointed at his father. "If you ever raise your fists at me again, I'll beat you fucking senseless," he said. "Got that?"

Neither adult said a word.

"Good," said Murray. "I'll get out of here." He went up to his room, packed a bag and left. He had cash from the holiday job he had worked after school and he was confident he would find a job in the computer business quickly, having seen the demand for personnel. He'd already talked to a couple of head-hunters and he had interviews lined up all week. He'd also looked at accommodation and found a cheap studio apartment, not particularly comfortable, but satisfactory for now. He knew he needed to talk to Peter Chang in England.

Sydney, Australia, November, 2019

"That's remarkably neat programming, Phil."

"Well, thank you Colleen."

Phil Murray had been a little nervous at first when he was assigned to a department headed up by a young woman, but his worries had eased when she had shown a technical ability that he found highly impressive. She was also a natural teacher and looked after all ten programmers in her department with attention to their professional growth and development.

"So you've been with us just three weeks?" she asked. "Where were you before?"

"At school in England."

"Ah, that explains the slight accent. North country, isn't it? I recognize it because my boyfriend is from Liverpool."

"Not far, Manchester."

She laughed. "I'd better not tell him that. He said there's a huge rivalry between the two cities, especially at football."

Murray decided he'd made a good career path, joining this computer organization after getting home. The working atmosphere was relaxed, dress code was casual, and the pay was excellent.

"Okay, Phil, that was your first project, you surely get a passing grade, well done. Here's the specification for another program, it's part of a suite for a television company in Sydney, quite complex. Bailey Hooper is in charge of it, go and see him and get the background." She handed over a folder and Murray left to return to his own cubicle to study the new program specification.

Just over an hour later, he decided he needed to discuss the new assignment and walked over to the cubicle of Bailey Hooper. The occupant had his back to him when he got there and Murray was intrigued to see the computer monitor alive with colourful characters. Motion stopped and Bailey switched to lines of coding to make some amendments. Sensing the presence behind him, he turned and grinned.

"G'day, Phil, grab a seat, with you in a moment." He returned to working on the lines of code as Murray took a seat next to him. After a few minutes, he turned back to Murray. "Colleen gave you the new spec, I see."

"She did. Can I ask you about a couple of details?"

For ten minutes, the two men discussed the technical requirements of the program and then Murray declared he was clear and ready to start work.

"What was that stuff you were working on when I came in?" he asked.

Bailey laughed. "One of the most fun projects I've ever worked on," he said. "We have a contract with one of the TV stations to produce educational cartoons for schools. This one's a real hoot. One of the guys in marketing found a book, *The Adventures of Gilbert the Farting Mouse.*" Really funny stories and beautifully illustrated by an artist in Coffs Harbour. He contacted the author and the artist and got permission to make a series of cartoons and then sold the idea to the television company who contracted us to make the cartoons."

"What software do you use for that?" Murray was fascinated by the idea.

"There are several," said Bailey. "The whole trend is called deep fake and I suppose it could be used for less pleasant purposes, because you can use pictures and videos of real people and show them doing anything. We use the top-of-the-line system, quite expensive and anyone using it here has to get a special access code."

"But can you buy it commercially?"

"Oh sure, quite pricey but available for download."

Murray stood up. "Thanks, Bailey, I'd better get to work on this program."

Bailey nodded and turned back to his monitor. Murray returned to his cubicle, deep in thought.

Back home that late afternoon he began to research the deep fake systems available commercially. To his surprise, some were available for no cost, some required a monthly fee, but none caused him any sticker shock. He finally opted for the one that seemed to have the most options and was widely used, and downloaded it. He looked forward to experimenting.

Over the following weeks, Murray spent every available hour at his computer, learning the complexities of the system. Gradually, he became more and more at ease with the wide range of facilities and began to experiment. The first results were disappointing. Movements of the characters were not natural and sometimes the faces he superimposed on bodies were not in proportion. Using imported voices and lip-synching to the characters in his videos was quite tricky. But he persisted.

Eventually he felt ready to show Peter Chang what he had done. He checked the time zones and one weekend evening, called Chang in Manchester when he would be out of bed but probably not yet out of the house.

"Hey, Phil, nice surprise," said Chang. "Good timing, it's nine in the morning here. What is, six in the evening there?"

"Correct. How's the life of the university student?"

"Bloody hard work. Assignment after assignment, hours at the computer, but it's all good stuff."

"Something to show you, mate. Sit back, I'm transmitting a little video I created."

He hit the key and waited for five minutes. The result was gratifying.

"Holy shit, Phil, where did you get that? I never fucked Alice Montgomery."

"That video shows you doing it. Did you enjoy it?"

"Christ, Phil, when did you do that? It's sexy as hell, I wish I had done it. She was gorgeous."

"Actually, it was quite easy. I downloaded a porn video from Porn Hub, I got your picture from our school yearbook and the same for Alice Montgomery from her school's on-line file. Then I played around a bit using this new system I bought and there you are! Groping Alice's tits while she gropes you. Ain't it grand?"

"It's bloody fantastic. It's giving me some ideas."

"Me too. How are you doing with our other project?"

"Haven't done anything yet. That guy Lloyd contacts me every week or so, asking when I'll be ready for some serious work, but I have to tell him, I'm swamped with university work."

"I can imagine. But it will be nice to earn some money. My parents aren't as rich as yours, I'm living in a tiny little studio apartment."

"Hang in there, Phil, the good times will come. But I have done one useful thing. I've developed a firewall better than anything the banks have. I'm going to download it to your system. It means we'll be able to talk freely without anyone able to get in and hear us."

"That'll be great, Peter."

"Okay, starting now. Keep working on those video skills."

"Will do. But Peter, I need your help."

"What's wrong, mate?"

"I've left home, it was getting too bloody difficult with that bastard of a father. I've got a small flat near work, but it's a bit pokey and I'm not exactly flush with cash. When do you think we can start operating and earn some dough?"

"Not long now. But I tell you what I'll do. I found a little bank in Leeds that had some serious weaknesses in their security system. I got into their accounts and nicked five hundred pounds and transferred it to the account I've set up in the Caymans, just as a test run. Send me your bank details and I'll set up a little subroutine that will get you into that Cayman account and transfer a couple of hundred dollars to you."

"Jeez, Peter, you can do that?"

"Damn right I can. And it wipes all traces of the transaction as well. The bank won't bother with a small sum like that, either."

"Thanks, mate, that will be a great help."

"And Phil, I'll keep working on this. When it's really safe, I'll send you the software for you to do a similar job for yourself."

"You're a bloody genius, Peter. I'll send you my details."

Murray disconnected the call with a feeling of great things about to happen.

Chapter 3

University Campus, Manchester, UK, November, October, 2014, five years earlier

"Mind if I join you?"

William Lloyd looked up from his book in surprise. His coffee breaks in the student refectory were invariably alone. He recognised the attractive young girl standing by his table as one of the students in his year but had never found out her name and she had never spoken up in classroom discussions.

"Of course," he said, folding his book away, intrigued by the interruption by a pretty girl.

She placed the coffee mug she was carrying on the table and sat down opposite him.

"You don't socialise much," she said.

"How do you know that? You've been watching me all of last year?"

"Actually, yes, I have. And I have never seen you have a social chat with another student. But what I have seen is that people ask you for help, you may give it, but the conversation ends there. No social chit-chat. You may be an advisor, but not a friend."

Lloyd froze. "And why have you been watching me?"

"Because you and I are the same. I don't chat much with other students either. They seem suspicious of me. And I can't see anyone warming to you in class, either."

He shrugged. "I can't say it bothers me much."

"Same here. I'm Anna-Maria Grassano."

"William Lloyd."

"I know."

"Okay then, Anna-Maria Grassano, what the hell is this? Why have you been watching me, how do you know my name?"

"Like I said, we seem to be alike. The students seem a bit scared of me, just like they seem scared of you. And yet when there's a debate in class, nobody seems able to stand up to you."

"I haven't seen you do much debating in class."

She smiled. "That's deliberate. I certainly pipe up in classes you don't take, but I like to watch your performance in the ones we both take."

"Once more, Anna-Maria Grassano, what's this about?" Lloyd was feeling a mixture of irritation and intrigue. He could recognise his strong attraction to this woman, she was certainly pretty enough, long dark hair, dark complexion, beautiful big eyes and a body that called up some hungers in him.

"I think you might be useful to us," she said.

"Useful? How? And to whom? Who is the 'us' you mention?"

She looked around the refectory. There was nobody sitting within earshot.

"The family business," she said.

"Which is what?" Lloyd felt some rising tension in the woman, and it caused his interest to grow. Something critical was happening.

"I'd better start from the beginning," she said. "My father is the boss. He lives in Palermo."

"Sicily... oh good grief, are you telling me this is a Mafia family?"

This time she laughed. "Got it in one, William."

"So what are you doing here, a student of History at a British University?"

"Getting a degree, like all of us, including you. But the business interests I think you can help are here, run by my Uncle Giorgio. He finds it strategically and economically better to be based here in the north and not in London."

"I can't believe you're telling me this. You're a member of an international criminal operation and you want to recruit me to work with you. How daft is that?"

"Not daft at all. I said I've been watching you. I've seen how you read people and beat them in debate. And I've seen how some of the students try and make your acquaintance, but you push them away. I think you could spot the strengths and weaknesses in people very quickly."

"And how would a Manchester-based Mafia business use that?"

"I have some ideas. Tell you what, there's a long weekend coming up. Why don't you come and spend it at my uncle's place and meet him and talk over the ideas we have. Anyway, I'd like to spend the weekend getting to know you better. I find you very attractive, William Lloyd."

Lloyd felt his excitement grow. Not only was this contact promising something sexually attractive, the idea of working with a Mafia family was intriguing. He felt no moral objections to it.

* * *

The ride into the Cheshire countryside had been exhilarating, from the first moment when she had handed the keys of the MGB to him, with a simple "You drive" and slid into the passenger seat with a breathtaking display of long legs under a short denim skirt, to the windswept drive in the open-top sports car.

"Good grief, it's a palace," said William as they pulled into the high metal gates that had opened automatically as Anna-Maria had pushed a button on the dashboard.

"No, just a country home of the obscenely rich," said Anna-Maria, laughing happily. "Pull up at the front door, somebody will take our bags and take us to our room."

"Our room?" said Lloyd, feeling a wave of excitement as he drove up to the massive building.

"We only need one," she replied.

As the car stopped, a man appeared at the front door. He walked down the steps.

"Welcome home, Miss Grassano," he said with a friendly smile.

"Thank you, Carlo." She pulled the lever to open the car's boot and the man began lifting bags and carried them up through the door.

"Let's go," said Anna-Maria and with another display of beautiful legs, slid out of the car. Lloyd followed, feeling overwhelmed by this display of wealth. He had never encountered a home with its own servants. He almost felt he was in some television drama of the lives of titled nobility. Anna-Maria took his hand and they followed the man and their bags, ending up in a room of extreme luxury with French windows overlooking extensive grounds with a small lake and a fountain. No other buildings could be seen.

"Thank you, Carlo," said Anna-Maria as what Lloyd assumed was a butler left the room.

"Impressive," said Lloyd, and stopped as Anna-Maria unbuttoned her blouse and unzipped her skirt.

"We've got an hour before we meet Uncle Giorgio," she said. "Let's make the most of it."

* * *

"My lovely niece says you might be useful to us."

Giorgio Grassano sat in an ornate, wing-back armchair. He looked about fifty in the estimate of William Lloyd, a muscular man of below average height, no obvious surplus weight. Blue eyes were the dominant feature in a face that was otherwise unremarkable, they sparkled, and William felt they could see right through him and read his thoughts. His speech was excellent, no trace of any accent that Lloyd could identify.

"That's what she told me," said William. "But I haven't yet seen just what it is that I could do." He sat in a regular armchair, nothing ornate and he was sure that it was a little bit lower than Grassano's seat. He felt like he was seated before a throne and Grassano was a king or a judge. It was all rather intimidating.

"She says you can read people well," said Grassano. "And you have the knack of drawing out people who seem to respond to authority or power."

"I don't know. I don't have many friends and the people who do seem to talk to me, I don't really like them."

Grassano emitted a small laugh. "It isn't necessary to like the people you can influence. What matters is the control."

"I don't think I control any of these people." Lloyd was unsure where this conversation was going.

"Anna-Maria thinks you do, but you haven't realised it yet. For many people, discovering the influence they have on others is a slow process and a wonderful thing to discover and develop."

Lloyd said nothing. The shock of realising that he could do this and that he wanted to be able to do it much better was startling.

"Are you going to marry my niece, William?"

The question shook Lloyd out of the inner thoughts.

"That's very early to say, Mr Grassano. We've really only known each other a few days."

"Anna-Maria says you are. And if Anna-Maria says something will happen, you can be absolutely certain it will."

Lloyd felt his face flush and a slightly panicky sensation of being drawn into something that could be wonderful but also not without its dangers.

"We still have two years of university, Mr Grassano. She is certainly a lovely woman and she has an incredible impact on me. But marriage is a little way off as yet."

"Alright, William, this is what I suggest." Grassano leaned forward in his armchair. "You continue at University, both of you. Meanwhile, we'll pay you enough money every month to ensure you can live well and look after Anna-Maria. In the meantime, I want you to examine all the people you find seeking you out. I want you to identify those who come from wealthy families, or those with influence, people who may themselves become influential and powerful in their own rights in future years. Also note those who show weaknesses that could be later applied against them, the ones who want wealth and power and will do anything to win it, the ones who succumb to sex too easily."

"You mean people who can be blackmailed?" Lloyd felt emboldened by the conversation, sensing the truth in what Grassano had said. He realised that he really could influence people and read them to learn what their internal motivations were.

Grassano smiled. "It's what we do, William. It's just one aspect of the family business. And I think you will be very useful to us. I can see that you have no moral difficulties with that."

Again, Lloyd sensed a new realisation in himself, this was true, he had no moral difficulties with using the rich and powerful for his benefit.

"I see that you have read me well, Mr Grassano. I will be happy to help you in this."

Grassano nodded. "And as you learn the family business, there may be other opportunities for you. In return, we will help you with your career, find opportunities for you and use the significant influences we have to ensure you can take advantage of them. So from now on, you can call me Uncle Giorgio. And now, I believe my niece is waiting for you."

The dismissal was obvious and Lloyd got to his feet.

"Thank you, er.. Uncle Giorgio."

Grassano nodded, but there was no indication that a handshake was to follow, and Lloyd left the room.

Sydney, Australia, March, 2020

"Phil, how's life in Australia?"

"Cooling off after a real hot summer. Hey, this video thing is great! Face to face conversation over half the world without time limits and it's not costing anything! How are you doing in Manchester?"

"It's hard work, I tell you! But I've got some interesting news you're going to love. You've switched on the firewall system I designed? I don't want anyone intercepting this."

"I have. This sounds interesting. What have you got?"

"There's something I've been working on," said Chang. "Remember I told you my dad is a heart surgeon. When I was home before the university year started, he showed me how pacemakers work, even gave me the technical specs on one of them and the blueprints. He told me that when the American Vice-President, that Cheney bloke had a pacemaker installed, the spooks were worried that somebody might be able to hack into it and cause all sorts of damage, or even listen in on top-level conversations with the president."

"I hadn't heard that."

"So what they did, apparently, was install a specially-made device without any communication facilities. So I started thinking. What if we could do that, hack into a pacemaker and control what it did to the heart?"

"But how would that help?" Murray looked puzzled.

"Well, one of the problems with hacking into banks and government systems is that they are bloody difficult for one, intensely monitored for another and if we did it, the police would start a major hunt. But if we could break into the pacemakers, we could then tell the patient to pay us big bucks or get killed. And we could give them a jolt to show we mean business."

"Holy shit, that's brilliant. Can you do it?"

"Not yet, but I'm working on it. First thing is to break into the system of a hospital that does pacemaker installations, identify the people who have them, get the serial number and then see how to get into the device itself. Might take some months."

"And that means they won't dare tell the cops or we'd kill them. Bloody brilliant, Peter."

"That's what I thought! Meanwhile, what are you doing down there?"

"I've got a lot more into videos. Like I did with the one of you and Alice Montgomery, you can make a video of somebody doing things without them knowing a thing about it. I've been making a few more of those, just for my own entertainment."

"What sort of things?" Murray could hear the laugh in Chang's voice.

"Some dead sexy stuff. I made one of myself screwing a movie actress, you couldn't tell it wasn't real. And I did one really ugly one of one of the worst right-wing politicians fucking a sheep. I was tempted to put that one on the internet, but I haven't learnt how to do that without leaving a trace."

"That'll happen soon. I'm working on all that sort of stuff using some of the code from the dark web, it's amazing what is there. I just have to finalise the code to make sure I don't get hacked. Another year, we'll be ready to do some serious money-earning. I reckon your video stuff will be something we can use when I've got this pacemaker thing worked out."

"I'll wait to hear from you."

"Great! Phil, got to go! I've got an assignment I have to work on."

"Good luck with it, mate!"

Manchester, UK and Sydney, Australia, June, 2021

"Hey, Phil, I think we're in business!"

Chang's face in the monitor showed more excitement that Murray had ever seen before.

"So what's happened?"

"That pacemaker thing, I've found out how to hack into them."

"Well, shit eh? That's amazing. Have you tested it?"

"I sure did." Chang was grinning widely. "And not only that, I had to find a way into a hospital system first, so that I could identify pacemaker users and I finally did that. Then finding somebody with a pacemaker was easy, I got the serial number."

"And you gave somebody a jolt?" Murray felt the excitement growing in him. He knew this was a world-first crime and could earn them a hell of a lot of money.

"Yeah, I broke into a hospital in London, identified some old codger and just gave him a small one. Then I watched the hospital records, he went back into the emergency room, but I'd wiped the trace in the hospital systems, the doctor couldn't find a thing and that's what he wrote into the old bloke's record. So I know it works, I think we're ready for the big time."

"That's bloody amazing. When can I try this?"

"Phil, I'm not sure you can manage this. It takes some expertise."

"Don't give me that crap. Look, I have to admit, I'm feeling a bit left out of all this. You're the one that worked out how to do it, you're the real hacking expert, I just feel I'm coming along for the ride."

"Oh hell, Phil, I'm sorry, I didn't mean that. You've found out how to do those amazing movies and we'll use those a lot. Look, tell you what. I'll identify a hospital that does pacemaker installations and I'll set up a standard routine for you to break in and identify people with them. Then we can start the real business."

"Okay, that sounds good. We've got to make sure we can't be identified, though."

"Yeah, I've been thinking about that. First thing, my routine blocks any trace of where the call is coming from, so that's safe. But why don't we wear a mask and use one of those voice distortion systems, you can download those easily enough."

"Sounds good, hey, why not use one of those Halloween masks, the one with the white face, evil smile with a thin black beard and moustache? You can buy those anywhere."

"Good thinking, Phil. Then everybody will think it's just one person doing this."

"Right. Will you let Lloyd in Manchester do this as well?"

"Maybe, not sure about that. We need to be sure we can trust him."

"Yeah, I agree, I'm not sure about him yet. Have you set up anything yet?"

"Not yet, but as you know, I've set up an account in the Caymans. When I've set up all the routines, I'll send you more details on how to take money from our victims' banks and transfer it to our account without leaving a trace of where it went or how it got there."

"Bloody beauty, Pete! I'll wait to get these details. You must be looking forward to graduation and getting back to Honkers. Has your dad got you an apartment yet?"

Chang's face showed irritation.

"No, the mean old bastard has gone back on that. He said his finances have taken a beating since the Communists began interfering in hospital management and I'll have to live at home until I get a job that pays well enough."

"That's a bugger. But you can probably buy a place yourself once you get going."

"I reckon. I'll let you know."

"Good luck with final exams," said Murray.

"Okay, gotta go."

Sydney Australia, June, 2021

Phillip Murray studied the details on the pages Chang had sent to him together with set routines for breaking into hospital records, locating a pacemaker and transmitting a jolt. The details of the coding were impressive and confirmed Murray's view that Chang was a truly gifted computer expert.

His nervous tension grew as he worked on performing his first blackmail deal using the impetus of a pacemaker jolt. He'd bought the mask at a costume shop a week before and downloaded the voice distortion system the day after. He knew he was ready to get to work.

First, the hospital. Chang had sent the first routine and Murray had installed it immediately. He entered the initiation code and sat back. It took fifteen minutes before a message appeared on the computer monitor.

"Enter password."

Chang had identified the password of the surgeon, Doctor Declan Short and Murray entered it. Although expecting it, he felt a surge of excitement when lines of data appeared on the monitor, with the heading, "Pacemaker Installations."

Murray studied the lines. They showed a patient name, a date, the serial number of the device and then several lines of medical data that Murray found little to comprehend. He selected a patient, a man named Craig Malloy, noted the serial number and then went into a secondary routine as indicated in Chang's notes, to display the personal details of the patient. He saw the address, a location in Windsor, west of Sydney, an email address and more medical data that Murray ignored. But what it didn't provide was a video address. Murray went back to the first screen and selected a second patient. This time, he found what he was looking for, a video address that he could use to call up the patient on his own computer. The patient was a man named Adrian Hogarth, seventy years old, living in Wollongong, a few kilometres south of Sydney. The details indicated he was a retired solicitor, so Murray decided he was probably in a good enough financial bracket to make the blackmail worthwhile.

Murray took a deep breath, donned the white mask and switched on the voice distorter. He entered the video code and sat back. It only took a minute.

"Who the hell are you?" shouted a man in Murray's monitor. The man was obviously elderly, almost totally bald with a severely lined face. His eyes were wide in shock.

"I'm the man who is going to take a thousand dollars from you," said Murray.

"Fuck off," raged Hogarth.

"Let me tell you how I'm going to do it," said Murray. His nerves were declining at the success of the call so far. Hogarth was reacting just as anticipated and Murray was thrilled at the sense of power he was feeling from the man's fear and shock. "I see that you had a pacemaker fitted six months ago," he continued. "If you don't agree to my instructions, I'll give you a nasty shock in that thing."

"Don't talk crap," Hogarth replied. The fear had been replaced by contempt. "Nobody can break into hospital systems."

"Well, now, Adrian, let me show you how wrong you are." Murray consulted Chang's notes and entered a three-digit code. He watched with satisfaction as the man fainted forward onto his desk and was motionless for a few seconds. When he returned to awareness, he stared at Murray's image.

"For god's sake, don't do that again," he whispered, his voice harsh.

"Well, I won't," said Murray. "Providing you do as I say. First thing is, have a thousand dollars in your account by Friday. Then I'll take it."

"You can't break into bank systems," said Hogarth.

"Didn't I just show you that I can break into hospital systems? I assure you, I really can break into anything. Now, are you going to have the money in your account by Friday? Because if you don't, I'll give you another nasty shock. And there's one more thing. If you go to the police, I'll find out and you'll be dead. And I know you'll go to the hospital and ask the surgeon about this, but they'll find nothing. Do you believe me, Adrian?"

The man put his hands over his face. "I believe you," he said.

"Good," said Murray. "Have a nice day." He disconnected the call and sat back, feeling a rush of exhilaration. He knew he could find Hogarth's bank details from the data shown in the hospital file and Chang had given him a routine for breaking into the bank system.

This was all going well, he decided. He saw big returns in the future.

Murray sat back with a feeling of immense power. He had done it! He had successfully blackmailed somebody into paying a sum of money under the threat of a fatal heart attack which he knew he could implement at any time he wanted. It wasn't the biggest sum in the world, but it proved he could do much better when he wanted. This was the true power of life and death and he held it. He felt the urge to go further with this new super-power. He used the routine Chang had given him and accessed the hospital computer from which he had taken his first victim's name. He slowly worked his way through the lists of pacemaker recipients over the last couple of years and finally saw a name he recognized. She was a far-right politician in the New South Wales parliament, renowned for her racist views. He took a deep breath, noted her computer video access details, donned the mask and went to work. A few minutes later he succeeded.

"Well, hello, lady fascist," he said as her startled face appeared on his monitor.

"Who the hell are you?" she snapped. "Get off my system."

"No, I don't think so," said Murray, smiling under the mask. "Couple of things I want to tell you."

"What things? Do you know who you are dealing with?"

"Oh, I'm very familiar with who I'm dealing with." Murray decided he was thoroughly enjoying himself. "You're a very nasty, fascist, racist bitch and you shouldn't be where you are. So here's a message. The indigenous people in a few parts of the country have put a curse on you. You're going to die quite soon."

"Don't talk crap, those people are always making threats like that, I couldn't give a flying fuck what they threaten me with."

"Such language, lady! Let me prove to you that their threat is very real indeed. Try this." Murray pressed the key and delivered a small jolt to the pacemaker. He watched as she fell forward on her desk and recovered just a few seconds later. She stared at the screen.

"What the hell did you do?"

Murray could see the fear in her face and her voice was croaky from the sudden stress.

"I showed you that you'd better pay attention to what Aboriginal people can do. That was the first warning. Any more of your hate-filled crap, you'll get another one. The third one will kill you."

The woman stared, her eyes wide. She was clearly frightened, but said nothing.

"That's the message," said Murray. "Have a nice day." He disconnected the call. "Holy shit," he exclaimed aloud. "You may just have done more for Aboriginals than anyone else in years."

He continued browsing through the names on the hospital computer, astonished at just how many people had received pacemakers in recent years from just one hospital in Australia. He came to a startled stop. It was his father's name. Murray had no idea that his father had experienced heart troubles and received the life-saving device. He checked the date. It was done during his student days at the school in Manchester. His communications with his parents during that time had been limited to simple reports of his education, sent only to his mother and she had replied with short comments, usually with some criticism or calls for more effort, but little about his home. He had no affection for either parent and considerable hostility towards his father who had always been a bully. Murray had spent his childhood terrified of him, never knowing when a beating would be administered for any reason his father could find, or sometimes imagine.

Murray stared at the screen. Everything he needed was there, the pacemaker serial number, his father's computer details, the possibilities grew rapidly in Murray's mind. He thought about what he could do, what revenge he might extract for the miserable years. After fifteen minutes, he disconnected from the hospital system. Attacking his father could wait. Anticipating how he would do it could provide much satisfaction for a while.

Cheshire Countryside, UK, February, 2022

"Uncle Giorgio, I may have a new business opportunity," said Lloyd. He could not yet get comfortable addressing a Mafia boss in that way, but his wife had told him her uncle would be badly offended if he didn't.

"That sounds interesting. You wouldn't have called me if it was not really viable."

"I believe it is. I have two young men who have shown they are expert at hacking into corporate computer systems, despite strong security."

"We already have expert hackers, William. What is special about these two?"

"What is special is that they are very young, just twenty-two, and they seem to have no scruples about what they can do. They will develop a lot in the next two years, but they will need some of the best equipment to develop further. I provided them with the initial gear, but it's time to upgrade"

"Where are they?"

"One is in Australia, the other is here at University but his home is in Hong Kong, but they met and developed their skills while at school in Manchester, which is where I met them, and then the Chinese boy has developed even more while at university."

"That will present no difficulty in providing them equipment. But this sounds risky, them being so young. How will they resist investigation by police if they leave some trace of their activities?"

"From what young Chang tells me, his skills involve leaving no trace of his work."

"That would be essential. What I recommend is that we wait until they demonstrate just how well they can cover their tracks and then give them each an assignment. If they pass that test, we should invest further in them."

"I agree. But let me tell you about the ideas they have for an unusual form of extracting money from victims."

"Go ahead."

"The Chinese kid believes he can hack into pacemakers after identifying suitable targets in the hospital files. That way, he can terrify the crap out of the target by giving them a jolt or two and then demanding money to keep them alive."

"Can that be done?"

"It can. These things all have network communication capabilities for remote monitoring by the hospital."

"That sounds promising, William. You have credit with me. You have worked well for us these years, you have given us many leads to people who can be manipulated, and we have profited from your efforts. And this has its attractions, it's a much simpler approach than a kidnapping for ransom and far less risky. If we target some people in government, we can perhaps extract future spending plans and get in ahead of them. This could be useful. Alright, William, go ahead. Buy them the equipment they need and see how they perform."

"Thank you, Uncle Giorgio."

"William, I will do this, but only because you married my niece. But if they fail and are found out, there must be no pointers back to my operation. You will buy their equipment in your own name and we will recompense you a little later."

"I will. Thank you, Uncle."

"Give my love to Anna-Maria."

* * *

Once more, Chang was disturbed in the student lounge by the appearance of William Lloyd.

"Mr Lloyd, what do you want?" Chang felt irritated. All the meetings with Lloyd in the past had been disturbing, even though they had led to financial advantages.

Lloyd sat down in the armchair next to Chang and looked around. Nobody was within earshot.

"It sounds like you have a seriously useful product now," he said.

"I have to do some refinements before I can use it," said Chang. "And I want to finish university and go home before I start it up properly."

"My people want it started up quicker than that," said Lloyd. "There's a lot of money to be made for all of us."

"And a lot of prison time to be served if we make an error and get found out."

"I have every faith in your brilliance, Peter," said Lloyd. "How soon could you be ready?"

"Maybe six months."

"Okay, take that, but be ready then. And when you have it done, I want to be able to use it. There's no reason why I can't make us some money also."

"No chance, Mr Lloyd. This takes real computer expertise. You'd never be able to handle the coding it takes."

"I could learn."

Chang laughed. "Maybe in ten years. That's how long I've been working on this and I'm supposed to be a computer genius."

"So how will Phillip Murray do it?"

"Phil's a bloody good computer man," said Chang. "He may not be in my class, but he can certainly learn the techniques from me. I've already given him all the instructions and the coding, and he's able to enter it without an error. I don't think you'll be able to."

Lloyd could see when he was beaten.

"Okay, Peter, but have this ready to go in six months."

"Maybe," said Chang. "I'll try but I have finals coming up, I need to get a good degree or my father will rip me a new one."

Lloyd nodded, got to his feet and left.

Phase Two

Outright War

Chapter 4

Taree, Mid-North Coast, NSW, Australia, October, 2022

Karl Jennings took three paces to the cupboard where his bottles of expensive single-malt scotch were kept and fell flat on his face. He had no idea if any time had passed since the fall, but blood was flowing from his mouth where a tooth had cut through the lower lip. Through the confusion and the fear that filled his body, one thought came to his mind.

That was not supposed to happen.

It was now eight weeks since his surgery to replace a defective heart valve and four since the surgeons had decided to install a pacemaker. This was the schedule the surgeons had given him before he could touch alcohol again.

Slowly he got back to his feet and returned to the lounge chair, pushing his handkerchief against his mouth to try and stem the blood, but it didn't work. Rather than bleed all over his lounge suite, he tried again, rose to his feet and reached his bathroom without falling, but as he stood at the basin, wiping his mouth with a hand towel soaked in cold water, it happened again. He fell, aware that he had fallen backwards against the shower stall, knocking the sliding door off its rail.

Confused and frightened, he reached for the pendant hung round his neck and pressed the button. Back in his kitchen, he heard the alarm of his emergency system go off and a few seconds later, the voice of the operator could be heard, asking if there was an emergency. He shouted as loudly as he could, "Heart attack, send an ambulance," then crawled to his front door, not trusting himself to stand again, and opened the door. He leaned against the wall by the open door, feeling sick with fear.

How was this happening? The surgeon had assured him that the pacemaker would control the heart rate and ensure a constant flow of the essential electrical currents in the heart ventricles. Was his pacemaker defective? It had worked perfectly since it was installed a month earlier.

He had no idea how long it took for the ambulance to arrive, but two men came through the door, checked him over, moved him to a stretcher and pushed him to the ambulance. He had a brief thought about the door remaining unlocked, but as one of the medics began gently questioning him about the episode, he forgot about the open door.

The small nurse who looked about fifteen years old applied a monitor to his chest over the pacemaker, held it there for half a minute then sat at her computer console and studied it intently.

"There's absolutely nothing wrong with the pacemaker," she said finally. "It's behaving perfectly, your heart rate is at a constant sixty beats a minute and there's no sign at all of a stoppage. According to this, everything has gone according to plan since it was installed."

"And yet I fell over twice, blacking out and I'm terrified."

"I'll call Doctor Hansen," she said and picked up the phone.

After studying the computer screen for ten minutes, the doctor had nothing to add.

"I'm baffled," he said, moving from the computer monitor to a chair alongside Karl. "There's no record on the system that anything went wrong, the pacemaker doesn't show a stoppage. Has there been any change in your medication?"

"None," Karl replied. "I've had no alcohol for two months, as I was advised and I was just about to have my first nip of scotch when the first fall happened."

"How long before the second fall?"

"Not sure, I don't know if I was out for any time, but maybe ten minutes at the most."

"And that was a couple of hours ago. There's been no repeat?"

Karl shook his head.

"Okay, let's give you something to calm you down and we'll keep you here overnight. If there's no change, you can go home."

After a peaceful night, Karl Jennings caught a cab home. The door was still open, but there was no sign of any disturbance when he walked in. Almost immediately, the phone rang. Karl picked up the handset.

"Hello," he said, not really sure he wanted to answer, as he was still shaken by the falls and stay in hospital.

"Welcome back home, Karl," said a metallic voice, the sort he had heard from the odd scam, threatening legal action if he didn't pay his out-dated taxes, or demanding payment for a debt. "I hope you had a peaceful night in hospital."

"Who the hell are you?" Karl's throat felt tight as he sensed a threat.

"I'm the person who caused your heart to stop twice last night."

Even with the robotic voice, Karl heard a small laugh in the speaker's words. He began to feel anger.

"Bollocks," he said. "That can't be done. You're probably just some scam artist who somehow knew I'd gone to hospital and why. Go fuck yourself."

"Oh dear. Karl, Karl, you don't want to play games with me. Let me prove my point."

And Karl fell flat on his face again.

Bondi, NSW, Australia, October, 2022

Veronica Caswell sat up in her lounge chair to reach for her coffee mug. She felt a tremble beginning in her left leg. It spread in seconds until her whole body was shaking violently. She lost awareness of her surroundings, only vaguely hearing her daughter calling her in panic. Then it stopped. She was lying full length on the couch, aware only of such terror as she had never experienced before.

"My god, Mum, what the hell happened?" Angela was bent over her, confusion and worry marked sharply in her face.

"God knows," Veronica replied. "I've never known anything like that before."

"I'll get you to hospital," said her daughter. "The pacemaker was supposed to prevent any problems like that, and it's been fine since you got it six months ago."

"Maybe it's got problems," Veronica replied. "Yes, get me to the ER and let's hope nothing happens while we're on the road."

"We're baffled," said the cardiologist. "The pacemaker shows no faults, it's working perfectly and there's no record of a malfunction. The ECG is perfect, no indications of anything wrong with you at all. You've experienced nothing like this before?"

"Nothing, doctor."

"The only possible thing we can think of is a small blood clot happening near the heart valve, but if that was so, it's gone. But we'll keep you in tonight, run a few more tests and if there's nothing showing, you can go home tomorrow."

He stood up, exchanged a few inaudible words with the nurse who had run the computer tests on the pacemaker, and left. A moment later, another nurse brought in a wheelchair and took Veronica to a ward with one other woman in a bed.

* * *

The phone rang as Veronica and Angela came into the house near Bondi Beach.

"Bloody hell, can't the company leave you alone for a couple of days?" muttered Angela and picked up the phone.

"Yes," she snapped, unable to hide her irritation caused by the anxiety of her mother's collapse.

"Good morning, Angela," said a robotic, non-human voice. "I bet you're glad to have your mother home again."

"Who the hell is this?" Angela's tone and volume were both raised. The voice on the phone was loud enough for Veronica to hear it and she looked at her daughter, the question in her eyes.

"Let me talk to your mother," said the metallic voice.

"You don't talk to my mother. She's had a horrible shock and she doesn't want to talk to some scam artist like you. So go fuck yourself."

"You'd better hear this, Angela. There's nothing wrong with your mother's heart, the pacemaker works beautifully."

"What the hell are you talking about?"

"That collapse last night, I caused it."

"You what?

"I caused it. Now, to prove my point, watch your mother."

Immediately, Veronica cried out in terror and she collapsed onto the lounge, shaking violently. The attack lasted just a couple of seconds.

"Oh my god," Angela exclaimed. "This can't be."

"Now, Angela," said the voice. "Do you believe me?"

"Mum, it's alright," said Angela. "There's nothing wrong. But some bastard is claiming he caused it." She put the phone back to her mouth. "Who the fuck are you?"

"I'm the person who can cause pacemakers to fail," replied the frightening voice. "I think I just proved my point. Now, let me talk to your mother."

Her hands shaking, Angela passed the phone to Veronica.

"Who the hell is this?" she demanded.

"I'm the person who caused your attack last night and the one just a few moments ago. So now you'd better listen to me, Veronica."

Veronica realised the reality but said nothing.

"So, Veronica," continued the unearthly voice. "You are the president of a successful data security firm, so you will certainly understand just how good I am at this. Your annual salary is $550,000 a year, which is why you can own a lovely home in Bondi with views of the ocean. Your bonus last year was a further quarter million. Am I correct so far?"

Veronica said nothing.

"No need for you to say anything. I've studied your books, everything, your bank accounts as well and I know what a wealthy woman you are. So, here's the thing. You will pay me a hundred grand a year from now on. Later, I'll give you the details of how to do it, but as you can probably understand, any efforts by you to trace the payments will get you nowhere. Now, if you object to this, or try and tell the police, you'll get several more shocks and one of them will eventually kill you. Do you understand me so far?"

"Yes," said Veronica, her voice barely a whisper.

"Good. I'll get back to you."

The connection was broken.

Forster, Mid-North Coast, NSW, Australia, November, 2022

Garry Henderson was enjoying his retirement. The hard-working, often frightening but usually exhilarating life in the military had ended some years ago, but it had been an easy transition to working with the security forces in Australia. Life in Canberra was pleasant and he usually got home in the evenings to enjoy developing his skills as a cook and consuming the results with a few glasses of wine. He felt he had earned these last years living on the Mid-North Coast with its almost ideal climate and the beach just a stroll away. The sizeable inheritance he had received from his father two years ago made life very comfortable.

When the phone rang, he picked it up, assuming it was one of the several elderly people he had met over his retirement.

"Henderson," he said, turning down the volume of his television set where he had been watching one of his favourite British cop shows.

"Good evening, Garry," said an ugly, distorted voice. "I hope you are having a pleasant evening."

"Alright, who's the joker?" said Henderson, feeling his irritation rising. The plot had been getting interesting with the British detective.

"No joke, Garry, I'm about to make an expensive demand on you," said the ugly voice.

"What the hell are you talking about? Get off the

phone and go and play your games somewhere else."
Garry was about to replace the handset when he
blacked out. When he returned to consciousness, he
was still sitting in his armchair, the telephone in his
lap. Bewildered, he stared at it as the terrible voice was
speaking. He lifted it to his ear.

"Did you like that little jolt, Garry?" said the voice.

"You did that?" Garry felt considerable anxiety.

"I did indeed, Garry. Now, here's what's going to
happen next. You have considerable income between
your army pension and the one you get from your time
with the spooks, never mind the enormous inheritance
your father left you and I want some of it. Here's what
you're going to do. Make sure there's five thousand
dollars in your chequing account by next week and then
I'll take it. Then we'll talk about an annual payment to
me of a hundred grand."

"Don't be stupid," snapped Garry. "You can't break
into banking systems."

"I've just shown you I can get into hospital systems
and I could stop your heart if I wanted to. So be a good
boy, arrange that bank balance and I'll take it. Later, I
may want some information about your life with the
Signals Directorate."

"Go fuck yourself, you bastard," said Garry and
hung up.

He was frightened, but he knew what he had to do.
He picked up the phone again and dialled his old office
in Canberra. An automated voice answered and Garry
left a short message about what had happened.

He resumed his television watching, unable to
subdue the deep anxiety he felt about the last few

minutes. Could somebody really do what that ugly voice has threatened? He had no intention of following the instructions.

He slept badly that night.

* * *

Garry stared at the phone as it rang the following evening. Panic ran through his body. But he knew that dreadful things could happen to him if he refused to take the call.

"Yes," he said, his voice harsh from tension.

"So you disobeyed my orders and called the spooks," said the metallic voice.

"I don't care what you do. I will not be bullied by some coward who knows how to hack computers. You don't get a cent from me."

"Dear oh dear! Garry, you're filthy rich, your dad left you fifteen million bucks, paying me a hundred grand a year is nothing to you. Anyway, I wasn't going to stay with that, the money is less important than some information you can give me about your job as a spook"

"Like I said, fuckwit, you don't scare me. You won't get money and you won't get military information. So fuck off."

"Oh, I think I do, Garry. But actually, I'm glad you're doing this. I needed an object lesson for my other clients. I hope you have your affairs in order."

A violent jolt hit Henderson and he shook like a leaf in a windstorm before blacking out.

Chapter 5

Chek Lap Kok International Airport, Hong Kong, December, 2022

Peter Chang left the Cathay Pacific airliner with some trepidation. Although he had lived in Hong Kong in his youth, he had been sent to England for his schooling since he was twelve and had only spent time in the city during summer vacations. After the years in the British culture, he no longer felt comfortable in a Chinese-Communist-ruled society. He had never known the pre-Communist days in British-ruled Hong Kong, but he had heard his parents speak about those times with nostalgia.

The meeting with the immigration officer was uncomfortable, as the officer seemed suspicious about the several boxes of computer equipment and the entries in Chang's passport, showing constant back and forth between Hong Kong and the UK, but after twenty minutes of questioning, he was allowed through to take the express train into the city and his parents' home in Kowloon.

The reception at home was not particularly warm. Peter felt that he had grown away from them after so many years in England and even though both parents had also been schooled in England, they had not been out of Hong Kong, other than trips to mainland China for professional conferences since they had returned before Peter's birth.

"You can have my old study as your room," his father said. "I added an extension to the house some years ago, as you know and that's where my office is now. When you get a job, you can probably get an apartment for yourself, but prices have risen sharply in recent years, so it might take some time."

"Thank you, father," said Chang. "I've got some pretty good computer gear that takes up some space, so I really do need a room."

His father didn't ask where the equipment had come from. He seemed pre-occupied with medical issues at the hospital where he worked, and Chang was relieved to take over the old study and set up his equipment that Lloyd had supplied him the previous year.

For two weeks, he did little but roam around the city, feeling disturbed at the sight of so many military forces in almost all public spaces. This was not like England. Nor was the television programming, which was far more subject to influence from the ruling Communists and far less entertaining than the British shows he had grown to love so much.

But finally, he settled into his private room at home. Although he told his parents that he had applied for several jobs in the computer industry, they seemed uninterested in his progress, both of them being fully occupied by their own professions. Chang began to feel ready to put his newly-developed talents to work.

To start, he identified a few hospitals in Hong Kong that performed pacemaker installations. There were several and he chose one of the biggest to try and hack into the computer systems. This proved fairly simple, as the hospital had computer systems that were common in the western world and the standard procedures he had developed were easily modified for the one he selected. After just one day, he was able to browse the lists of recipients and he noted several obviously wealthy people, including two who lived on the road up to the Peak and would have to be multi-millionaires, probably billionaires to afford such a location. The models of pacemaker were all manufactured in the west also, and he knew he could attack those with ease, after having had the details from his father.

Then he had an idea that made him smile. He could do something about his hostility to Communist philosophies and the mainland rule of Hong Kong. He switched his research to hospitals in mainland China and quickly identified one that specialised in servicing top government officials. Again, he had no difficulty in accessing the computers, as these were also supplied by western manufacturers, but then saw that, as expected, the files were written in the primary dialect of mainland China, Mandarin, rather than the Cantonese dialect of Hong Kong.

However, this presented only small challenges to Chang. While the two dialects were very different and a speaker of one would not be able to comprehend the other, Chang knew that, like most Cantonese speakers, he could read the Mandarin script without much difficulty. Carefully, he went through the lists of pacemaker recipients and while he found that most of those done before 2016 had been given western-manufactured devices, many of the later recipients had been given the first Chinese-manufactured model. He looked through the list, seeing few names he could recognise. But at last he saw one, a high-level government official whose name had appeared in a recent newspaper article.

Chang smiled to himself. This would be hugely satisfying. He noted the serial number of the device. There was no point in trying to access the man's computer, they would not be able to speak to each other, but anyway, this was just to be a test run. Assuming the technology of the Chinese-manufactured pacemaker was similar to the rest of them, Chang prepared his assault. Taking a deep breath, he initiated the routine with a jolt big enough to kill the man.

He had no way of knowing if he had been successful. Deciding to watch the local news stations for the next few days to see if any reference would be made, though realising it was unlikely, Chang went back to setting up his equipment.

Two days later, with the main government news program on the television in his room, his heart jumped as an item appeared.

"A senior official in the financial planning department, Ah Too Wong died from a heart attack," said the young female announcer. She went on to pour lavish praise on the official and his patriotic service to China, but Chang couldn't care less about that. He had now successfully tested his technology in Communist China on a Chinese made device and satisfied his personal hostility to the ruling force in Hong Kong.

Peter Chang slept well that night.

Cheshire, UK and Bondi, NSW, Australia, February, 2023

Phillip Murray regarded the screen of his computer with trepidation. Calls from William Lloyd were rare, and this was the first one he had received since settling back in Australia. He took a deep breath and accepted the call.

"Yes, Mr Lloyd?"

"Good evening, Phillip. It's what, seven in the evening there?"

"Correct. How can I help you, Mr Lloyd?"

"I just wanted to see how you were doing, now that the system in fully operational. Have you completed any exercises yet?"

"Just two. I took a bit from some old codger and that's gone into the Cayman account as you have instructed. And just for the hell of it, I gave a jolt to some evil bitch of a politician and persuaded her to change her policies."

"Okay, I understand how that might satisfy you, but no more of those, understand? This is all about serious money, not personal satisfaction."

Murray nodded but felt some irritation about being ordered around like this.

"Did you have any difficulty doing these exercises?" asked Lloyd. "When I talked to Peter back at University, he said it was an extremely complex, difficult process that took serious computer skills. How did you manage?"

Murray laughed. "Developing it took the sort of genius Peter has. I could have done it with a lot of practice, but Peter sent me a set of routines already pre-programmed, so all I had to do was enter the hospital code, which was easy to find, look up a pacemaker code and then it was all automatic. Hell, even you could do it."

"That's interesting," said Lloyd. "Okay, Phillip, keep up the good work."

Lloyd disconnected the call.

"Fuck you," muttered Murray.

"Peter, I've talked to Murray and he tells me you've set up the entire process as an automatic routine that anyone could run."

Chang went silent for a moment. "He wasn't supposed to tell you that," he said. "It's still a risk for a novice to do this."

"Well, he did and I want to be able to do the same."

"I'll say it again, Mr Lloyd, this is too risky."

"Peter, let me remind you again of who we're working for. If I can do these projects, we can earn a hell of a lot more money. I want those routines and I want to conduct a few operations."

"What if I say screw you, and Phillip and I go off on our own?"

"Be careful, Peter. If even a whiff of that gets to my people, you won't last a week. They get very unhappy with people who turn on them."

Peter Chang was silent for a few moments.

"Okay, I'll send you the routines," he said. "But for fuck's sake, follow the steps very carefully."

"Thank you, Peter," said Lloyd. "I'll look forward to getting the information."

The screen went blank. Chang sat silently for a few moments, letting the anger subside.

"Fuck you," he muttered.

Chapter 6

Police Station, Mid North Coast, NSW, Australia, May, 2023

"This is Detective Inspector Melanie Carter. How can I help you?"

Melanie's phone had rung soon after getting to her desk. She had begun reviewing the latest reports of crime in her region and developing a priority schedule to investigate them. Her life had been fairly quiet for a few weeks since her last case, a series of murders with bodies buried in a field on the Mid-North Coast.[1]

"My name is Declan Short," said the voice in her ear. "I'm a cardiologist at Saint John's Hospital in Newcastle."

"And why are you calling me, Doctor? "I'm a long way from Newcastle."

"It's about the recent death of Garry Henderson. He was found dead in his home in Forster late last year."

"Again, Doctor, why are you calling me? You should be calling your nearest police station."

"Normally, yes, Inspector Carter. But I'm very familiar with some of your previous work and I think you may be the most appropriate person to call. This is in your area, after all."

---

[1] See "The Death Gambit" by Michael Davies

"We may have to get back to you on that. But, yes, I remember the case of Garry Henderson. The Coroner recorded a death caused by equipment failure. Apparently, his pacemaker failed, and he suffered a massive heart attack. Do you have something to say about that?"

"I do. I was the surgeon called to testify. I told the Coroner that we had tested the pacemaker intensively and found no fault in it. We found no record of any failure and if it had stopped for any reason, that would have been recorded. The manufacturer repeated the tests with the same result. These things are highly sophisticated computers."

"The Coroner discarded your testimony, Doctor."

"She did, despite my objections."

"So what makes you choose to call a police detective on the subject?"

"In the last few weeks, there have been two cases of patients coming to an emergency room at their local hospitals with cases of temporary blockages to their heart functions, causing blackouts and collapse. Both patients had pacemakers installed at this hospital some months ago, the same with Henderson. Their cases were referred to us and we ran all the standard tests of the devices. No faults were shown. Both returned home after overnight stays and the full battery of tests, neither has suffered any such event since, none that they have reported, anyway."

"What are you implying, Doctor?"

"There has been a lot of discussion in recent years about the possibility of hacking into pacemakers and other devices that are implanted in a patient. One new development is an insulin pump that measures the blood sugar and automatically pumps insulin when needed. Another example is a device to prevent sleep apnoea, it's a recent development."

"I thought people used a breathing pump for that? My uncle has a CPAP machine and he sleeps with a mask."

"It's the most common approach, but internal devices are being developed and they all have the same characteristic, they communicate with the hospital's computers and can be monitored by the medical staff. It hasn't happened yet, but hacking into these things is definitely a possibility and we haven't found a way to prevent it, not that anyone really believes it to be likely. But if you do some reading, you will find that when Dick Cheney was Vice President of the USA some years ago, it was a definite concern. The pacemaker he had fitted was specially modified to remove all communication facilities."

"How easy would it be to hack into a device like that?"

"So far, it's been considered almost impossible. It's believed that it could only be done when very close, say ten metres at the most away from the patient. But these three events make me wonder if some clever hacker has found a way to get into the device remotely. The fact that all of them have occurred relatively locally, to people who had the implant conducted at this hospital suggests something is wrong."

"Let's say you have a point, Doctor. How would somebody identify pacemaker recipients?"

"By getting into the hospital computer records. That would take considerable skill, we have the best protection systems money can buy, much the same as banks and government departments. I doubt anyone could do it."

"Doctor, are you implying that the death of Garry Henderson was not a fatal failure of his pacemaker, but possibly deliberate?"

"Detective, in some ways, we have similar jobs. We look at facts, we evaluate possibilities and conclude a course of action. It may be further evaluation or it may lead to specific treatment. In my professional opinion, the failure of the device is not a possible cause of death, especially after both we at the hospital and the manufacturer found no evidence of failure. Add two other episodes of unlikely failure of the pacemaker and my diagnostic nose starts twitching."

Melanie laughed briefly.

"Doctor, you have stirred my interest. Will you send me the details of the other two cases, so I can contact them?"

"I will, but I worry that if these are all cases of possible blackmail, talking to them might be a risk."

"I'll see if I can work around that."

"Thank you, Detective Inspector. I'll send you the contact details."

* * *

"Boss, I'm convinced the surgeon has a point. Three episodes of serious heart attacks, one fatal, when not a single fault can be found in the pacemakers. Like the doctor said, it makes my detective's nose twitch."

"But can these things be hacked?" Chief Superintendent James Willoughby looked interested.

"So far, we think only by somebody very near to the victim, but as the doctor said, they are sophisticated computers and it's well within possibility. Apparently, it's enough to cause the authorities around the world some worries. And then there's another issue."

"Which is?"

"I've researched all three of them and they're all very rich," said Melanie. "The dead man was worth about fifteen million bucks, an inheritance from his father about ten years ago. Veronica Caswell is the Chief Executive Officer and majority owner of a software company, a most successful company specialising in data security and what is termed business continuity planning. Karl Jenkins is a worry. He's something senior in the government, the Australian Signals Directorate to be precise and he would have access to a lot of high-security material."

Willoughby leaned forward on his desk.

"All of them ripe for blackmail, it would seem. Do the spooks in ASIO share your concerns?"

"Yes, sir, they're wide open to blackmail. As to the second, ASIO and I don't have a working relationship, I have no idea what they think."

"And all this would have had to be conducted by somebody highly skilled in computer technology, more skilled than almost everybody, if this is what is happening."

Melanie said nothing.

"Okay, Inspector, open a file on this, but keep it to yourself for now. We all know the standard threats these people make, go to the cops and you're dead. Check their bank records, see if any large payments have been made. Somehow, you'll have to talk to the two survivors, but work out some way of doing it without raising the blackmailer's suspicions, assuming there really is someone behind it."

"I have an idea about that," said Melanie. "But I think I can test that thesis first."

* * *

Veronica Caswell stared at the phone, but finally forced herself to pick it up.

"Veronica Caswell?" said the woman's voice, a perfectly normal female voice and Veronica felt a flood of relief that it was not the inhuman, robotic voice of before.

"Yes," she said.

"This is Detective Inspector Melanie Carter, Criminal Investigation Branch."

Relief was replaced by panic.

"Go away," she shouted. "Please don't call me again."

She slammed the phone down and began trembling.

"Interesting," said Melanie and dialled another number. "Mr Karl Jennings?" she said when the phone was picked up. "This is Detective Inspector Melanie Carter, Criminal Investigation Branch."

"Oh my god," exclaimed the voice at the other end. "For god's sake, go away and don't call me again."

"My oh my," muttered Melanie as the phone was slammed down. "I'd say the good Doctor Short and his diagnostic nose was quite right to twitch. And so to Plan B."

The doorbell rang at the home of Veronica Caswell. This was a common enough event and she felt no worries as she peered through the spyhole and saw a teenage girl waiting outside. She looked quite ordinary, plain tee-shirt, jeans, dark brown hair in a ponytail. Veronica opened the door.

"Hello," she said.

The girl smiled. "Hi," she said. "My dad asked me to give you this." She handed an envelope to Veronica. "He said not to stand near your computer when you read it. See ya," she said and walked away.

Curiously, Veronica closed the door, opened the envelope, and found a typed note inside.

"Dear Ms Caswell," she read. *"I am Detective Inspector Melanie Carter, Criminal Investigation Branch and I suspect you are being blackmailed by somebody who can hack into your pacemaker. I realise you must be frightened by the computer skills of this, so we can't speak on the phone or communicate by computer means, but I believe we can help you. That was the daughter of one of my colleagues, Diane who called on you and even if your home is being watched, she would not arouse suspicions. But if we speak well away from any electronic devices, you will not be overheard. Can I ask you to meet me at Bondi Beach at 2pm tomorrow? Buy an ice-cream and sit on the*

sidewalk by the southern end. I'll join you. There are no audio pickup capabilities in your pacemaker, so we will not be overheard. All I will ask from you is what the person has demanded of you and how payment is to be made. After that, I will not need to communicate further, we'll conduct the investigation with high secrecy."

Veronica felt a sour taste of fear in her mouth, but also a small sense of relief. She knew she would make that meeting.

The doorbell rang at the home of Karl Jennings. After a small surge of panic, he decided to answer it. His threat would not be coming to the door. He checked through the spyhole and saw a boy of about twelve or thirteen, wearing the blazer of a high school in the city.

"G'day," said the boy when the door opened. "My uncle asked me to give you this." He handed over an envelope. "He said don't read it anywhere near a computer." He turned and walked away.

* * *

"It's confirmed, sir," said Detective Inspector Carter. "Blackmail, at least of the two living victims. I talked to both of them, away from their homes and from any intrusion. An electronically distorted voice has called them after inflicting at least one heart stoppage. Jennings had one attack, went to hospital and was cleared to return home after a night in the emergency ward. But then he got another call after getting home and a warning attack when he told the robot voice to get fucked. The demand is for fifty thousand a year paid to an overseas bank in the UK. We're trying to track down that account, but it's being blocked. Same story with Veronica Caswell, cleared at the ER after an attack, went home, got another call, demanding a hundred grand a year in the same process and had a second blockage as a sort of reminder."

"And Henderson?"

"I checked the records. Henderson did actually call his old office in Canberra to say he was being blackmailed and threatened and he died the next day. At least, that's what seems to have happened. I checked his call log and there was a call to Canberra."

"Okay, Melanie, get to work and see what you can find out."

Melanie stood up and left the office.

A few minutes later, the telephone on the Chief Superintendent's desk rang. He picked it up.

"Front desk here, sir. You're about to get a critical visitor. I couldn't stop him."

The door opened and a man stood there. He walked in and took a wallet from his jacket pocket and displayed an official badge.

"Gordon Porter, ASIO," he said. "We're taking the investigation of Garry Henderson off your hands. This is now a matter of national security."

Chapter 7

Canberra, ACT, Australia, June 2023

ASIO Special Agent Gordon Porter sat before his large computer monitor. Two faces on the screen looked back at him.

"Thank you for coming, Mr Knight and Ms Simmons. I believe we have a potential security risk for all our countries, possibly others too and we should discuss it."

"From your message, I have to agree." Jacqui Simmons looked like a well-cared for, fifties woman, immaculate hair style, a complexion that appeared almost perfect, despite the computer screen quality and almost invisible but highly effective make-up. Bright blue eyes dominated the attractive features that reflected high intelligence.

"Same here. This was a good call, Mr Porter." Jerome Knight resembled a senior television newsreader, dressed in a dark blue suit, white shirt and a blue and white tie in a perfect Windsor knot, all topped by a classical face displaying wisdom and maturity. "Why don't you start by giving us the details of your concerns?"

"Thank you, both. My department is positive that the involvement of the CIA and MI6 is essential and will be a great help. In the last few months, we have had three cases of blackmail aimed at wealthy individuals, one of whom had been an agent in our Signals Directorate. All three suffered dangerous heart stoppages, though all three had pacemakers installed. The attacks were accompanied by blackmail demands, two of them for money, the third for information of a secret nature. That one was aimed at our security man. He put himself at risk by calling us but died of heart failure some hours later. The other two survived and the local police were able to talk with them. All three pacemakers were installed by the same surgeon at one hospital in New South Wales, all three were examined in detail by him and by the manufacturers and no fault was found. We have concluded that one agency, whether a single person or a group conducted all events and has developed the ability to hack into implanted medical devices like these which have communications capabilities with the hospital systems."

"That's interesting," said the American. "I remember that when then Vice President Cheney had a device implanted, there was great concern about him being hacked in this way. In fact, we removed all communications facilities from his device, which meant difficulties in monitoring it, but this was preferable to some external group having this ability."

"Most authorities are concerned about this," said Porter, "and are researching solutions, but it seems they haven't found one yet. Are you aware of any such events occurring in the USA?"

"Not so far," said Knight. "But if they were only civil blackmail cases not involving security people, we wouldn't easily have heard of them."

"But I have," said the Englishwoman. "Not a security issue, but there was a case just a few weeks ago where a senior executive of a large corporation in Manchester died of a heart attack. He'd had a pacemaker installed a year ago. The Coroner ruled death due to failure of this device. I read about it at the time, because my uncle was due to have one and I was interested. There was no mention of examinations by surgeons or manufacturers, though."

"We had the same coronial review," said Porter. "But that was because we got to her and ensured that result. We did not want the perpetrator seeing that his efforts had been suspected. It might be that the local Manchester police had done the same, for the same reasons."

"I'll check on that," said Simmons. "This seems to be something new. It implies that the person behind it had hacked into the hospital computer systems to identify pacemaker recipients and that requires superior skills. We're involved because of the international espionage aspects, but it falls into the purview of the National Crimes Agency who specialise in such cases. They have some very clever people who can investigate this."

"That sounds logical," said Porter. "I know the NCA, they have a formidable reputation."

"And if there is a case elsewhere, such as here in the USA," said Knight, "somebody is using the global communications systems. This person is one hell of a hacker. It's reminding me of somebody."

"Me too," said Simmons. "We had an extraordinary case last year that involved your country, Gordon. You may have read about the tenth Baron Percivale and his scandal. To escape it, he fled to Australia with a new identity and the assistance of both governments. But he died and his daughter inherited the title and the assets, or at least, believed so until it was revealed that her father's second wife, the daughter's mother was illegitimate, as his first wife was still alive and they had not divorced. However, in a way that nobody has yet been able to work out, all the baronial assets were sold off and the money given to several charities. Our people say it was the most sophisticated example of hacking they had ever encountered and still have only suspicions of who did it."[2]

"I remember all that very well," said Porter. "And I suggest we are all thinking along the same lines."

"Allen Miller?" said Knight.

"Allen Miller," said Simmons.

Porter nodded. "Allen Miller," he said.

* * *

Cheshire Countryside, June, 2023

"Dammit, Anna-Maria, I feel so bloody useless." Lloyd took a gulp of his scotch and stared moodily at the empty fireplace.

Anna-Maria turned from where she was arranging flowers in a vase and came and stood next to him.

"William, why would you feel like that? Uncle Giorgio is perfectly happy with your work and we're making nice money from it."

Lloyd looked up at her, unhappiness written all over his face.

"I know, but all I'm doing is pointing out kids at the school who seem good opportunities for Uncle's people to work on and extract money from them. I don't do anything useful, myself."

---

[2] See "The Death Gambit" by Michael Davies

Anna-Maria sat down next to her husband on the Queen Anne sofa and put her hand on his shoulder. "William, dear, I think I understand. Do you have any ideas of what else you could do?"

"I'd like to find some business line that could make us a lot more money and make Uncle Giorgio think I'm more than just a useful serf." He took another sip of his scotch and stared into the glass.

"He certainly doesn't thank of you that way, William, he told me so. But is there anything you could think of?"

"There's something that has been on my mind." Lloyd put the empty glass on the side table by the sofa and sat up from the disconsolate slump of before. "Two or three years ago, I met a couple of kids at my school. One of them a Chinese kid from Hong Kong had already shown a lot of ability in computer hacking. While I watched them, he broke into the systems of a business in town and stole an expensive dinner voucher and used it to take the two of them and two girls from the local school to dinner. I thought then, that was bloody brilliant for a kid of eighteen and neither of them saw anything wrong in what they did. I bet they're still developing that and it's something we could use."

"Sounds interesting, William. Tell you what, do you know where those boys are now?"

"I know where the Chinese kid is – right here in Manchester at the University. He told me before he finished school that he had a place there."

"And what about the other one?"

"He was Australian, and I know he went back there. I don't know if he was going to university or not, he didn't say."

"Then what I suggest is that you find the boy at university and see where he's at with that skill. I agree, it could be useful. When you're sure of what they can do and that they'll work with us, then talk to Uncle Giorgio. I know he'll be impressed."

"You're sure? I know I'd really like to do something bigger than I'm doing now."

"I'm sure of it and I'll be very proud of you, even more than I am now."

"Good, in that case, be a dutiful wife and pour me another scotch."

She laughed. "Just this once, dear husband."

Falls Church, Virginia, USA, June, 2023

Boon Lee Ng packed his briefcase, his mind working overtime. He had several cases on his mind, most noticeably the analysis he was conducting for a corporation in Chicago with nearly a billion dollars to invest in projects around the world. His commission would run into the hundreds of thousands if he did this well, and so far, his success rate indicated that he would. He felt fit and healthy, quite unlike his condition a year ago when he had been taken to the hospital by ambulance with a severe heart attack. Emergency surgery and a pacemaker implanted solved the problem and he felt fitter than he had in years. The strict diet and exercise routine he had followed since then had taken sixty pounds off him and he resolved to keep it off.

A tremble began in his left leg, spread rapidly to his whole body and he blacked out, luckily falling onto the lounge in his living room. He gradually came to, lying on the couch, sensing waves of panic and much confusion. His cell phone buzzed. Automatically, he reached for it and placed it to his ear.

"Yes," he croaked.

"Back with us, then," said an awful, inhuman voice.

Struggling to comprehend, Boon Lee said nothing.

"I imagine you're pretty shook up by that little episode," continued the robotic voice. "And no doubt wondering how it happened, since you've had no problems after your pacemaker was put in last year."

Boon Lee's head began to clear. "Who the hell are you?" he demanded.

"I'm the guy that just hacked into your pacemaker and stopped your heart for a few seconds."

"Don't talk crap. Nobody can do that."

"Well, I can. And just to prove it, here's another one, just a little one, don't want to kill you yet."

Boon Lee's body shook violently, but he didn't black out. He remained aware of his surroundings and how his body shook, but after only a few seconds, he recovered full consciousness.

"Now do you believe me?" said the toneless voice.

"What do you want?" said Boon Lee, his voice barely a gasp.

"One million dollars."

"I haven't got a million dollars."

"Don't try my patience, Boon Lee. You have this lovely house down by the lake in Falls Church, it's worth nearly two million alone. You have eight million and change in various investments and last year, you earned over eight hundred thousand in commissions. You can find a million bucks in loose change! So here's the thing. Get the million dollars available in the bank, and I'll take it from there, and I assure you, nobody will be able to trace it when it goes. And another thing. If you go to the cops, you'll die. Do you believe me?"

"Yes."

"And one more thing. If I'm forced to kill you this way, nobody will realise what happened. It will be put down to equipment failure, but nobody will be able to find any signs of it, so the hospital and the manufacturers will be greatly embarrassed."

Boon Lee said nothing.

"Okay," said the voice. "Time for you to head off to work. You have to earn all that lovely money. I'll be in touch."

Boon Lee struggled to his feet, his world in chaos.

Richmond, Middlesex, UK, June, 2023

The chairman of one of the biggest accounting firms in the world was having a quiet breakfast with his wife. This was his favourite time in the day and although they didn't speak during the meal, his wife knew that he was deeply immersed in going through the outstanding issues he would face during the day and left him alone, happy that he had the intelligence and dedication to trust her. They would talk it all over when he got home and they shared a quiet drink in the lounge room.

She was right, he was deeply involved in the issues he would face in the next twelve hours. The associate firm in South Africa was showing declining revenues with increasing rates of client failures. The London management consulting department was not as profitable as the audit department and some of the partners were expressing hostility to the fourteen-person operation, none of whom was an accountant. But he knew how much the slightly unconventional group contributed to the service the firm gave its clients and he would fight the partners who wanted to close down the consulting arm. A partner in the US firm had been arrested for sexual misconduct in the office and that office would have to go through the complicated issues of removing him from the partnership, and some embarrassments would reflect on the whole US operation. He anticipated a full day.

The phone rang, shattering the peaceful atmosphere. Both looked up in irritation.

"It's six thirty," said Kaarina. "Could one of the foreign offices have a problem?"

"Possibly. I'll take it." The chairman stood up and walked over to the telephone.

"Good morning, Paavo Hukkinen," said a metallic, inhuman voice. "I'm sure I haven't called too early, knowing your morning habits."

"What are you going to tell me, you silly bastard? You're the Inland Revenue Service? How about some huge bill I haven't paid? Go away, I've heard all these scams before."

"Let's see," said the ugly voice. "You are the chairman of the international accounting firm, Gottfried, Farmer, Reidweg and Deanshaw, known as GFRD for short. You transferred to London two years ago when you were promoted from the top job in the Helsinki firm, your wife is Kaarina and here's the critical point, you had a pacemaker fitted four months ago after the cardiologists detected a slight problem. How am I doing so far?"

"What the hell do you want?"

"Nothing complex, Paavo, just a million pounds."

"*Runkata,* go fuck yourself. You don't get a penny."

"Paavo, I don't know what that means, but I can safely assume it's a deeply offensive Finnish word. But never mind, may I suggest you sit down?"

"Why?"

"Because I'm about to show you how serious I am and why you will pay me a million pounds."

Something in the voice made Paavo sit down, feeling tension rising. A second later, his body began to shake violently, and he blacked out, just as he heard his wife scream in panic.

Later that day, after a check by the emergency ward at the hospital and a discussion with the cardiologist, Hukkinen was convinced the threat was real. There was no failing in the pacemaker and the medical staff were completely baffled by the incident.

Paavo was not a man easily panicked. His father had flown Saab Draken fighters in the Finnish air force and his grandfather had fought in the brutal winter war against Russian invading forces during World War Two and had served with distinction. On returning to his office, he hand-wrote a letter, sealed it in an envelope and looked up the address of the nearest police station. Then he summoned one of the trainee accountants from the audit department. When she arrived, he led her out of the office into the corridor and handed her the envelope.

"Jessica, take this to the police station on the envelope. Tell them it must go to the detectives without being opened. Then come back. Do not ever talk to anyone, not colleagues, not friends, not family about this. Believe me, I will owe you a big favour for this. I'll clear this with your supervisor."

She looked back at him without expression.

Yes, Mr Hukkinen," she said and went to get her coat.

Thirty minutes later, Hukkinen got a phone call.

"Just got your letter," said a man's voice. "Meet me in an hour on the Embankment. I'll recognise you."

Hukkinen replaced the phone without replying.

* * *

"This must be one of the oddest meetings I've had in my years on the job."

The middle-aged man leaned on the railings of the embankment overlooking the Thames. The scene was the usual busy activities as boats of various sizes worked their way up and down stream. Across from where Hukkinen and the detective stood, the impressive SIS building, headquarters of Britain's MI6 dominated the view.

"Whoever is doing this must be one of the cleverest hackers in the business," said Paavo. "This is the only way I can think of to keep out of his view."

"You weren't so stupid either," said the detective. "It was quite a shock to open your letter and the first thing I read in capital letters was *'Keep away from any computers when you read this.'*"

"Probably overkill," said Hukkinen. "But he seems to have hacking skills beyond the ordinary."

"So it seems," said the detective. "And I did as you asked, also, I shredded the letter."

"Thanks for taking me seriously. This seemed the best way to tell you what was going on."

"I chose the location well," said Detective Inspector Burrell. "It's one of the few places where the cameras have a blind spot. Now, tell me everything that's happened."

Chapter 8

Mid North Coast, Australia, June, 2023

Gordon Porter took a seat across from Willoughby's desk and smiled pleasantly.

"Before we start, Chief Superintendent, turn off your computer and disconnect it from the network and turn off your mobile phone."

"What? Why?"

"Please do that before we continue," said Porter. "You will understand soon."

"Good grief," muttered Willoughby but did as he was asked. "Now what?"

"Garry Henderson was one of us," said Porter. "And he called us as soon as he received the first threat, as he was required to do. As you have learnt, the caller used an electronic distortion device. Somehow, the attacker learnt of this contact and killed Henderson with a fatal jolt to the pacemaker. We can only assume that, as the post-mortem showed no fault in the device."

"What did he want?" asked Willoughby.

"Nothing I can reveal to you," replied Porter. "But it was stuff that would harm Australian security if it fell into the wrong hands. So you will understand why we have to take over this investigation. It's also the reason why the Coroner was persuaded to give the verdict she did. We do not wish it known that Bill was murdered and let the killer know that we're aware."

"We understand," said Willoughby, his initial hostility fading. "What about the other blackmail cases?"

"Obviously the same bastard," said Porter. "But they are police matters and the police will investigate them and we need to keep each other up to date so that we do not interfere with each other's investigations. But there's another issue here, you may not like."

"I thought there might be." Willoughby tapped his desk in irritation.

"I had a chat with our opposite numbers in the UK and the USA. While there have been no attacks on any of their members, there have been similar blackmail efforts directed at elderly, wealthy individuals recently fitted with pacemakers. Just one in each country, but more may be expected. Whoever is doing this is just starting this new operation, but we all agree, the level of hacking is exceptional, so much so that we think we know who's behind it."

"Can you tell us?"

"Not yet, but I will, very soon. However, you won't be totally detached from the case. The reason the surgeon from Newcastle called this office is because he knew of the past cases managed by your Detective Inspector Carter. He didn't know all the details, especially the assistance she had from outside sources."

"Ah," said Willoughby. "Now I know why you're here."

"When I've talked to DI Carter, we'll continue to liaise with you and brief you on developments. But we don't want you investigating it yourselves, you might confuse other lines of inquiry that aren't public."

"1 suppose we understand, but you must see that such a limitation is frustrating as hell," said Willoughby.

"I do, and there's another facet to this. Given the talents of this individual, all communications must be kept off the computer network. He has shown his ability to connect to a specific computer and listen in to the discussion, regardless of the firewalls and other safety factors. We'll set up a post office box and send all information by snail mail for you to pick up. You must reply in the same manner. I also must tell you, never discuss the matter in this office. Always go outdoors or use an area where there is no connection to your network. The same at home, do not discuss the matter on the telephone or by any electronic means like email."

"I think I know who you're talking about," said Willoughby. "So I agree with the precautions you've demanded. You've had no further contact with him since DI Carter last dealt with him?

"None at all. As you know, the FBI hunted for him for years while he was in the USA. Then he vanished, created a new identity for himself that fooled every check that could be made and lived in Australia for some years. DI Carter and her team were able to identify him, but just as Immigration went to arrest him, he vanished again. He has since communicated with the police, to assist in uncovering a serial killer, but nobody has been able to locate him, and he's been quiet for a year or so."

"A real bloody wizard, it seems," said Willoughby.

"Very much so," said Porter. "Chief Superintendent, we'll be in touch. Now I must go and talk to the one person who may be able to help us."

* * *

"This doesn't sound like Allen Miller," said Detective Inspector Melanie Carter. "He's not a killer, he's a thief, but a Robin Hood style thief. He's poured millions into charities, and he's only stolen from rich people, corporations and governments."

"Not entirely true," said Porter. "He's kept millions as well and he did kill that woman in your previous case[3]."

"That's true, but she'd organised several murders by her associates and Miller took it upon himself to

---

[3] See "The Ninth of the Month Murders" by Michael Davies

stop her. And he had committed identity theft or as described in his short story, digital death, with his exceptional hacking skills, but that was part of a game. He cleared it up a day later and sent a significant sum to that man's account in compensation."

"All true, Melanie, but this episode calls for skills we haven't seen before. Pacemakers and other devices can be hacked, according to the experts, but only from within a few metres. This man, if it is Miller, has found the ability to hack them from any distance. It's brilliant and that's why we thought of him at once."

"Why would he do this?" asked Melanie. "He doesn't need the money and as I said, he's not a casual killer, nor a blackmailer."

"Can you contact him? Maybe he can show why he's not the culprit."

"I don't have any contact details," said Melanie. "But hey, let's try something." She switched her computer back on after following Porter's order to turn it off, and tapped the monitor, smiling at Porter. "Allen, are you there?" she asked.

"Of course I am, you silly detective." Miller's face appeared on the screen. "Good morning, Melanie. And you too, Special Agent Gordon Porter, how is your day?"

The shock on Porter's face was obvious and his irritation was not helped by Melanie's outburst of laughter.

"Good god," the ASIO agent exclaimed. "How long has he been listening? And does he listen to all your conversations?"

"Only since Melanie turned the computer back on," said Miller. "And no, I don't listen to all Melanie's chats, my system is triggered to notify me if my name is mentioned and then I join in and listen. But otherwise, I don't listen into her conversations."

Melanie watched as Porter obviously struggled for self-control.

"There's no point in getting angry, Mr Porter," she said. "We can't control what Allen does, but so far he's behaved relatively ethically."

Porter cleared his throat. "Okay, Miller, I'll take Melanie's word for it. One question then. Are you the man conducting these attacks on people with pacemakers for blackmail purposes?"

"No, I am not."

"You've stolen millions and killed at least one person. How can I take your word for anything?"

"That's your choice," said Miller. "I've retired from the hacking business and blackmail has never been my thing. Frankly, I'm seriously pissed off that you suspect me."

"Not just me, but a lot of people here, in the USA and in Britain," said Porter. "The consensus was that you were the only person they could think of who could break into hospital medical systems and hack pacemakers remotely."

"I'll take that as some sort of compliment," said Miller. "But like I said, I've retired. I have a shitload of money, so I have no need to blackmail anybody and yes, I did kill somebody once and you know the background to that, so I feel no remorse for that event. But once again, I am not responsible for this business."

Porter seemed to relax.

"Okay, if Melanie speaks for you, I'll accept your word for now. So will you help us find the person responsible? You must be the most qualified of anybody to assist us."

"Yes, Mr Porter, I'll help. I'm disgusted at what has been done and I'm frankly, deeply offended that somebody is apparently almost as good as I am at this business, but using it in this manner."

"Thank you, Mr Miller. Will you give us a contact where we can get in touch with you and update each other with developments?"

"No," said Miller.

"No? Why not? How can we work together if we can't communicate?"

Porter's irritation was showing again.

"You've got some clued-up people in ASIO, just as the CIA and MI6 do," said Miller. "I'm not going to give them any chance of locating me and have you suddenly show up at my door with guns and handcuffs."

"So how the hell are you going to help us?" demanded Porter.

"I'll deal with Melanie and only Melanie," said Miller. "I'm sure your assistant spooks will try and tap into her computer and trace me that way, but I assure you, they'll fail. She can contact me just by saying my name aloud by her computer, just as you saw and I can contact her in my own way, but that's the only communication that will take place."

Porter relaxed again.

"So be it," he said. "I'll send Melanie everything we have so far, so you'll see it also. And I'll make sure that she's in the loop with all our agencies, here and overseas."

"Sounds good," said Miller and his face vanished from the computer screen.

"I think that means we have to do something rather critical with you, Melanie," said Porter.

"Oh? That sounds like things might get difficult," replied Melanie.

"Probably. I have asked the Australian Federal Police to set up a specific anti-terrorist squad to deal with this new situation. They've agreed. But now, with Miller refusing to deal with anyone but you, it seems rational that you should be seconded to this group."

"I can see that," said Melanie. "It puts a lot of responsibility on my shoulders, rather above my pay grade, don't you think?"

Porter smiled. "I do. So I'll be requesting that you be given the acting rank of Chief Inspector for the duration of the case."

Melanie tried not to show any reaction.

"That seems appropriate," she said.

"It does," said Porter. "Congratulations, Chief Inspector Carter. You'll be contacted when you're required for the meeting of that group."

"Something interesting has happened," said Melanie. "Let's have coffee and I'll tell you about it." She waved at the waitress in the little café in which they were seated, well away from other occupied tables. Orders taken, Melanie leaned forward, as did the other two.

"I got a letter this morning. I am seconded to the Australian Federal Police for a time with the rank of Acting Chief Inspector. They decided this case must be a Federal matter, given the people being attacked in several states, especially a Federal officer and we're the single contact with Miller who is thought to be the person best qualified to help in the hunt. They will ignore his illegal methodologies and they hinted at pardons for his other crimes while in Australia. So I'm to be the official liaison with him. I'm going down tomorrow. Jack, can you come too?

"Wouldn't miss it for the world," said Jack.

"Alex, you'll hold the fort here," said Melanie.

Alex nodded.

* * *

Canberra, Australia, July, 2023

Melanie looked round the table. Five pairs of eyes looked back at where she and Jack sat together.

The usual problem, she thought. *Senior blokes, ogling my boobs, impossible for them to accept that I might be competent, even though I look like some Victoria's Secret model. I must remember what Jack once told me – I'm actually a super-dominant. I may need it.*

"Thank you for coming, Acting Chief Inspector Carter," said the senior man at the table. He had introduced himself as Chief Superintendent Blake Harvey. "This is an extraordinary case with serious international repercussions, and we value your help."

"Thank you, sir," she replied. "I will help as much as I can."

"Welcome also to Professor Jack Savage," said Harvey. "Your work is well known to us, and we appreciate your assistance."

Jack nodded but said nothing.

"May I speak, sir?" asked one of the others at the table. He looked in his thirties, medium height, well dressed as were all the AFP Officers. A large forehead was well-displayed by the bald patch that extended back to his crown. He looked irritated.

"Go ahead, Bert," said Harvey.

"Inspector Albert French," said the other. "I have to ask, why do we need the help of a relatively junior State police officer? We're the Australian Federal Police and this is the anti-terrorism group. What does she have that we don't?"

"She's senior to you, Bert," said Harvey. He looked amused. "Would you like to rethink that question or perhaps rephrase it?"

"She's acting in that rank," said French. "My question remains."

Time to check out Jack's observation of my super-dominance, thought Melanie and stood up.

"What I bring to the table is a hell of a lot of experience in serial killers," she said. "I suspect more than you have. I also bring to the table the services of Professor Jack Savage, who has assisted the police forces of several states as arguably the best police profiler in decades. We have worked together for some years. And finally, what I bring to the table is the complete cooperation of the best hacker in the world, Allen Miller. We have talked with Miller and received his assurances that he is not responsible for these events. But he won't work with anyone but me. Does that answer your question, Inspector French?"

She stared at the other officer and watched as his eyes switched from looking back at her to looking down at his hands and his posture seemed to crumble a little. His mouth opened a couple of times.

"Er... yes, Ma'am," he replied and sat down, his face flushed.

"Thank you," said Melanie and returned to her seat. She looked down and saw Jack give her a thumbs up gesture under the table. She fought the impulse to laugh out loud. *You've still got it, girl,* she thought. She looked round the table and saw that the expressions had changed. She decided she might now be accepted as a real police officer.

"This is early days," said Harvey. "All we know so far is that somebody, one or more persons, has discovered how to hack into implanted pacemakers and cause heart stoppages leading to death as a blackmail method. We also know that it's not who we suspected, Allen Miller, long considered the best computer hacker in the world. Which makes the potential criminals a very short list. It seems the hackers are attacking people for financial returns and in one case, also for government information. The latter example may indicate further cases of that nature. We have decided that the police will work closely with the security forces, in our case ASIO, but also with MI6 in Britain and the CIA in the USA."

"One massive worry is that the media will hear of this," said a middle-aged man to Melanie's right.

"This is true," said Harvey. "You're right to be worried, Keith. And if they do, there's nothing we can do about it. The good old days of being able to slap a Schedule "D" on the media and keep them silent are over. We can only ask them to moderate the hysteria when they do find out."

"It could cause mass panic all over the world," said the man named Keith. "How many thousands of these things are in use all over the world?"

"About 700,000 new ones a year now but they started in the 60s," said Harvey. "But if and when they find out, we'll have to cooperate, but give out as little information as we can." He looked slowly round the table. "Okay, meeting closed, people. Chief Inspector Carter, Professor Savage, thank you for coming and letting us get to know you both. We'll be in contact when we need to meet again, but meanwhile we will both share whatever information we get, right?"

"For sure," said Melanie and stood up, well aware that every male eye was focussed on her as she and Jack left the room.

Phase Three

A New Stage in the War

Chapter 9

Cheshire Countryside, UK, August, 2023

William Lloyd had never got over the slight spasm of worry he felt when he heard Giorgio Grassano's voice over the phone. It was a reminder that he was involved in one of the greatest organised crime groups in the world and was always under observation for his performance. But this time, his fear was alleviated almost at once.

"William, you have been doing some good work for us," said Grassano. "The family has profited from your assistance in identifying likely candidates for our attentions."

Lloyd knew that meant that many of the young people at the school he had identified as likely candidates for blackmail of their parents had fulfilled his aims and the family had applied pressures either through blackmail or simple threats to earn significant sums.

"Thank you, Uncle," he said, hiding the slight gasp of relief he felt. "It has pleased me to help my wife's family."

"And profited you, also, of course," said Grassano.

Lloyd thought he detected a vein of mockery in the Mafia boss's voice but said nothing.

"And those two young men you recommended to us have proved enormously valuable," continued Grassano. "They have contributed to our coffers from their share of the work they do. That's considerable genius there, William, we are most grateful."

"Thank you, Uncle," Lloyd said again. "I always thought they would prove valuable."

"Indeed they have. But I've been thinking, and I believe they could raise their game by a large amount with a slight change in focus."

"I'm interested to hear what you have in mind," said Lloyd.

"Getting a few thousand certainly helps, but it's time we used the genius they have shown by changing the target and calling for returns of far greater value. I want you to tell them to start targeting people in the high echelons of government or security and demand invaluable data from which we can profit enormously."

Lloyd was startled. He hadn't thought of this approach.

"That's brilliant, Uncle. But surely that will have higher risks. Such people would have great resources to assist them."

"The fear of death conquers all, William."

"Actually, I have something to add to that, Uncle. The Australian boy told his friend that he has developed great skill in creating scenes involving people which are indistinguishable from real life. What if we ask him to create scenes of high-level people, like politicians or top executives apparently involved in serious sex play or such like? I suspect such people fear disgrace more than death."

There was a short pause on the phone. Lloyd held his breath.

"William, I bow to the master," said Grassano. "That is truly brilliant, I congratulate you. Get onto your colleagues and tell them to get started. Have the Australian identify likely candidates and develop suitably destructive films."

"Can they continue to extort money from them as well as useful data?"

"Certainly, under the same terms they have had from the start. The money must be sent to the family accounts in the Caymans and they will receive the same returns as before. But if we make profits from the data they obtain, they will be suitably rewarded."

"I'll tell them that, Uncle."

"Good. Advise Anna-Maria when they are ready to begin the new operations, she will tell me."

"I'll do that, Uncle."

Lloyd put down the phone, breathing a sigh of relief that he had placed himself in Grassano's good books and would not have to talk to him again for some time.

* * *

"Peter, I have some new instructions for you."

"What new instructions? I thought you were the only ones who know us and what we're doing. Who are you to tell us to do something differently?"

Lloyd could clearly hear the irritation in Chang's voice.

"You may be my only channel, Peter, but remember who I report to. And they're the ones with new instructions."

"Yeah, I know you're in deep with some crime mob and that's who funded us all this equipment, but it still gives me the shits that I have to pay the proceeds into their bank account and then get just a portion of it back."

"Remember that Phillip and I both get a share from this and you would not have the protections and support without the people behind us. These people have a lot of influence with the people who might be your enemies."

"I suppose so." Chang didn't sound fully convinced.

"Peter, don't even think about striking out on your own. Believe me, they'll soon find out who you are and where and you won't like what they do."

"You'd tell them?"

"Of course I would. You think I want my fingernails being pulled out or a couple of toes chopped off with garden shears?"

There was a moment's silence from the speaker in Hong Kong.

"Okay," said Chang at last. "What are we going to do?"

Lloyd outlined Grassano's instructions and added further requirements for Phillip Murray in Australia to develop suitable films.

"Okay, we'll do it." Lloyd could hear the resentment in Chang's voice but knew that the younger man was frightened by what he had heard and tempted by the money.

Falls Church, Virginia, USA, September, 2023

James Deverall knew that the awful, inhuman voice would stay in his memory for many years. The first call had come in his home telephone in North Virginia one sunny Friday morning, just after his wife, Cherie had left to take their six-year-old daughter to school.

"About to leave for work, James?" said the distorted voice in his ear. "I imagine your secretary at the China Desk in the CIA will make you a coffee as soon as you arrive."

"Who the hell is this?" snapped Deverall. He was unnerved by the call, both because the voice was quite frightening and because nobody outside of work knew of his position with the CIA.

"No need for you to know that, James. But I know all about you, your wife Cherie and your gorgeous little daughter, Zoë. She's just six, right? And I imagine you had some social problems working on your doctorate in Asian Affairs at Princeton. Hard for a black man working with those whitey academics in such a rarefied field, was it?"

"Listen, you bastard, you're making one hell of a mistake playing this game with me," said Deverall. "This is the CIA. You think we won't be able to track you down? We don't like jerks like you threatening us."

"One more thing I know about you, James," said the hideous voice, ignoring the comment. "You had a new heart valve installed six months ago and then a pacemaker. Now, this is what I can do with your pacemaker."

Deverall felt a sharp pain in his chest, and he blacked out.

When he recovered, he found that he was sitting on the floor, his back against his armchair, his phone still in his hand. The metallic voice spoke again.

"That lasted just a couple of seconds, James, but believe me, I can make it permanent with just a touch of a button. So here's the thing, James. I want some information from you. It's stuff right in your area of expertise and I'll send you a list of requirements to your work computer. I promise you, nobody will be able trace where my messages are coming from and they'll only stay for a few seconds. If you try and tell your bosses, believe me, I'll kill you. Do you understand?"

Taking a deep breath and struggling to control his fear, Deverall managed to say, "Yes" in a croak.

"Good," said the voice. "Time for you to leave for work. You don't want to make Cherie suspicious by being here when she gets home. You're a man of strict routine and you need to stay that way."

Saying nothing, Deverall got to his feet, picked up his briefcase, found his car keys and left the house for the drive to the CIA headquarters at Langley.

He knew exactly what he had to do.

London, UK, September, 2023

Shirley James was feeling blue. Her husband Craig, was away again, this time a three-week tour of Europe to sell-out audiences who loved his playing of the Rachmaninov piano concertos and the works of Chopin. While financial returns were excellent, she was left alone during these increasingly frequent absences, and they were proving stressful. But her work at the Russia Desk of MI6 was engrossing, even if that too was becoming more and more demanding after Putin had invaded the Ukraine and thrown the whole world into confusion. The need for a pacemaker had been sudden and frightening, but after six months, she never noticed its presence.

But now she did.

The jolt in her chest threw her forward onto her desk, her face bruising from the computer keyboard. She had no idea how long she was blacked out but as she came to, she felt an overwhelming sense of fear. Was she about to die? How would anyone find her? How would Craig learn of it?

The telephone rang, driving a painful dagger through her head and she forced herself to pick it up. Working for the British security services for some years had taught her never to ignore the telephone and the training was firmly drilled into her.

"Good morning, Shirley," said the voice in the phone. It was ugly, a distorted voice using electronic means to disguise the speaker. It sounded robotic, inhuman. "How do you feel after that little shock?"

Shirley's fear increased. She could imagine a scenario where a security officer of her seniority would be attacked for blackmail, there were many examples in the files of MI6. She said nothing, struggling to regain her composure.

"Now, believe it or not, Shirley, I caused that little episode. I can do it again at the touch of a button and I can make it far worse if I want to, and I will want to if you try and tell your colleagues. You won't survive that, I assure you. In a few days, I will call again to tell you what I want you to do. If I see that your phone is tapped, I will kill you immediately. Do you understand?"

Deciding not to answer, Shirley put the phone down. She had to get to work.

* * *

Canberra, Australia, September, 2023

Hugh Russell, senior agent in the Australian Signals Directorate, drove into Canberra, his mind in a turmoil. The shock to his pacemaker, followed by the terrifying threat by a disembodied, distorted voice had frightened him beyond anything he had experienced in the jungles of Vietnam.

But he knew what he had to do. And he knew the risk he faced. Slowly, he worked out a plan.

Langley, Virginia, USA, September, 2023

James Deverall walked into the office of his superior. He said nothing in reply to the friendly greeting from the man he had known for three decades, but placed a sheet of paper on the desk. Raising an eyebrow in query, the other man picked up the sheet. It read:

'DO NOT SPEAK – I AM SURE YOUR PHONE AND YOUR PC ARE HACKED. MEET ME IN THE SECURE ROOM.'

Deliberately, the senior agent fed the sheet into the shredder by his desk, stood up and the two men walked down the corridor to the secure room. It was used for meetings where no chance could be taken of eavesdroppers, hackers or any other possible breach of security. The walls and ceiling were thickly soundproofed, there was not a telephone, nor a computer terminal of any sort and the room was swept for bugs several times a day.

"What the hell is going on?" asked the older man.

James took very few words to explain.

"Fuck," said his boss.

* * *

Feeling her insides crawling with worry, Shirley James reached her office, scrawled a message on a sheet of paper and walked to her superior's room. Placing the paper on the desk, she held a finger to her lips as her boss stared in astonishment. But she fed the paper into her shredder and joined her colleague in the soundproofed room that had no computers, no telephones, not even a power point and was scanned for bugs at least four times a day at random intervals, a room almost identical to the one at the CIA.

The two women stood in the middle of the room as Shirley spoke.

"Oh Christ," said the senior woman.

Chapter 10

Canberra, Australia, September, 2023

Three faces looked out of the computer monitor on Gordon Porter's desk.

"It suggests that our hacker has moved from financial rewards to something far more dangerous," said Jerome Knight of the CIA. "The latest attack was on one of our best China experts."

"Was any demand made?" asked Porter.

Knight shook his head. "Just a warning of future demands to be made and met, or else. Our man was given a nasty jolt to his pacemaker and told his life was at risk if he told anyone."

"The same with a specialist in the Russian Section," said Jacqui Simmons. "She did the right thing, told us by using the secure room. No demands as yet, but threats of death if she doesn't comply when they come."

"Same here," said Porter. "I hope to god whoever is doing this is unable to break into this network."

"Damned impossible," said Knight. "We've got the most secure systems in the world, something the Israelis developed, and I know you have the same. We're safe."

A fourth face appeared on the screens of all of them.

"I don't think so," said Allen Miller. "You've probably just killed three top agents."

* * *

James Deverall's phone rang in his car. He touched the button on his dashboard.

"You fool," said the awful, metallic voice. "I warned you."

James blacked out. His car swerved across the road into oncoming traffic and hit a heavy truck. The vehicle was slung forward and crashed into a car a few yards ahead, skidded to the side and hit a tree. The truck slammed on its brakes and came to a screeching stop as did most of the other cars on the road.

The driver reached for his phone.

* * *

"Stupid woman," said the robotic voice in Shirley James' phone. "You're no use to me now. I did warn you."

Shirley collapsed to the floor of her kitchen. The smoke from her kitchen warned her neighbour who called the fire station.

* * *

Hugh Russell reached for the phone on his desk.

"You fucking idiot," said the ugly voice. "You're dead."

Hugh fell forward onto his desk, his body shaking violently.

It was an hour before anyone came to his office and found him.

Chapter 11

Cheshire, UK, October, 2023

"Uncle Giorgio says he's delighted with what you are doing with the boys," said Anna-Maria. She had come into Lloyd's study to bring him his regular evening scotch and found him at his desk.

Lloyd turned to greet her, accepted the drink, took a sip and placed it by the computer.

"What are you doing?" she asked.

"I'm going through the list of people Uncle has asked us to consider as targets for the boys to attack."

"He didn't tell me about that," said Anna-Maria. "What's it all about?"

"The family has told me to have the boys step up the business, not just blackmailing for money, but now to get high-level information they can use for seriously big hits."

"Wow," she said. "That sounds great. Who have you got so far?"

"Some people in the British government, the Australian government and a couple of spooks in the American security services."

"Does it have to be Chang and Murray who do it?"

"For sure. Chang's the one who developed the secure systems and he's still the best hacker we've got. He showed Murray how to do it as well."

"But can't you do some of this?" Anna-Maria seemed disappointed.

"I could," said Lloyd. "Chang sent me the same set of sub-routines he gave Murray, so that all I need to do is enter the name of the target person and it will do all the hacking into that person's computer."

"What about disguising yourself?"

"Dead easy. Look what I bought in the mall the other day." Lloyd reached under his desk and pulled out a mask of a horrible face, the one commonly seen at parties and rallies, a huge wide smile, a frightening, malignant expression.

"Ooh!" she exclaimed, feigning terror. "That's great. What about the voice?"

"Also easy. I downloaded a program that distorts the voice. Chang and Murray have used these a couple of times and it makes it impossible to identify us."

"This is really fun, William. How you plan to use all this?"

"I've already done a couple of trials, just small stuff, calling up a couple of wealthy people I knew in Birmingham. I got a few thousands from them."

"I'd love to try this myself. Could I do something?"

Lloyd laughed. "I thought you would. Tell you what, there's a bloke in Australia, works for the Prime Minister's Department." He pointed at a name on the computer screen. "Uncle wants to get some stuff from him. The suggestion is that he gets a call on his computer, gets a warning jolt and then told we'll contact him later for some government information. How about you make that first call? Chang will call him later when Uncle has told him what information he wants, but the two voices will sound exactly the same, he'll never tell the difference."

She laughed. "I'd love to. What do I do?"

"I just call up the program Chang sent me. If that bloke answers, he'll see you, but you'll have the mask on and I'll set the distortion program going. Just tell him we can kill him at any time, give him a small jolt and then tell him we'll get back to him for some information."

"How do I give him a jolt?"

"Easy, press the number one for a small jolt, which is what you'll give him as a warning. Two is a severe one that could knock them out for a while, three will kill them. make sure you only press one, we need this man for later use."

"Sounds easy." She put the mask on, waved him away from his desk and took his seat. "Let's go," she said.

Canberra, Australia, October, 2023

James Falwell found his work fascinating, engrossing and sometimes exhausting. Working in the Prime Minister's office meant he was in daily contact with some of the most powerful people in Australia and knew almost everything about the inner workings of the government. Some of the information scared him, occasionally disgusted him, but mostly he loved the fact that he was part of the government, regardless of which political party was in office.

He was up early that morning, well before seven, knowing he had a full day ahead of him. The Cabinet was meeting at eleven and he still had to put the finishing touches to a briefing document he had prepared. He was staring thoughtfully at the computer monitor, weighing up the phrasing of one part, when the document was replaced by a face. It was not a human face, it was a mask, a white mask with a wide, thin smile and a thin beard and moustache. Falwell could make out the eyes behind the mask, but not well enough to tell the colour.

"Good morning, James," said a voice. Like the mask, it was not human, but a distorted, electronic voice.

"Who the hell are you?" he snapped, feeling anxiety

run through him. He had been assured that the security system on his computer was foolproof, nobody could break in. Despite the fear caused by this intrusion, he remembered the instructions of the security experts who had installed the firewall on his computer. He pressed the button hidden under the edge of his desk.

"I'm the man who is going to get all your secrets," said the robotic voice.

"Like hell you are," said Falwell. "Get off my computer. The security people will trace you in no time and you'll be in a cell soon after."

"No chance," said the voice. "Let me demonstrate why you'll give me what I want."

Falwell's heart briefly stopped and he fell forward on his keyboard. He had no idea how much time had passed when he recovered, but his computer monitor showed no more than a minute or two.

"You see, James," said the voice. "I know you had a pacemaker fitted a few months ago and I can stop it any time I want. Next time I call you, I'll tell you what I want from you."

The evil face vanished and Falwell's document returned to the screen.

Shaking, Falwell took a few minutes to try and recover his composure and finish the paper.

Cheshire, UK, October, 2023

"Hooo-*eeee*! exclaimed Anna-Maria as she took off the mask, revealing sparkling eyes and a wide, excited smile. "William, that was *fantastic*. I've never done anything like that before. Seeing him get so frightened and knowing I was the one causing his heart shiver, that was just the *best*."

She picked up William's half-empty glass of scotch by the side of the computer and sank it in one gulp. "Jesus, William, I've never been so turned on in my life," she said. "Let's go to bed."

Chapter 12

London, UK, October, 2023

Cabinet Minister Rodney Barker-Swanson looked in satisfaction in the mirror as his wife brushed down his Saville Row suit. He checked the Double Windsor knot in his Marylebone Cricket Club tie and smiled.

"Got to look good for a major speech," he said.

"And you look magnificent, my dear," she said, standing back to check her handiwork. "I have no doubt the whole of Parliament will be impressed, especially the Prime Minister and you will put the fear of god into those dreadful queers and sexual perverts who are destroying this country."

"I believe you are correct, Prudence," he said. "Now, let me check my emails once more and a final run through my speech before the limousine arrives."

"I'll make some more coffee," she said. "I'll bring it in fifteen minutes." She walked to the door and quietly left.

The Minister sat down at his desk and brought up his emails. He was not expecting anything new, but he wanted to read through his speech once more. Instead of the emails, a face filled the screen. It was actually a mask, white, with black eyebrows, wide mouth and a thin, black beard and moustache.

"Good morning, Minister," said the intruder. The voice was dreadful, metallic, distorted, alien, and the Minister felt a deep disturbance in his gut. "Not what you were expecting, I imagine."

"Who the hell are you?" Barker-Swanson's voice was harsh from the shock.

"Your worst nightmare," said the evil mask in the screen.

"What? Explain yourself, you perverted criminal. How dare you break into my system? It's supposed to be completely secure."

"Nothing is secure to me, Minister. I was reading your speech as you wrote it last night. You really want to say all those unpleasant things to the country?"

The Minister was too shocked to reply.

"You're really going to attack all the poor gays and lesbians and transgenders and demand that they be rounded up and put in prison? That's not very nice, is it?"

Barker-Swanson found his voice. "They're destroying the country. All this same-sex rubbish, men and women having sex before they're married, these homosexuals, they should all be killed."

"Well now, Rodney, that's all a bit extreme. I want you to watch something, I'm sure you'll find it interesting."

The frightening face shrank to occupy just a corner of the screen and something else took its place. For a moment, Barker-Swanson struggled to make out what was happening. Finally, he realised it was a large room, filled with couches, all occupied by naked bodies, always two at a time. With increasing horror, he realised some of the pairs were both men or both women, all engaged in violent love-making, emitting cries of passion. Into the middle of the screen came two men, both naked. With a gasp of dismay, he realised one of the men was himself. The two men stood with arms round each other's shoulders and the unknown second man smiled into the camera.

"Hello there," he said. "Let me introduce you to my lover, Minister Rodney Barker-Swanson. Isn't he handsome?"

The two men turned to each other and exchanged a passionate kiss. Barker-Swanson felt nauseated.

"That can't be me," he stammered. "I've never done anything like that."

"Well, Rodney, you know that and I know that, but when I broadcast that on social media, do you think anyone will believe you? Technology is so wonderful, isn't it? One can create anything these days."

"That will destroy me totally," said Barker-Swanson. "What do you want?"

"For now, Rodney, you won't make that speech. Frankly, it doesn't matter to me whether you do or you don't, this is just a little demonstration of the power I have, but I'll keep that little movie safe and secure for possible future use. And now and again, I'll call you and tell you what I want."

"You want money? How much? I'll pay anything."

"Oh Rodney, Rodney, I have as much as I need and don't you think I can take whatever I want from banks and corporations any time I want? No, what I'll want some time soon will be information about what your government is planning, or I'll tell you what I want you to propose to your cabinet. Anyway, I think your transport is here. Remember, not that speech! And of course, I hardly need to tell you not to discuss our little matter with anyone, not the Prime Minister, not any of your colleagues, not the spooks, nobody. Otherwise, have a nice day."

The screen went blank.

Chapter 13

Washington DC, USA, October, 2023

Senator Dwight F. Kendricks III played at his computer on a quiet Sunday evening. His wife was away at a general meeting of the local branch of the Daughters of the Revolution, and he had the house to himself. He treasured these evenings, the only time he could access the pornography channels and watch his favourite topic, lesbians making love to each other with a variety of toys, while he consumed a large amount of his vodka and tonic mix.

To his dismay, the extraordinary scene faded and was replaced by an evil-looking mask staring straight at him. The Senator sat back with a small gasp of shock.

"Good evening, Senator." The voice was distorted, ugly, obviously the result of an electronic security device. "Are you enjoying the adventures of Amy and Delilah? They are rather lovely, aren't they?"

"Who the hell are you?" spluttered the Senator. "This is a secure line, get the fuck out of here."

"Oh you poor, dumb thing," said the electronic voice. "You think that the firewall the FBI installed in your computer could keep an expert out? I assure you, I've been reading your emails and checking on your viewing habits for weeks. Why is it that members of your party are such ignorami with technology?"

Kendricks felt a cold, sinking feeling in his gut. "What the hell do you want?" he grated.

"Not a lot," said the mask. "Not for now, anyway. I just want you to watch this speech you appear to have made. For a devout hater of abortion, queers, same-sex marriage and coloured people, it's quite fascinating."

The mask shrank into the bottom, right-hand corner of the screen and was replaced by a scene of a crowd watching a man at the podium. Initially, the camera appeared to be at the rear of the venue and the speaker was not easily identified, but the focus quickly centred on the speaker and grew closer until Kendricks recognised himself. He couldn't think of just when this was taken.

"My fellow Americans," said the image of the Senator. "It's time I told you some facts about myself. The first thing is that I'm a total fraud."

A buzz of interest ran through the auditorium.

"What the hell is this?" exploded the Senator, rising to his feet and knocking over his glass of vodka. "I've never said anything of the sort. What the fuck are you playing at?"

"Do calm down," said the distorted voice. "Keep listening and watching, it gets a lot better."

Despite his rage, Kendricks resumed his seat.

"Back when I was a student at Illinois State," continued the image of the Senator, "I got three women pregnant. I told all of them they had to get rid of it, I was not going to be charged with rape, which it really was. I paid for all three abortions. Later, soon after I got married, I had an affair with our African-American maid and the same happened. She had an abortion at my expense before I got rid of her."

The buzz in the auditorium grew louder.

"It gets worse," continued the image on the screen. "I was always attracted to children, I couldn't help it, both girls and boys. I have molested several children in my time, but paying them and their parents to keep quiet has always saved me."

Kendricks rose to his feet again, in absolute terror.

"I've never done any of those things," he shouted. "I've never said that. How the hell did you get that?"

The mask emitted a laugh and returned to filling the screen.

"Dead easy," the appalling voice said. "It's quite simple technology. Anyone can be shown to have said anything. And while you might claim that, just imagine the results if I broadcast that on all the various social media outlets."

"For god's sake, what do you want?" Kendricks' voice was reduced to a whisper, recognising his entire life could be over, subject to national disgrace, evicted from the Republican Party with no chance of redemption.

"For now, nothing," said the mask. "This was just to let you know that I can do it and I must admit, I did enjoy making that little movie. But at times, I'll call you and let you know what I want. It could be your vote in the Senate for a Bill you don't like at all and your party would oppose, or something similar that would result in very unpleasant reactions in the Senate and among your voters. It will be such fun, for me, if not for you. Meanwhile, I don't have to tell you that if you try and pass the details of our little chat to the President, or FBI or anyone in Congress, I'll release that movie to the world. Good night, Senator."

The mask disappeared, replaced with the scenes of lesbian love-making that had been there before. But Kendricks had no further interest in watching. He turned the computer off, picked up his glass from the floor and refilled it with vodka, draining the contents in one gulp. He repeated this several times before staggering off to bed.

* * *

Canberra, Australia, October, 2023

Gordon Porter visited the desks of his direct reports. With each, he left a handwritten note that he had prepared beforehand. Saying nothing, he placed the paper in front of his subordinates. It said, *'Secure room, ten minutes.'* His staff were well trained in the ways of security services, they said nothing, simply nodded at Porter and prepared to leave their desks. A few minutes later, they were all in the soundproofed room that was bare of all communication devices and had been swept for bugs just fifteen minutes earlier, as instructed by Porter with a similar silent command.

"We've got a feral hacker loose," said Porter. "At first, we and our brethren in MI6 and the CIA assumed it was Allen Miller, such was the degree of skill required to do what was being done, but I am assured by Miller himself that he is not guilty."

"You spoke to Miller?" One of the agents voiced the astonishment that they all showed in their faces.

"I did, courtesy of Detective Chief Inspector Melanie Carter, you've heard of her, and she is the only person Miller will deal with. But to update you, I had a short three-way chat with Jerome Knight of the CIA and Jacqui Simmons of MI6. Somebody has learnt how to hack into pacemakers and cause heart problems and there have been a few cases of blackmail being applied to certain individuals. These names came up as one of them was a colleague of ours in the Signals Directorate, Garry Henderson who reported immediately to his office. The other two were civilians who contacted the police, all three had pacemakers fitted in recent months. All three died soon after."

"Good god, boss, you mean the hacker was somehow listening in to the conversation?" The speaker was a middle-aged man with almost pure white hair. "Our international networks are supposed to be tighter than a duck's arse."

"That's what we thought. But it was Allen Miller who broke in to make his point. We're leaking."

"That's rather alarming," said the agent.

"Thank you for understating the case," said Porter to a low round of laughs around the room. "But the attack on Bill Henderson indicates that the hacker may switch his attacks to secret service individuals, possibly people in high government circles and similar in at least the UK, the USA and ourselves. That means maximum   alertness   and   careful,   secure communications between us."

"But if...."

Porter cut short the objection from the other agent.

"Exactly," he said. "That's why we're here. And this is how we'll proceed as information of similar attacks reaches us. First, you write the information by hand. You take two photocopies, as we know the photocopiers are not connected to the network and cannot be hacked. One copy goes in the safe, the other comes to me. Any such documents will be taken by diplomatic bag to our colleagues in Langley and London by the next available airline. Similar discussions are taking place there and we'll receive any information the same way. That's slow, but it's secure. If you want to discuss the matters, we do it here, nowhere else. Somehow, some time, we'll get something that may point to whoever is doing this. And here's what I want you to do."

He paused and looked round his staff. He could see that he had their full attention.

"Walk around the offices. That means here, Defence Department, Parliament House and as many social gatherings of pollies and others that you can get to. Find excuses to have casual chats with everybody who may have access to information that we would not want leaked. You've all been trained, look carefully for signs of stress. If you see any, somehow manoeuvre the person outdoors, well away from any computer device, try and find a location with surrounding noise and turn on your localised mobile phone signal blocker and see what you can get. Okay, that's it, get your lazy arses back to work."

The agents left the room silently, clearly lost in thought about the possibilities of what was happening.

Chapter 14

London, England, October, 2023

Cabinet Minister Rodney Barker-Swanson always felt a wave of terror any time he sat before his computer at home. Since the call from the evil mask that had somehow broken through the claimed impenetrable fire wall that the security people had installed, he was frighteningly aware that his career and his whole life were now at the mercy of somebody who could destroy him with ease if he didn't obey whatever commands would be given him. He had spent many hours trying to work out what he could do if and when the crisis came.

This Sunday morning, his fears rose up and smashed him as the mask appeared on his monitor.

"Good morning, Minister," said the mask. The tones were as before, distorted, metallic, unidentifiable. "I trust you are enjoying this fine English day."

Swanson's hand was still on the mouse. He took a deep breath and slowly moved the cursor to a newly-installed icon. *Would the caller be able to recognise the movement or what it signified?* Swanson prayed silently, but there was no reaction.

"And so, Minister," continued the ugly voice. "Time for you to do something for me and save your career. You will prepare for me a summary of the top five biggest financial expenditures the British Government is planning for the next financial year."

"What the hell do you want those for?" said Swanson. His voice was grating, raw with tension.

"I have clients waiting for them. They pay well and I get considerable other benefits from servicing their needs."

"And if I don't get them?"

"Rodney, Rodney, don't be more stupid than your normal self. You know what I can do to you. A day or two after I release that action movie of you, you'll have to resign from Parliament and that lovely income, the pensions that come with it, a potential knighthood and all the other goodies, all will be gone. So will your wife, the home, everything. Your life will be total crap. To be honest, the only thing left for you will be to take a hot bath and slit your wrists."

Swanson knew very well how true that forecast would be.

"And when I have all that?"

"You have ten days, Rodney. I'll call you then, have the information in big letters on regular computer paper and you'll hold each sheet before the camera."

Swanson nodded. He knew that he was about to risk everything, but he also knew where his duty lay. "I'll do what I can," he said.

"Better succeed, Minister. The alternative is too awful to consider."

The mask disappeared and Swanson realised he was sweating. He moved the cursor back to the icon where it had been, pressed the button and pulled the flash memory drive from its slot. He had to take a shower.

Jacqui Simmons advanced on Swanson where he was standing by the entrance to the MI6 building.

"I'm..." he began, but she put a finger to his lips.

"I know who you are. That's why I'm here and not a more junior person. It was wise of you to come wearing a mask from Covid days and a floppy hat. Come with me."

Two minutes later, Swanson was in the secure room. He looked around him. The room was bare of furniture other than a round conference table that could seat a dozen people. There were no computer terminals, no phones, no pictures on the wall.

"Take a seat," said Simmons. Her voice was curiously deadened, devoid of depth and Swanson assumed the room was sound-proofed. As he sat down, she took a seat across from him as four people walked in and also sat down.

"These people are all MI6 and completely secure," said Simmons. "You don't need to know their names, but they know why you have come. I commend your courage, Minister. But I am curious. There is no record that you have had a pacemaker installed at any time in your life."

"A pacemaker? No, of course not. Why do you say that?"

"Interesting," said Simmons. "Not a pacemaker. This is new. What threat has been applied?"

"You seem to know a hell of a lot about why I'm here," said Swanson.

"We do. A white masked individual has appeared on your computer monitor and demanded something of great value. The voice is seriously distorted. But you don't have a pacemaker, so you were not subjected to a jolt to the heart to show you what will happen if you don't do as you're told."

"This has happened elsewhere," said Swanson.

"It has."

"The threat is a made-up video of me taking part in homosexual orgies. It looks completely realistic, but it is most certainly fictitious. If I do not provide certain information, that video will be broadcast around the country on social media. It will destroy me."

"That's new," said Simmons. "Have specific demands been made?"

"After the first call, I installed a recording application," said Swanson. "Luckily, when he called this second time, I already had my hand on the mouse and I was able to start the recording without him noticing."

Swanson took out the USB device and laid it on the table. Simmons nodded at one of her agents who left, returning a few minutes later with a laptop computer. He placed it on the table, switched it on and inserted the USB.

"That computer is totally without communication facilities," said Simmons. "This room is soundproofed. Okay if we play this?"

Swanson nodded and watched as she started the recording. Despite his own knowledge of the false images, he couldn't help but feel awful embarrassment as the scene played out.

"Again, please believe me," he said, his voice hoarse from the tension he felt. "That is totally fictitious."

"Not to worry, Minister," said Simmons. "We know how such films can be made, and an expert examination will show that it really is manufactured."

"I hope so," said Swanson.

"Some things I can tell you," said Simmons. "This has happened in the USA and Australia. The other events have been related to pacemakers, threats of hacking into the devices and causing massive pain and in some cases, death. This blue-mail, as we call it is a new development."

"I'm risking everything by coming here," said Swanson.

"We know, and we are going to do everything possible to help you. In Australia, a similar demand was made on somebody in a similar position to yours. The ASIO people bodged up some faked information that sounded quite real and that was shown to the blackmailer. The threat there was interference in the pacemaker and we managed to avoid that. But the information provided caused some international tensions and we've already prepared some faked stuff for when it happened here. And now it has."

"You've been expecting me?" said Swanson, feeling a mix of worry and relief that help might be on the way.

"It was only a matter of time before somebody in a position like yours was attacked. So we went ahead and thought out what sort of high-level information might be demanded and prepared some possible scenarios. Here's what we will give you. We will indicate several high budget government plans. One will show a plan to invest heavily in Littoral Ships for the British Coastguard. These are ships designed for coastal patrols, flat-bottomed, very fast and several countries use them, mostly for drug interdiction. A second plan will purport to start building a new satellite town in the Midlands, designed for the internet era with ultra-fast networks, fully equipped with shops, cinemas, schools, etc., to permit almost everybody to work from home without the need to commute to the major cities. There are a few more and their value will be to see who reacts to them. That will help identify who sells them that information."

"Good grief," said Swanson. "I had no idea that this crap was taking place around the world. So you're already dealing with ASIO and the CIA?"

"We are. It's a very dangerous situation. Somebody has technical skills beyond almost anything we've encountered before."

"Almost?"

"Initially, as this began, we all tended to assume it was a man who has demonstrated these talents in the past. But let's say we are now sure it's not him, in fact he's helping us hunt down the hacker."

"But what if you don't find him and the bastard does broadcast this film all over the world?"

"We'll prepare a detailed group of experts who will make it a point of loudly and frequently proclaiming in all media that the film is faked. It should make the point."

"God, I hope so."

"Okay, Minister, we'll give you the documents on the way out. We'll escort you to a very small exit which we know is not covered by traffic cameras, so nobody will be able to see you, but put on the hat and mask again, just in case. Thank you again for coming, you've been a massive help."

Chapter 15

Canberra, Australia, November, 2023

"I'm delighted you could both come down for this," said Gordon Porter.

"Wouldn't miss it for the world," said Melanie. "This is a real chance for a breakthrough in this awful business."

"And as Jack has known Professor Ruth Blackston for many years, she pretty well demanded you be here, Jack."

"Since student days," said Jack. "I was finishing off my doctorate when Ruth got her bachelor's degree in linguistics. We dated for a year or two."

"So she told me," said Porter. "Your reputation was a bit wild and woolly in those days, she said."

"That's interesting," said Melanie. "Jack, you need to tell me about those days some time."

"Possibly," said Jack. "Or not."

"Okay, let's head into the secure room," said Porter. "Ruth's all set up in there."

He led the way from the lobby where Melanie and Jack had undergone full security checks and opened the heavy door that was the only entrance to the secure room. Seated at a table with a variety of electronic equipment was an older woman in casual jeans and sweater, a headphone over her ears and a notepad and pen at her side. At the entrance of the three people, she took off the headphones and stood up.

"Hey, you old bastard, it's good to see you," she said and walked into a bear hug from Jack.

"It's been a few years," he said and kissed her cheek. "You done good, kid, Australia's leading expert on linguistics, no less."

"You haven't done too badly yourself," she replied. "I knew you'd be okay, once you stopped the binge drinking and womanising."

"Hey, no secrets," he said with a wide smile.

"And this is Detective Chief Inspector Melanie Carter," said Ruth, smiling and taking Melanie's hand. "I've heard a lot about you and the two cases you and Jack worked on."

"He was a major factor in breaking those cases," said Melanie. "We couldn't have solved them without him."

Jack looked embarrassed. "Hey, this is work. Ruth, sit down, show us your stuff."

All of them took seats around the table of electronics.

"Since the last contact with the hacker, we've identified three different voices recorded by victims," said Porter. "And you may not know this, but the vendors of the distortion software provide the keys to restore the original voices. Those keys are provided to the authorities but not sold commercially. Doctor Blackston has already run the restoration systems on all the voices and is now going to try and make a detailed identification of the speakers. She's done this sort of work for various police organisations in the past, we're hopeful we'll get a good idea of who is doing this stuff."

Ruth put on the headphones and turned to the table, pressing a switch and a male voice came from the loudspeakers. She listened intently for several minutes, watching the graphs on different screens and replaying the recording three times before sitting back and taking off the headphones.

"As your agent first indicated, Gordon, the speaker is Chinese. His English is immaculate, but there is a small indication of Cantonese intonation, suggesting he is or was a resident of Hong Kong for much of his life. But there is also a trace of Lancashire in the vowels. My suggestion is that he either got an undergraduate degree at Manchester University, Salford University, or a similar institution in that area, possibly after his last school years at a high school in Manchester. It probably took five to ten years to develop that quality of English, so possibly even a post-graduate degree at the same university. He's young, under thirty, so my view is that he was sent to England in his teens, having already learnt English at school in Hong Kong, spent perhaps two or three years at school there before going to university, gaining a bachelor's degree and then possibly a Master's. It's a common profile of a wealthy Hong Kong family and it's quite likely that one or more parents have a similar history from the days before China took possession of the city state."

"That certainly narrows down the choices," said Porter. "Excellent, Doctor Blackston. Can you tackle the next one?"

She nodded and resumed her position, listening with extreme concentration to a second voice. Even without the training in linguistics, one thing was clear to Melanie, and it was no surprise when Ruth turned back to face them.

"Australian, obviously," she said. "This is another young man, under thirty, origins the Eastern Suburbs of Sydney, possibly Bondi, Coogee or that area. Again, well educated, may well have been a student at one of the best schools in the region, maybe Sydney Grammar School, but like our previous candidate, has spent some years in England. But look here…" She pointed at a line on a graph on one of the computer monitors. "There's just the faintest trace of Manchester in those vowels. The strong Australian accent tends to hide such a small indication, but I suggest it's possible that this young man also spent time in Manchester."

"Probably one of those vast numbers of young Australians who did the standard trip," said Melanie. "I know so many of them. They go to England, live in the area that became known as 'Kangaroo Valley' because of their numbers, often travel round Britain and Europe in a minibus and then come home again."

"But this guy is not one of the financially limited kids," said Porter. "Like the other bloke, most likely from a wealthy family. Jack, any thoughts on that?"

"I think so," said Jack. "But let's hear the third speaker, it may cast more light on this mob of killers."

Ruth nodded and turned back to the table, again spending several minutes listening to the voice. Finally, she turned back to the group.

"English," she said. "An interesting mix. He's not as young as the other two, I estimate in his forties or fifties. Midlands origins, Birmingham region, Solihull to be exact, a fairly wealthy area north of the city. His grammar and intonation are good, suggesting a high school education, possibly university. There's no sign of major influence from any other regional accent, so it's likely he's not a well-travelled man. However, once or twice, there was the faintest hint of something else. It could be Manchester, but I cannot be sure. If he only went to Manchester in his more adult years, the influence would be far less. Again, like the Australian, the Midlands accent is a strong one and not easily modified by other influences. So he could have spent time in Manchester as a young man, possibly at university, then moved elsewhere for a number of years and the Lancashire influence would have been lost. I can't detect enough there."

She moved her headphone well away and relaxed back in her seat. "Jack, I think this now calls for your thoughts," she said. "How can two wealthy, educated young people get to be serial killers, why are they working with a middle-aged man who may be the main influence? I know that serial killers are your area of expertise and I know that you and Melanie have worked on two big cases involving such psychopathy."

Jack stirred from what seemed to have been deep concentration during the entire process.

"Quite a few ideas come to mind and there's an echo of the first case Melanie and I worked on. I'll come back to that in a moment. But first, let's look at the standard profile of the serial killer. Mostly male, commonly they grew up in uncaring families, little affection shown by parents. Even if they were given the advantages of wealth, they didn't get parental affection or support, in fact, the opposite was often true. One or both parents were bullies, most commonly the father was a physical bully, beating the child frequently as a way of avoiding the reality of his own weakness and cowardice. The mother would be cold, distant, concerned mostly with her own interests, maybe her business or other social involvements. This upbringing as a child can often lead to a tendency to anxiety, depression and a strong sense of anger at the world. These scars could become the start of the killing drive, but if left alone, the child would probably never fall into that pattern of behaviour, though the scars would remain."

He paused for a few seconds.

"The fact that Ruth indicated they are both young men adds a further indicator. For all their technical brilliance, they are very naïve and arrogant. They have clearly never thought that they might give themselves away in any manner. They don't know that the distortions can be reversed, they never thought that the victims might be able to inform the police or their superiors in a way that couldn't be detected. Both have come from wealthy, cold families, the classic examples of serial killers, lacking in empathy or any feeling of vulnerability for their mistakes."

"And the third person?" Porter was clearly fascinated by this.

Melanie smiled to herself. She knew what was coming and she knew that Porter would soon recognise it.

"While most people grow up with a reasonably balanced view of the world," said Jack, "many develop the characteristics of dominant personality or subservient personalities. The latter are commonly damaged personalities, the damage coming either from unhealthy childhoods as I described, or some form of trauma at any time, as children or as adults, say from wartime experiences. Dominant personalities tend to seek out the subservient ones to satisfy their need to control others and they can often drive them to actions that they would normally never commit. Melanie and I worked on a case where a single dominant character, a woman was able to control a group of subservient people and persuade them to kill innocent people as a form of project."

"Ah!" exclaimed Porter. "That case, the leader of a writers' group who somehow corrupted her group to kill people as a literary project."[4]

"That one, indeed," said Jack.

"And Allen Miller was one of that group," said Porter. "He played along, committing a case of identity fraud as a form of "killing" but later repaired the damage and paid the victim compensation."

"And then killed the woman who was so dominant," added Melanie.

---

[4] See "The Ninth of the Month Murders" by Michael Davies

"I wasn't involved in that case," said Porter. "It was strictly a police matter with no international security ramifications. But I learnt about it after meeting Jack and Melanie in their next case."

"That was also a matter of a serial killer, or actually, a whole family of multiple generations of serial killers," said Jack. "But again, there was a dominant personality influencing a subservient one to commit murder. Interestingly, in most cases, it was the wife who drove the husband to be a serial killer[5]. Gordon came into it because of international security matters."

"So you think this third person, the middle-aged bloke from Solihull could be a dominant who has been able to corrupt the two kids?" asked Porter.

"I do," said Jack. "And it seems probable that the Chinese kid is a genius who studied information technology at university."

"Could he have become as good as Allen Miller?" asked Porter. "Miller took a decade or more to reach that level of skill."

"But that was in a time before computers were an everyday feature of our lives and the dark web was a resource that gave shortcuts," said Jack. "Miller went to work for a computer company as a young man and learnt his skills there, then spent some more years honing them. This kid grew up with computers, it could be his parents were in the business, it would have taken a lot less time."

"This is a huge help," said Porter. "But it doesn't identify the crooks. One problem is that they may not

---

[5] See "The Death Gambit" by Michael Davies

even be living in the same country. The internet makes it possible to work closely as a group while at opposite ends of the earth."

"But they would have met up at some time, almost certainly in England, if the older bloke was not well travelled," said Jack. "And long enough to become influenced by him. At some stage, the three of them were physically in the same area, possibly had some sort of working relationship and the common factor appears to be the Manchester region."

"One thing may help us," said Melanie. "As Jack said, they may be tech wizards, but still didn't know that electronic distortion devices have a key to them, and we've been able to identify much of who they are. And they didn't think that somebody might intercept the banking transactions as Miller did."

"Nor does it seem to have dawned on them that the government defence details might have been faked for them," said Porter. "They may be brilliant, but they are also possibly young and stupid."

"Not so much stupid as inexperienced and too obsessed with their own brilliance and the game they're playing," said Jack.

"It's a fact," said Melanie, "crimes are mostly solved when the crims make a silly mistake. We have to hope this happens here, too."

"Meanwhile, we also have to hope that they don't get so frustrated by being blocked, or if they learn that the security information they were given is fake that they kill the victims," said Jack.

"We have some ideas about that," said Porter. "Let's hope we can prevent some of the damage."

Washington DC, November, 2023

Senator Kendricks sat stiffly in a chair in the party leader's office.

"This recording was sent to every Senator last night," said the leader. "What the hell is this all about, Dwight?"

Kendricks tried to moisten his dry mouth. "A few weeks ago, somebody broke into my computer system, wearing a mask and using a voice modifier and told me I had to make a speech in the Senate supporting some standard liberal ideas. If I didn't, that crap would be broadcast on social media all over the country. I thought it was just a threat, nobody could do that and I couldn't say the sort of stuff that he demanded."

"Well, he didn't spread it around the country," said the leader. "But he might as well have done. Trouble is, most senators would realise it was a deep fake media creation, but enough staffers and other people saw it and they've already spread it out on their social media accounts. The worst part is that whoever did this also attached a sample of the sort of stuff you were watching. That's what has fucked you, Dwight. You've become an object of utter derision by everybody in the USA and the foreign media have already picked up on it."

Kendricks felt frozen, unable to think.

"You'll have to resign immediately," said the party leader. "We'll put out a statement about bad health and try and say the deep fake video was created by some liberal activists out to attack you, but there's no way you could continue as a senator. Your state governor will appoint a replacement until the next election, but that's it, Dwight. You're finished."

Kendricks stiffly stood up and walked out of the office. His mind was in a state of shock and he barely noticed the turned-away faces and subdued laughter from others in the corridor. Somehow, he made it to his office.

"Get me home," he croaked to his secretary. She nodded and picked up the phone.

The Washington Post, November, 2023

Senator Dwight Kendricks was found dead in his home this morning. Death was by an overdose of a drug as yet unidentified. The senator appeared to have taken his own life, following revelations of a speech confessing to numerous offences, including rape, payment of abortion surgery for several women and the rape of children. While these revelations were found to be made in a deep fake video created by persons unknown, the video, circulated to senators of both parties, also included attached recordings of pornographic material that the senator was watching on his personal computer.

The Republican party leader declined to make any comments beyond expressing his anger at the attacks on Senator Kendricks and thoughts and prayers for his family.

Manchester, UK and Bondi, NSW, Australia, November, 2023

"What the hell was that for, Phillip?"

William Lloyd was furious. He had taken a tongue lashing from his father-in-law about the death of the US senator who had been a useful asset to the American Mafia and was feeling frightened at the possible repercussions.

"I just didn't like the bastard," said Murray. His face in the computer monitor held a smirk that made Lloyd even more angry.

"Nobody liked him," said Lloyd. "But that was no reason to do what you did. What's worse, what did it give us? Did you get any money from him? Any state secrets?"

"I got a shitload of satisfaction," said Murray. The smirk was even bigger.

"What you got us, you fuckwit, is a full investigation by the FBI and a bunch of experts investigating the senator's computer. If they find any trace of who sent that video, they'll be onto you and demanding your extradition to the USA for trial. They might even demand the death sentence."

Murray's smirk vanished and he swallowed nervously.

"Peter's firewall is too good. They'll never break through that. Anyway, his system wipes all traces of the origins of the call, nobody could find those."

"You'd better bloody hope so, Phillip. Because I tell you, if they do identify you, the people I work for will deal with you very firmly. You'll never make it to the weekend, you'll be dead within hours."

Murray's face went noticeably white.

"In future, Phillip, don't do anything like that again without a direct order from me and it will be to obtain some financial benefits or leverage for all of us. Do you follow me?"

Murray nodded without speaking.

"Good," said Lloyd and disconnected the call.

Chapter 16

Royal Air Force Air Command, High Wycombe, UK, December, 2023

Group Captain Ivan Messing loved his life. Even though his current posting was desk-bound and not in command of a Hercules station as his previous posting had been, the work was intensely satisfying. He played a significant role at the heart of the Royal Air Force Command structure, and he could think of nothing that suited him more. All his boyhood dreams had come true, he had flown the greatest fighters in the world and then the magnificent Hercules in some of the global trouble spots. Every time he donned his uniform with the four stripes on each sleeve and the hat with the gold trimming on the peak, he could not stop himself grinning in pride at his image in the mirror.

His mobile phone rang. He looked at the screen but saw only the message, *"Out of region."*

"Group Captain Messing," he said, thinking that it was probably his wife or one of his two sons, but not taking the risk of being informal.

"Good morning, Group Captain," said a weirdly distorted voice. "I trust you are hard at work planning the defence of the realm against all hostile forces?"

Messing laughed out loud. Both his sons had a bizarre sense of humour and while this was unusual, he was sure it was one of them.

"Okay, Brad," he said. "Or is it David? What do you want?"

"It's neither, Group Captain," said the voice. It was metallic, not human. "It's somebody who will make your life hell unless you do what I say."

Sensing the menace in the voice, Messing took a deep breath to try and control the surge of worry, but said nothing.

"So how are you enjoying life behind a desk, Group Captain, instead of soaring in the wild blue yonder at the controls of a Hercules? It must be so boring."

"Who the hell are you and what do you think you're doing?" said Messing.

"Who I am is not for you to know. But here's what I want. I am reliably informed by one of my clients you are working on plans for emergency reactions by the RAF in the event of an invasion of a certain Middle-Eastern country by a foreign power."

Messing felt the shock run through his system. Such plans were top secret and were always maintained in a current state. He had been assigned the updates to this one some weeks ago. He still said nothing.

"No response, Group Captain? So let me tell you the whole thing. You will prepare a summary of the key points of your plan and in ten days, you will get a call from me on your home computer. I will instruct you to hold each page up before the camera so I can copy them."

"And if I don't?"

"Ah, he speaks! If you don't do this, Group Captain, I will send to your wife and then to various top-ranking officers in your command structure, a wonderfully entertaining film of you having wild sexual relations with some rather well-known public figures."

"Unlikely, seeing as I have never done anything of the sort." Messing began to feel easier. This was just a crank call, though how the caller had got the details of what his assignment was remained a worry.

"Group Captain, you are out of touch. I can create such dramas just at my desk here and nobody could ever tell the difference between fact and fiction. Just think what such a film could do to your marriage and your career. Bang goes the upcoming promotion to Air Commodore, your wife leaves you and you have a horribly expensive divorce ahead of you."

"I suggest you simply go and fuck yourself, whoever you are. I've got work to do."

"Then may I suggest that when you get home, you look at your home computer. Then we can talk some more. Good afternoon, Group Captain."

The call was disconnected. Messing tried to laugh it off, but couldn't help feeling worried.

Soon after six, Messing returned to the house assigned to him for the duration of the posting. After the usual warm greeting from Gillian, his wife of twenty years, he excused himself briefly to check on his computer.

The film was already starting as he sat down at his desk. In utter shock, he saw himself, quite naked, indulging in active sexual behaviour with two men, then switching to what seemed like the rape of a naked young woman. Her screams of pain were clear against the background noise of several other naked bodies engaged in highly active sexual behaviour.

Messing sat back, thinking of the next steps. But he came to the only possible conclusion within minutes. He got up and went to the lounge room where Gillian was reading the daily paper. He kneeled before her and took her hands. She looked astonished then smiled.

"Gillian, do you trust me?" he said.

She leaned forward and kissed his forehead. "After twenty years, I've never had any reason not to," she said.

"Then I want you to come and look at something." He got to his feet and pulled her upright, leading her to his study. "This was sent today," he said and stood next to her, his arm round her waist.

She watched the twelve-minute display, showing no reaction until it ended.

"That's not you," she said calmly. "You may be unusually fit for a man of your age, but you still have a bit of a dad bod, not the six-pack that man has at his gut. And whoever made this doesn't know about the tattoo of your RAF wings on your upper left arm, nor the rather sexy hairy back. So, dear husband mine, that's a fake. Clever technology, it's got your face alright, but the rest of it is not you. So what's going on?"

He realised he'd been holding his breath and finally let it out. "Somebody's trying to blackmail me into passing air force secret material."

"What are you going to do?"

"It's pretty obvious."

"Yes, it is. Okay, come and have a drink, dinner will be ready soon and you can tell me all about it."

"There's no doubt, marrying you was the best thing I ever did," he said and pulled her to him in a tight hug.

* * *

Messing stopped at the doorway, gave the mandatory first salute of the day, received the friendly nod from Air Vice Marshal Ralston and stepped in. He placed a sheet of paper on the desk and stepped back.

Ralston raised one eyebrow, then studied the paper. He stood up, donned his cap and followed Messing out of the building to the carpark. He took the driver's seat of the blue Air Force vehicle and waited while Messing took the seat next to him.

"Where to?" he asked.

"The apron," said the Group Captain.

Without expression, Ralston drove the short distance to the dispersal area where a squadron of fighters was deployed, several of them with engines powered up, beginning to taxi out to the runway. The noise was extreme.

"Ivan?" said the Air Vice Marshal.

"I'm being threatened. A caller yesterday, the voice distorted by computer technology, told me he would circulate a pornographic video featuring me to my wife and probably most of the Command senior officers."

"What did he want?"

"The complete plans in the event of a foreign invasion of Israel."

"I assume that wasn't you in the video?"

Messing laughed. "My wife reviewed it and pointed out the physical discrepancies between the actor and me. They got my face all right, but not the rest."

"Clever," said Ralston. "I knew that technology was available, and it was only a matter of time before somebody would try this. Any ideas?"

"The caller said 'his clients' wanted the information. I'm assuming one of the regular hostiles."

"Saudi, North Korea, Iran, Russia or China, yes. Ivan, we've got plans for just about every military contingency and we've even looked at this one. But that threat obviously involves international entities and that takes it out of our remit. Here's what you do. Head down to London, go by rail, second class, wear civvies. Pay for the ticket by cash, don't use your forces travel card. If this character can hack into computer systems like this, he could perhaps find out you were heading to London. Go to the MI6 building in Vauxhall. I'll advise somebody there that you're coming."

"This really has been looked at," said Messing. "Okay, Sir, I'll head off in an hour."

"Good man. Come and see me when you get back. Now, let's get back to the office, this noise is splitting my head in two."

* * *

Wearing plain jeans, a blue sweater and a football club cap, Ivan Messing walked into the MI6 building in

Vauxhall. Uncertain of what to do next, he stood unmoving. A few moments passed, then a middle-aged woman approached with a friendly smile.

"Good afternoon, Group Captain," she said. "We were expecting you."

"So I was told."

"It's a situation we've been anticipating for a while, so I think we can help you. Come with me." She led the way down a corridor, opened a door and waved him in. "This is a secure room," she said. "Nobody can hear what goes on in here. Now, take a seat, tell me the whole story."

When Messing had completed the details, the woman sat back.

"Time for me to introduce myself," she said. "My name is Jacqui Simmons, I head up one of the counter-terrorism units here. You recorded the call, I assume?"

"Standard Operating Procedure for calls from outside the station."

"Ah, those wonderful SOPs," she said. "They save us so much time. Let me have the recording."

Messing handed over the flash drive and Simmons opened up a laptop computer and inserted the drive.

"This PC has no communication facilities, so nobody could hack in, even if the room were not as secure as it is. Now, this may interest you." She touched a key, and the ugly, distorted voice came out. Almost immediately, the words were repeated but in normal tones.

"That's not a facility available to the public," said Simmons. "But we spooks have it. That voice is an Englishman from somewhere in the midlands, we believe Solihull, near Birmingham, according to a top linguistics expert in Australia."

"This has happened in Australia as well?"

"And the USA," replied Simmons. "We don't know who this man is, yet, but we do know that he has associates in Australia and Hong Kong."

"Good grief!" Messing was a man normally capable of controlling his emotions, but the implications of what the MI6 agent was saying frightened him.

"And so to what we do, Group Captain. This is a massive upgrade in potential problems, but I see some opportunities. Go back home, I need to talk to a couple of people. When I have the results, I'll get back to you."

"I've got ten days to reply."

"Don't worry. You'll have a wonderfully realistic and perfectly rational report for our man in Solihull well before then."

"Sounds good." Messing stood up as the door opened and a man waved to him to be led out of the building.

* * *

"It's pretty serious when you can ask the Defence Secretary and the Chief of Defence Staff to meet with you, Ms Simmons."

The tall man in the immaculate blue suit looked relaxed in his armchair. Opposite him, a muscular man sat cross-legged in a similar chair, the one broad and three narrow stripes on each sleeve demanding attention.

"Secretary, Admiral, thank you for agreeing to it. I believe this is critical."

Receiving nods from both men, Simmons related the full story of the blackmail attempt on Group Captain Messing. There was a small silence for a moment when she finished. The Admiral broke it.

"That gives us some interesting decisions and also opportunities," he said. "The first choice to make is do we report massive military support from us and the Americans and so scare the crap out of any nation considering such action? Or do we say there will be little or no help from us, and maybe convince the attackers that there's no hurry to invade and wait a few more years?"

"Or maybe tell them that now would be a good time to invade?" added the Defence Secretary.

"The interesting question is who wants this information?" said the Admiral. "My strongest opinion is Iran, destroying Israel is their primary policy. Iraq is not up to it anymore and Egypt might like the idea but they've taken beatings from Israel in the past and won't have the balls to try again."

"And not Saudi," added the Defence Secretary. "They depend on American military hardware and general trade too much to offend them. My suggestion is to make up a fake report to submit to these people, indicating huge military support from both countries, all plans in place. Then we will probably see who reacts to this and that will be useful."

"Agreed," said the Admiral. "So, Ms Simmons, take this down. Tell them that we are training Israeli fighter pilots in large numbers. They don't need it, those blokes are better than anyone, but add that the RAF has developed whole new air combat techniques with some variations in armaments. And say we will have four squadrons of Typhoons available for immediate despatch to Israel and the Yanks will have six squadrons of F-35 Lightnings. In addition, we will send thirty General Atomics MQ-9 Reaper drones."

"Thirty, Admiral?" The Defence Secretary laughed. "We've only got nine."

"Yes, sir, that's the official public information, but these bastards won't know if that's true or not."

"What are they?" asked Simmons.

"Drones," replied the Admiral. "Very nasty drones, long range, very dangerous."

Simmons added more notes to her pad. "How true is all that?" she asked.

"You don't need to know, Ms Simmons," replied the Defence Secretary.

She nodded and stood up. "Thank you, gentlemen," she said.

Chapter 17

Canberra, Australia, December, 2023

Porter looked up at the tap on his open door. One of his agents, Peter Stone merely looked at him with both eyebrows raised but said nothing.

Porter nodded and stood up. He went to the desk of each of his agents and raised his hand. All of them understood and within a few minutes, they had gathered in the secure room.

"Peter, you have something?" asked Porter.

"I do, boss," said Stone. He didn't bother consulting the sheets of paper he had brought with him. "I followed your suggestion over the last three weeks, I managed to have some informal chats with a few members of parliament, two Senators, a couple of very senior civil servants and three of your colleagues, boss, senior members of ASIO management. All were happy to chat, all seemed relaxed, had no difficulties talking to an ASIO agent like me. But one of them, a top official in the Prime Minister's department was not as happy. He seemed quite tense, couldn't wait to get away, spouted some stuff about an urgent meeting. I've talked to this guy before, never had a problem. And I checked later, there was no meeting within his department, he spent the day in his office doing routine stuff."

"You think he's been targeted?" asked Porter.

"It's a fair bet," said Stone.

"Let me have your notes," said Porter.

Stone passed across a single sheet of handwritten notes and Porter studied it for a few moments.

"Yes, I think you have something here," he said. "Not conclusive, of course, but he does seem nervous about something, He's certainly senior enough to know pretty well everything the Prime Minister and most of the Cabinet are doing, so he'd be a good target for our hacker, if indeed the hacker is involved. The man's name is Falwell. But for now, I want you to ignore him totally, don't go and talk to him, don't mention the name outside this room, we don't want him to get suspicious if suddenly ASIO agents go and talk to him. But this is interesting timing."

He paused and extracted another single sheet from his jacket pocket.

"This came from MI6 by King's Messenger this morning. Two cases, one definite, one possible. The definite case is a bloke who heads up an international accounting firm. He got the first threat on a phone call, the same stuff, electronically distorted voice, said he'd be demanding a million pounds. Later, he got a face in a mask appearing in his home computer, telling him to have a million pounds in his bank account and it would be removed by chappie. But this guy, he's Finnish, was pretty bright. He handwrote the details on a paper, had it taken to a police station, requesting a meeting outdoors away from cameras or anything else. A detective met him and got the details, then sent the story to MI6 in the same way, handwritten note by personal delivery."

"Pretty clever, those Poms," said one of the agents.

"Indeed," said Porter. "Meanwhile, our fellow security people in MI6 have been doing the same as you for the last few weeks, casually chatting to likely targets of an international hacker. They've had a visit from an RAF Group Captain in the Air Command Group who had received another of those calls over the Internet, same thing, mask, distorted voice, demands for defence information. His history shows great competence, he flew Hercules for some years and was decorated for his performance under fire in Iraq, so not somebody who would get nervous easily. Our contact at MI6 had a chat with the Defence Secretary and the head of the military, an Admiral, and they're doing something interesting, I'll tell you all later. So here's what I'm going to do. First, these papers go in the company safe. A copy of the one that Peter produced will go to London and Langley by diplomatic bag. Now I have to talk to our civilian supporter. I'll update you all later."

When all his staff had left, Porter left the building and walked a kilometre to a small park, found a bench and took out the cheap telephone he had bought at a supermarket three weeks earlier. He dialled a number, let it ring twice and disconnected. Thirty seconds later, he dialled again, let it ring twice more and hung up. Then he sat back and waited.

* * *

Melanie Carter was about to pick up the telephone on her desk, but after two rings, it went silent.

"Ah," she said and waited. Thirty seconds later, the same happened. She left her office and walked two blocks to a shopping centre which had two public telephones in the mall. She entered a number and let it ring.

"Porter," said the voice.

"Carter," she replied.

"Three possible targets," said Porter. "James Falwell in the Prime Minister's department here, Group Captain Ivan Messing in Royal Air Force in the UK, Paavo Hukkinen in London, head of accounting firm, GFRD."

"Got it," said Melanie and hung up. She walked back to her office, tapped her PC monitor and said, "Allen," then returned to the public phone in the shopping mall. Ten minutes later, it rang and she picked it up.

"Deborah?" said the voice which she recognised as that of Allen Miller.

She repeated the details Porter had given her and hung up.

* * *

Gordon Porter switched off his phone and extracted the SIM card. He walked back to his office, found a pair of scissors and cut up the tiny card into four pieces, placing them in his jacket pocket. He unlocked the drawer of his desk, an unusually secure drawer with a unique key and took another SIM card from the box containing several, noted the number and inserted the card in his phone. Later that day, after getting home, he placed the pieces of the previous SIM card into his microwave oven and cooked them until they had melted then placed them in his rubbish bin. He went to his desk, wrote the new number of his phone on a small card, inserted the card into an envelope and addressed it to Deborah James at a PO box near Melanie's office. It would eventually be collected by a teenage girl, the daughter of a patrol car officer.

"Let's go visiting," said Melanie. "You can drive."

"Oh right!" said Detective Constable Alex Welland. Only twice had Melanie let him drive her Gordon-Keeble and the experience had delighted him, even more than his time behind the wheel of a police patrol car.

"Jack's place," she said as they walked outside. "No discussions until we get there. I don't know if our phones can be tapped."

"Understood," he said and unlocked the car door for her. The Gordon-Keeble predated remote electronic door locks by some decades.

The drive was passed in silence, broken only when they parked outside the home of police psychologist, Jack Savage.

"This must be serious," said Jack as he came to the car door.

"Alex, leave our phones in the car," said Melanie and dropped hers on the passenger seat.

Jack understood. "I know the very place," he said and led the way into his spacious garage which housed a tractor, a motorboat, a motorcycle and two cars. Closing the door behind him, Jack walked to each vehicle and switched on the engine. The noise was almost painful.

"Okay, nobody outside could penetrate that racket," said Jack. "So, what is it?"

When Melanie had finished running through the events of recent weeks, she studied the faces of the two men, laughing at the astonishment on both of them.

"Somebody is out-doing Allen Miller?" said Jack. "You're all certain it's not Miller himself running a double bluff?"

"Whatever else Allen is," said Melanie, "he's not a serial killer. And mostly, he's relieved large corporations and governments of big sums, he hasn't blackmailed high-ups for state or corporate secrets."

"That's true," said Jack. "This sounds like somebody almost trying to prove he or she is better than the master himself. Let's stick with "he" until we know better. It's likely to be somebody who knows about Allen's work and thinks he could be better. The dark web would be full of Miller's exploits. I didn't think one could hack into medical devices like pacemakers."

"It seems the medical profession has been worried about it for some time and there's a lot of work going on to tackle the problem," said Melanie. "But so far, the view is that hacking into these things is only possible from short distances, though this sort of thing has always been seen as a future danger."

"And now it's not," said Jack. "Have you had contact with Miller?"

"He talked briefly to ASIO when Porter came to my office," said Melanie, smiling at the memory of the agent's shock when Miller appeared on her monitor. "He's agreed to help, but he'll only talk to me."

"Not surprising," said Jack. "Presumably you've worked out some secure ways of communicating with each other that nobody can hack into?"

"We have," said Melanie and described the procedures she used.

"Good," said Jack. "Seems like there's not a lot we can do until Allen reports back on his efforts to find out who's doing this."

"Sounds about right," said Melanie.

"Right. Let's shut this noise off and go inside for some coffee and apple pie," said Jack.

A few minutes later they were seated securely in Jack's lounge, carefully talking about safe subjects like the new Alpaca kids, Jack's granddaughters and the chess tournaments that Alex was competing in.

Chapter 18

Thames Embankment, Vauxhall, London, December, 2023

"What the hell is this?" muttered Kent Williams. "I didn't think people could get inside MI6 headquarters."

"And mostly, you'd be right," said the pleasant man, one of seven accompanying the group of visitors. Williams' military experience automatically made him look for a holstered automatic pistol inside the man's jacket of his well-tailored suit but he was unable to see one. "Very few outside people ever come here. But this is an unusual situation," continued the security agent.

Williams' temper was rising after the third passage through an X-Ray gate, the second detector sweep of his body from hair to his wing-tip shoes.

"Are we ever going to get somewhere?" he asked. "How long do we have to be examined like bugs? I'm a busy man, this is ridiculous."

"Patience, Mr Williams," said the agent. "At least you're in your home country. All your associates here have had to come through British Customs and Immigration, which is extra stress."

"I suppose," said Williams with grudging acceptance. "Now what?"

"A very secure room," said the agent. He waited while the other visitors were all finally through the security measures, then led the way to a door with no indications of its use. He slid a magnetic card down a slide, entered several digits to a keypad and opened the door, standing aside to allow the visitors to enter. Williams knew the two Americans and the Irish woman, but while he knew that he had spoken by video to the Belgian woman, he had never met Monique Theilemans in person. The Indian and Chinese men were unknown to him. But from his briefing, he knew that all of them were Chief Executive Officers of companies like his, major manufacturers of pacemakers and other medical equipment. He wondered what the hell was going on.

The room was small, holding no more than ten seats round a table, with another table against the wall, holding cups and saucers and two pots holding hot water. Instant coffee, tea bags, milk and sugar completed the display, identical to so many that Williams had attended at executive meetings. Several of the attendees moved to the table and began making drinks for themselves. Nobody spoke. The tension in the air demanded silence.

The door opened again, and a woman entered. The air of authority around her commanded the attention of everyone. Williams estimated that she was in her fifties, immaculately dressed in a dark blue business suit, white blouse and no obvious ornamentation. Her hair was shoulder length, auburn and looked silky smooth, framing classic features. Williams thought she was enormously attractive, but somehow cold and unapproachable.

"Good morning, ladies and gentlemen," she said, "Please take your seats."

Almost like schoolchildren at the start of class, the seven executives took places, still without a word being exchanged.

"My name is Simmons," the woman said. "And of course, you are all wondering why we have asked you here. I'm sure you have all recognised that you are Chief Executive Officers of companies that manufacture the majority of pacemakers installed around the world, ninety two percent, in fact. So let me start by saying the situation is severely dangerous and your cooperation in avoiding international damage and scandal both to your businesses and to our countries is essential."

A small stir round the table. Williams felt the tension rise, his interest peaking and all the irritation he'd been feeling dissipated like morning mist in the breeze.

"In recent months," began Simmons, "several deaths have occurred in people fitted with pacemakers, all of them manufactured by your companies. The American company that made one of them will know about one case in Australia because they were asked to investigate but found no failure in the device. Despite that, the coroner returned a verdict of technical failure."

"And we registered a serious protest," said one of the men. Williams knew him as Arnold Peterson, they had met on occasions at business conferences.

"Yes, you did," said Simmons with a small smile. "And you had every right to, because there was no failure in your device." She held up a hand as Peterson looked set to speak. The air of command silenced him. "Now let me explain why. The Coroner did so at the request, perhaps I should call it the *demand* of the Australian Security Intelligence Organisation, known as ASIO. The victim was murdered by some unknown person who had hacked into the device and stopped the man's heart."

"What? That's not possible." The loud exclamation came from the Indian CEO. Williams didn't know his name.

"And that is why we are here," said Simmons. "I'm sorry to tell you, Mr Anand, it is certainly possible, and it has been done several times. Let me tell you about the other cases. The first example was in Australia, and we only learnt of it because the victim, Garry Henderson, was a member of the Australian Signals Directorate. He first received a phone call from a speaker using electronic distortion, demanding a large sum of money and for later, some intelligence data. To emphasise the point, the man received a temporary jolt when his pacemaker was stopped for a few seconds. Very bravely, Henderson informed his superiors and was killed the next day with complete heart failure. That showed that whoever was doing this was able to hack into communications systems, even the computer on the superior's desk and hear the conversation."

"Good god," exclaimed the other American, a woman in her mid-forties, Williams estimated.

"Yes, Ms Faversham, it's that serious," said

Simmons. "As we in MI6, the CIA and Australia's ASIO have now begun to share information, we have learnt of several other cases involving security organisations as well as others which were blackmail for financial returns. We think that those were test runs by an unknown hacker who has developed the means to attack pacemakers from any distance. And that is why you are here. And that is why we are in a secure room, completely soundproofed and totally without any communication facilities at all, no phones, no computer terminals, no devices of any kind that could be hacked and the room is shielded so mobile devices will not work."

Silence hung in the air like a threatening storm cloud.

"Shouldn't this just be a police matter?"

Williams recognised the Irish CEO, Michelle Curren. The dark, thin face showed no emotion, but Williams sensed some irritation in her.

"No, Ms Curren, it should not." Simmons spoke with calm courtesy, but the intention was clear. Almost, Williams felt that had he been spoken to that way, he'd have been ready to stand in the dunce's corner. "As I said," continued Simmons, "blackmail efforts have been directed at security personnel and this represents national security problems for all of us."

"So what do you want of us?" Williams felt it was time to speak up, though he had a good idea of what the answer would be. "Why have you brought the CEOs of the world's main manufacturers together in this most secret of locations, fully insulated from the world?"

"So far, Mr Williams, you and your associates have recognised the potential problems that we have now revealed, but you have done little to find a solution." Simmons had an almost glacial calm about her. "But now I must ask all of you to begin serious research and development to insulate your devices from this problem. Whether that is some form of insulation against hacking, or some form of encryption of the signals that cannot be read by an outside agency, that is for you to determine. But let me be clear, this is a global problem that could adversely affect every country on earth. Nobody has the resources that you have."

"I don't see why we have to do this," said Ms Faversham, the American. "This is a hell of a lot of time and money to be spent, all at our own costs. This seems to be a national security problem, so will our respective governments cover those costs?"

Simmons smiled. Williams felt that he would rather face a beating than be the recipient of one of those smiles. It was quite chilling.

"Ms Faversham, may I remind you of the prime American culture of free-market enterprise? It's called competition and minimal government intervention. Imagine if one of your competitors does produce an interference-free device. Who do you think will sell their products, them, or one of the organisations that hasn't bothered to try? Imagine the effect on your bottom line and your future as the CEO if you choose to ignore this call."

The American woman seemed to deflate like a balloon with a leak.

"So no, Ms Faversham, there will be no government support of this project," said Simmons. "Your own survival depends on your setting up the project with maximum importance."

"This may be your problem, it's not ours." The Chinese executive finally spoke. His English was flawless, the accent of the finest British universities.

"Why is that, Mr Tang?" asked Simmons.

"We solved this problem years ago," said Tang. "We developed technology superior to any Western systems and there is no way anyone could do as you have described with our devices."

"That is most interesting, Mr Tang," said Simmons, showing no emotion. "Would your company be willing to share your technology with the rest of the world and let us reach your stage of advancement?"

Williams smiled to himself, detecting a faint trace of sarcasm in the British agent. He felt that she probably did not believe Tang's claim.

"No, we would not, Ms Simmons," replied Tang. "We have no desire to make the Western nations safer. And we will no longer market our equipment outside of our territories and let you work out what we have developed."

"I understand, Mr Tang." Simmons obviously wrote him out of further discussion. She looked round the others. "I hope you understand how critical this is. Can I believe that you will all begin serious development to counter this threat?"

She looked at each of the executives in turn, staring them in the eye and did not look away until she received a nod or word of agreement. At the end, she stood up.

"Thank you all," she said. "You will be shown to the exit by our agents."

She walked out, as seven agents walked in and fifteen minutes later, Williams found himself on the Embankment, smelling the odour of the River Thames and the motor traffic of London.

* * *

Canberra, Australia, December, 2023

Gordon Porter walked past each of his agents' desks, nodding at them. Ten minutes later, they were in the secure room, looking with interest at Porter.

"I received this by King's Messenger fifteen minutes ago," he said, touching the single sheet of paper on the table before him. "As you know, MI6 held a meeting at their HQ building last week, to which were invited the Chief Executive Officers of the biggest international manufacturers and suppliers of pacemakers and similar equipment. The meeting was in their secure room, similar to this one. The objective was to brief them on recent events and ask them to begin serious research and development of ways to insulate the devices from hacking. All agreed, except one, Tang Koon Yee of the Chinese company. He claimed that they had already solved the problem and their equipment was secure."

He looked down at the paper and then round the room.

"Simmons has advised us and the CIA that she has since received word that three senior members of the

Chinese government have disappeared from sight in recent days. Our information is that all three had been fitted with pacemakers in the last year. Two days ago, a message appeared on Ms Simmons' computer. It said, and I quote here, *'Tang Koon Yee was lying through his arse. He told his Communist Party about the MI6 meeting, not realising that I could hear that briefing in Beijing. I decided to demonstrate how wrong he was. Three of his people are now dead.'* Ms Simmons said that the best efforts of MI6's technical experts were unable to trace the source of that message or how it got through the building's firewalls."

He looked round the room. "Any ideas?" he asked.

"Interesting that our hacker could understand the conversations Tang had," said one of young agents at the desk. "Does this indicate that he can speak fluent Mandarin?"

"Possibly," said another. "But automatic translation software exists. You can carry several languages on the average smart phone. I've got French, German and Spanish on mine. I'm sure there's a Mandarin-English system available."

"Or Mandarin to whatever language our chappie speaks," said the first agent.

"Probably Cantonese," said Porter. "We have no idea of the identity of our chappie, but remember that the linguistics specialist said he was a Hong Kong citizen and Cantonese would be his native language. I imagine that Mandarin-Cantonese translation systems would be common, especially now that China has taken control of Hong Kong."

"One suggestion," said a third agent. "As we identify people being attacked this way, can we ask them to come here, to this room and tell us what's happening and what information is being demanded? Then we can brief them with modified information for them to give to chappie and do less harm."

"Good thinking," said Porter. "Always make the request on a notepad, away from other eyes, not spoken. Let's at least try and minimise the damage until we solve the technical problem."

Chapter 19

Canberra, Australia, December, 2023

James Falwell was at his desk when the ugly face appeared again. For a moment, he felt a twinge of worry, remembering the hideous, distorted voice that had appeared on his monitor several weeks ago, the prelude to the shock and blackout he'd experienced, feeling like a thump over the heart. But he sat forward to hide the movement of his hand and he pressed the button under his desk again.

"Good evening, James, are you well?"

Falwell sensed the cold shiver run through his body as that evil, robotic voice sounded in his ear. But he worked at controlling his reactions.

"Oh, good evening, scumbag," he replied, trying to sound unconcerned. "So have you stopped your marathon wanking session to get back to me? What themes do you choose for these episodes? Do you dream of fucking Victoria's Secret models? Or little boys? Not that you're able to do either, of course."

"Oh dear, James, you do like to take risks, don't you? As I showed you so convincingly last time, I can kill you at any moment. So why do you think you can insult me like that?"

"You may kill me, douchebag," said Falwell. "But that's no loss to the world. And one thing is sure, one day we'll find you and depending on which country does that, you'll face either life behind bars or a bullet in the head."

"Tsk, tsk," said the voice. "I think you need to be reminded of who's the boss in this arrangement."

Falwell felt the jolt in his chest and collapsed to the floor, not blacking out. He leaned back against the armchair by which he'd been standing, breathing hard. Despite the pain and the shock, he felt a small wave of exhilaration at the recognition of a tone of irritation in the other voice, despite the distortion.

"So, are you back with us, James?"

Falwell slowly and painfully dragged himself up right and resumed his seat at the desk.

"Alright, filth, what do you want?"

"You know, James, keep this up and I may just want to see you dead. You know I can do that at the touch of a button, don't you?"

"I said, what do you want?"

"Well, alright, seeing as you are being so insistent, here's what I want. Your Prime Minister, Defence Minister and Defence Chiefs are preparing a new defence spending program and new strategies for implementation in three months. I know that the details will be discussed in a secure room. I want those details. You will write the summarised details on no more than two sheets of paper and when I call you, you will hold those sheets in front of your computer monitor at your home."

"What the hell will you do with that?"

"That's my business, James. I might buy stock in armaments companies, or just sell the details to China, maybe North Korea or Indonesia. Now, do I have your agreement, or do you want to get another reminder of what I can do to you?"

"I'll do it. It will take a few days."

"You have a week."

"Go fuck yourself," said Falwell and the call disconnected. He climbed back into his seat , picked up the phone and dialled a three-digit number. "Plan A," he said when a male voice answered.

"Roger," said the voice and the connection was broken. Falwell blessed his intelligence and forethought in having developed a plan for just such an event.

* * *

Next morning, Falwell drove as usual to Parliament House, drove to the underground parking area and parked inside a line of five spaces over which a tent had been erected. A car sat in four of the spaces, each with a driver at the wheel. On climbing out, he was met by a young man.

"This way, sir, please leave your phone in the car," said the man. "Somebody will drive it and the phone will indicate its location, which will not be yours." He led Falwell to an ordinary family sedan. He opened the back door, Falwell climbed in and lay down on the floor, pulling a blanket over him. The tent opening was pulled aside and all five cars drove out of the parliament building, each heading in a different direction on reaching the main road.

* * *

Accompanied by a silent agent, Falwell was shown into the secure room at ASIO headquarters in the Ben Chifley Building. The others were already present, and Falwell nodded at the agent who had interviewed him a few weeks ago.

"I hadn't realised I'd given myself away so easily," he said.

"Actually, you hid it rather well," said the agent with a smile. "But it's something we get trained to look for."

"Take a seat," said Gordon Porter. "You have the recording?"

Falwell handed over the flash drive that he had removed from his computer that morning and Porter inserted it into the computer sitting in front of him.

"The room is proof against any signals coming or going," he said. "And this computer is not connected to any network. Let me assure you, this conversation is secure."

"I'm betting my life on it," said Falwell without expression.

Porter nodded and played the conversation between Falwell and the ugly voice.

"One thing that is not known by the general public," he said when the conversation was over, "is that while distortion systems like that are available to computer users everywhere, they are not the same versions as sold to security organisations like ours. We use them for reasons I don't need to explain to you, but the difference is that the commercially available systems are required by law to have a key to them, though the buyer doesn't know that and doesn't have access to the key. When we know that key, we can return the distorted version to the original. We have keys for all commercially-available systems and what I'm going to do now is test that recording with all the ones we have. The system will test just the first few seconds of that recording against each key and when a match is found, we'll play the entire conversation. Stand by."

The room went silent for a few minutes until Porter spoke.

"Okay, we have it. Let's hear this."

He pressed a key, and a new voice replaced the ugly, mechanical sound that had haunted Falwell's dreams. The voice was male, possibly a young man, thought Falwell, and very well spoken.

"Any thoughts?" asked Porter to the room at large.

"We'll run it through the analyser," said a young woman. "But I'd say that was a man in his twenties, possibly early thirties. Not a native English speaker, but well educated in the UK, almost perfect diction. At first hearing, I'd suggest that this is the Chinese resident of Hong Kong that we heard before from the previous tests by Doctor Blackston."

"Excellent," said Porter. "Nikki, take the flash drive give it every test you can. Meanwhile, Mr Falwell, we'll work on a set of mythical defence budget details for you to give our crook. You'll get those by a personal delivery from some young person who has no connection to this office or yours."

"Thank you," said Falwell. "Naturally, I hope your security protocols are as successful as you have indicated. I like my life."

"I'm sure of it," said Porter. "Now let's get you back to your office."

Thirty minutes later, Falwell climbed out from under the blanket to find himself in the Parliament parking ground. Two cars were already back in their spots and as he waited, the others arrived. He took a deep breath and returned to his office, fervently hoping that the decoy cars had successfully kept the hacker from discovering where he had been.

Chapter 20

Falls Church, Virginia, USA, January, 2024

Boon Lee Ng sat back in shock at his home office desk in Falls Church as the hideous mask appeared on his computer monitor. He had been laying out the strategy for the massive investment by his client and his concentration had been so deep, the appearance of the mask caused a huge confusion on top of the fright.

"Good evening, Boon Lee," said the alien, robotic voice. "I trust you are enjoying the lovely evening in Virginia? Such a beautiful part of the world you live in."

Lee Ng took a deep breath. "What the hell do you want?" he said, his voice harsh with the tension.

"I told you before, I want a million dollars. Now I know you tried to tell me you don't have it, but I'm quite certain you do. I know where all your investments are, I know what your average billings are, and I know the value of that lovely house near the lake. So here's what you are going to do. You have ten days to convert some of your assets to cash, one million dollars, in fact. Then you will simply leave that cash in your bank account. I'll take it after ten days."

"And what if I don't," said Lee Ng.

"Don't be stupid," said the distorted voice. "You know what I can do to you. I'll make you suffer quite badly. You'll get just the one chance and if you don't follow the instructions the second time, you'll be dead minutes later. And here's the funny thing, Boon Lee. If that happens, I'll actually take the assets and convert them to cash myself. I really can do it, but I'd rather play this game. It's so much fun. Do you understand me?"

Boon Lee knew he was beaten. "I'll do what you say," he said.

"Such a good boy," said the mask and vanished.

Richmond, Middlesex, England, January, 2024

Paavo Hukkinen's computer emitted the gentle warble to indicate he had a video call.

"That's odd," said Kaarina. "Usually, these urgent calls come by phone."

"Damned inconsiderate," said Hukkinen, putting down his coffee cup and standing up. "I'll be back as soon as I can." He walked out of the dining room to his study and sat at his desk. His computer monitor showed an ugly mask, the eyes of the human behind it just visible.

"Good morning, Paavo." The voice was the same inhuman, metallic voice that he had heard before. "Remember me?"

Hukkinen said nothing, remembering the pain and terror of the heart attack inflicted on him by the speaker.

"You don't want to talk to me, eh? Well, I can understand that."

Even through the metallic distortion, Hukkinen could detect the mockery in the speaker's voice.

"It's time for you to pay the bill, Paavo. Remember what I told you last time we spoke? I want a million pounds and here's how you're going to give it to me. You have ten days to liquidate some of your assets. Now I could actually take those assets myself, believe me, but this is being nice to you. Have a million pounds in your chequing account within ten days and I'll take it. Okay?"

"That's impossible," said Hukkinen. "Nobody can break through the bank's security systems like that."

"I'm sure you believe that, Paavo, but I'm not anybody. So here's the deal. Have the cash ready for my removal or suffer the same consequences you suffered last time. And again, don't tell the police, don't warn the bank, don't do anything but follow my orders or your lovely wife will have to arrange your funeral."

The mask disappeared.

Canberra, Australia, January, 2024

"Good morning, Mr Falwell, and how is your day going?"

Even though he had been expecting it, the appearance of the mask in his monitor sent a pang of fear through Falwell. He said nothing.

"Not being sociable, eh, James? Well, I can understand that."

Even through the electronic distortion, Falwell heard the mocking tones of the speaker. He studied the mask. Only the eyes were visible, but nothing remarkable could be deduced from those.

"So, James, do you have the information I asked for?"

"I do."

"Such a good boy you are, James. It's a pleasure dealing with you. Let's have a look."

Falwell took the first of two sheets he had been given by ASIO and held it up before the camera.

"Excellent," said the ugly voice after a few seconds. "Now the next one."

The process was repeated.

"That's lovely," said the mask. "I'm so glad you behaved yourself, dear man. Much as I enjoy causing pain, it's better in the long run if you simply do as you're told. Good night."

The mask disappeared from the screen.

Falwell poured himself a large scotch and prayed that the false trail had worked.

Mid North Coast, NSW, Australia, January, 2024

"So are the spooks keeping you informed, Melanie?"

Allen Miller's face had appeared in Melanie's computer monitor as she was talking to Alex and Jack in her office. She felt it was no coincidence. She had experienced a lot of Miller's sudden appearances.

"Allen, why are you calling me here? We've no way of knowing if the hackers have accessed my system."

"Let me tell you what I've done, Melanie. I'm no slouch when it comes to secure systems, so I developed a new firewall and installed it in your computer this morning. We're quite secure."

"I do hope so, Allen. But I can't help but feel a bit nervous about this."

"Relax, Melanie. If anybody can break through this firewall, I'll retire for life. Now, about my question. Have the spooks kept you informed?"

"Yes, they've kept their word, as far as I can tell," Melanie replied. "They're doing an excellent job of keeping their actions hidden from the hacker."

"I agree, but the trouble is, they don't know everybody our little genius is attacking. One of the victims was clever, though and found a way to tell the cops about the blackmail without it being visible in any way. His name is Paavo Hukkinen, he's the global boss in London of one of those humungous accounting firms, offices in almost every country and our little genius has demanded a million pounds from him."

"Yes, MI6 was told about that," said Melanie. "They told ASIO by King's Messenger and Gordon Porter told me in a handwritten letter."

"So I got into Hukkinen's computer and listened in on the conversation with the hacker. It was interesting. First, I recorded the distorted voice and I'll get back to you on that. Then I started tracing the origins of the call."

"What did you find?" Melanie felt excitement, this could be a breakthrough.

"Nothing." Miller's voice reflected anger. "This bastard is clever. I tracked the communication back through Singapore, Kuala Lumpur, Tokyo and then I hit a brick wall. He used all the tricks I've used, but somehow, he put up a wall. He's giving me the shits, Melanie, I can tell you."

Despite the disappointment, Melanie laughed.

"That can't have happened to you much, Allen."

"Correct, but it only makes me try harder. However, back to the other known victims. I broke into the computer of James Falwell and heard the demands. That's a good ploy, feed false information to the hacker and see who gets it. But back to the voice. I have the same keys to distorted voices that the spooks have, and I ran the programs. Something interesting came up. First thing, I didn't recognise the voice and I thought it might have been somebody I've tutored in the past."

"So it's a new player?" Melanie was intrigued.

"Hang on a second." Allen's voice showed some tension. "From your previous information, I got into the computer of the RAF Group Captain Ivan Messing and I heard the demands made on him. I ran the same program on this voice and the result was interesting."

"What's that?" asked Melanie.

"They're not the same person. And here's the other thing. I found that Falwell had received a call just warning him before he got the calls demanding information. He'd recorded that one too, though he didn't bother giving it to MI6, probably because he assumed it was the same person. It wasn't. One of them is a woman."

Chapter 21

Richmond, Middlesex, January, 2024

After nine days of silence since the last communication with the blackmailer, Paavo Hukkinen's personal computer warbled at him during his breakfast. With a sigh, he moved to his study and sat down before the monitor. The ugly mask looked at him.

"You're a dead man, Paavo. You know what I told you, have a million pounds in your chequing account within ten days."

"I did, you bastard. It was there by yesterday and you took it in the evening."

"I didn't take it, Paavo, don't lie to me. It's not there and you're going to suffer."

"Look, dimwit, if you can access my bank account as easily as you say, have a look. You'll see that one million pounds was placed in my account yesterday morning at nine and was taken out again some ten hours later. I didn't take it, so it must be you who's lying."

"Wait," said the electronic voice and the mask disappeared. Two minutes later, it reappeared.

"You seem to be right," said the robotic voice. Even with the distortion, Paavo could hear the anger in the tones. "Somebody else got in there ahead of me. This is unacceptable. So I won't kill you now, but you must see just how upset this has made me. You will get further instructions in a few days."

Hukkinen felt the jolt in his chest and blacked out. When he returned to awareness, his face was on his keyboard and the monitor was blank.

* * *

"That's an interesting development," said the detective as they leaned on the railing by the Thames. "I'll get the details to the spooks across the river over there," he continued, pointing at the MI6 building across the river.

"MI6?" said Hukkinen. "Since when did they get involved?"

"Since MI5 told them."

"Okay, now I'm confused. Who told MI5 and why?"

"I told them, using the same method you used to tell me. This seemed to be a major league crime and I thought that it was likely to have happened with other rich people. I was told by my boss that they returned the compliment, sent a hand-carried note to my office telling him that you're not the only victim, but there are others in top government and military, here and in the USA and Australia. That makes it MI6's business."

"Good grief," said Hukkinen.

"They added one other instruction," continued the detective. "They think they know who got in ahead of our man, but they'll investigate further. But seriously, Paavo, they ordered all of us to keep completely silent about this. Not a word."

"I understand. And when he gets back to me? I can't find another million pounds that easily."

"Let us know at once. We may know more by then."

The two men shook hands and went back to their offices.

* * *

Mid North Coast, NSW, Australia, January, 2024

"Melanie," said the voice in Melanie's computer monitor.

"What have you got?" she said, closing the file of current crime rates in her area.

"Paavo Hukkinen's million pounds," said Allen Miller.

"Explain," said Melanie, not sure whether to laugh or feel shocked.

"I got into his account and watched as he paid a million into it. I assumed this was for our masked crook, so I took it first. This should throw the bastard off his breakfast and might give us a lead to him."

"It's going to upset him, that's a fact. And it will get worse if he finds out that the secret details of Australia's defence spending that ASIO fed to Falwell are fake."

"It looks like the spooks in Canberra are being kept fully aware of what's going on in the UK and USA," said Miller. "And they're keeping you in the loop as promised."

"It's a bit scary," said Melanie. "This is well above my pay grade."

"I'd say Hukkinen and the others with pacemakers will be more frightened. Our man may take it out on them."

"It's frightening, that's a fact."

"Anyway, one bright note," said Miller. "Let your contact know what's happening and that I'll return Hukkinen's money in a few minutes. Now I'll keep a watch on the account and see if I can get a trace on the next transaction to take it again."

"Let's hope so. Good luck." Melanie waited a few moments for Miller's face to vanish from the screen and made another call, knowing both her computer and the ASIO systems were now secure.

"Porter," said the voice at the other end.

"It's Miller who took Hukkinen's million pounds," said Melanie.

"We suspected so," said Porter. "He's thrown down the gauntlet okay. I hope Hukkinen survives this."

"Miller said he'd return the money immediately and then watch what happens. Maybe he'll be able to trace the removal when our man takes it."

"Maybe," said Porter. "He could be proving useful."

"I'll let you know if I get any more," said Melanie and terminated the call.

* * *

Canberra, Australia, January, 2024

After receiving a coded message from ASIO, James Falwell followed the same routine as before, climbing into the back of one of the five cars lined up under the tent in the parking lot of Parliament House and was driven out. Four of the cars took random routes through the city but the car containing Falwell went to the major hospital. In the underground parking lot, he was transferred to a stretcher, his face covered and wheeled up into the hospital. After first being taken to a private ward, he was stripped naked and carefully washed by two nurses, to his intense embarrassment before being moved to an operating theatre.

"Hello," said the nurse. "The remote monitoring system reported a fault in your pacemaker, so we're going to replace it. Are you okay with that?"

He studied the face, the lower part covered by a mask. From what he could see, she was a beautiful young woman and he wished he could see her full features.

"That's fine," he said.

A few moments later, he faded into bare consciousness as he was lifted onto the operating table. Dimly, he heard the conversations between nurses and a surgeon and at some point, woke up, still lying on the table.

"All done," said the same nurse. "Let's get you back to recovery."

Two days later, he returned home.

Thames Embankment, London, England, January, 2024

"Why have you called me out here?" Hukkinen was puzzled and somewhat irritated. The day had been busy, as usual when he received the handwritten note that had been delivered to the firm's reception desk by a teenage boy.

"Those blokes over there told me to," said the detective, pointing at the MI6 building across the river. "We've worked out a way to save your life."

"That sounds nice," said Hukkinen. "How the hell are you going to do that?"

"Don't be sarcastic," said the detective. "Here's how."

As he spoke, the ambulance arrived at the spot where they were standing.

"In," said the detective. "You're getting a new pacemaker, one without any communication facilities. I'll tell your office you were taken ill and you'll be back in a day or two."

Two days later, Hukkinen returned to work, the new scar on his chest itching but otherwise causing no difficulties.

Canberra, Australia, January, 2024

James Falwell was working from home, three days after the pacemaker had been replaced. The day was full, more than two hundred emails since the previous evening, about normal for the Prime Minister's office. The mask appeared on the screen. Falwell sat back, a sick sensation in his stomach. *What if this hadn't worked?*

"Falwell, you lying bastard, you tried to cheat me." The electronic distortion could not hide the fury in the speaker.

"Is that so?" replied Falwell. "How did I do that?"

"You know very well how you did it. You must have gone to the Prime Minister or ASIO about this without my knowing and you were given fake information. You made me look a fool to my client."

"Well then, that's the best news I've had all year," replied Falwell.

"Don't play games with me, Falwell, you're going to be dead in a few minutes."

Falwell didn't reply. Despite his outward calm, he felt scared, not certain of the replaced pacemaker and its immunity.

"Goodbye, Falwell," said the mask.

A few seconds passed. Falwell felt nothing.

"What the hell have you done?" raged the robotic voice. "Why isn't this working?"

"Beats me," said Falwell, relief flooding through his body. "You appear to have fucked up. Goodbye for now. We'll get you eventually."

The mask disappeared from the monitor. Falwell got up and made himself a fresh cup of coffee, trying to still the trembles that persisted.

Richmond, Middlesex, England, January, 2024

"So I see you replaced the million pounds, Paavo," said the distorted voice. The mask in his screen showed no expression. "That was very wise of you, or you'd be dead by now."

"I didn't replace it, fuckwit," said Hukkinen. "Somebody else took it to show you that you're not as bright as you think you are, but then he replaced it for my sake."

"Who took it? What the hell are you talking about? Nobody else could have broken into your account."

"Well, it seems you're wrong, little man," said Hukkinen. "Somebody most certainly did take that money and then replace it. The bank manager is going crazy with worry about it and he informed the police, but there's nothing they could find. So somewhere out there, there's a player who can do what you did and now he's on your trail. We'll find you soon."

"You're lying, Hukkinen. There's nobody else that can do that. You're lucky you put the money back in time, or you'd be dead by now. As it is, I'm going to teach you a lesson."

"Go ahead, little turd," said Hukkinen and sat back in his seat.

Several seconds passed, the mask continuing to glare at Hukkinen.

"What's happened?" shouted the ugly voice. "How are you still conscious?"

"Because you fucked up, shit-face," said Hukkinen, smiling. "You're not as clever as you think you are. Somebody is on your trail now, and when we find you, you'll end up in prison and I'll get my money back. Goodbye, idiot."

Hukkinen turned off the computer, realising he'd been frightened ever since the face had appeared. The relief he felt now was like waking from a nightmare.

Chapter 22

Newcastle, NSW, Australia, January, 2024

Doctor Declan Short was at his computer, reviewing the case files. He had two pacemaker surgeries that afternoon and then three the next day, and with the usual rounds of patients in the recovery ward, his days were always filled. But it was intensely satisfying work, knowing that with his efforts, people were given a new lease on life after the pain and difficulties of heart problems.

The details on his screen faded and an ugly mask appeared. It was white, with a wide mouth in an evil smile. Only the eyes were human, but not easily seen, being set back from the covering.

The surgeon sat back with a gasp. "What the hell..?" he said out loud.

"A good choice of words, Doctor Short," said a voice from the monitor. It was distorted, an electronic twisting of a human voice, impossible to identify as male or female. "Because now I'm going to give you hell."

The surgeon said nothing. The menace pouring out of his screen froze him.

"So you replaced the pacemaker in that spook with one without communications," continued the voice. "And you think that's going to stop me?"

Short remained silent not knowing what the mask was talking about.

"Well, tough shit doctor, because there are a lot of your patients still with the normal devices. I know all of them. All I had to do was get to the hospital records,

identify people you had given the devices to, check the
serial numbers and I can give all of them a very nasty
shock. In fact, Doctor, five of them are going to die and
it will be your fault. So think of that, Doctor, you are
directly responsible for the deaths of five innocent
people. I hope you never sleep again."

The mask vanished, leaving the surgeon breathing
hard, a sense of utter horror filling his body. He picked
up the phone and called the detective he had spoken to
the first time.

* * *

In Coffs Harbour, William Gaines was sitting on a
bench by the beach, enjoying the mild air and the
colourful scenes around him as young people walked
around in skimpy clothing. The jolt hit his chest and a
few seconds later he was dead.

In Wauchope, Lesley Freeman was entering the
coffee shop on the main street when she collapsed on
the pavement. She didn't hear the screams from the
people around her because she was dead as she hit the
ground.

In Collaroy on the northern beaches of Sydney,
Garry Lewis was crossing the road when he stopped,
gasped and fell on the road. Two cars screeched to a
halt, only just avoiding hitting him. But he wouldn't
have known that because he was dead.

In the far west of the state, in Broken Hill,
Raymond Potter was sweeping the floor of the Pro Hart
museum when he collapsed on the floor. He didn't hear
the commotion this caused because he was dead.

Angela Maynard was driving her Toyota down her road in Newcastle, about to turn into her driveway, when she died. The turn was incomplete, the car continued at an angle to the traffic flow, she missed a car coming towards her but smashed into the brick wall at the front of the apartment building, knocking down the bank of letter boxes. The other car stopped, the driver pushed the button on his stereo which was paired to the phone and called the police.

* * *

London, England, January, 2024

"So you saved Paavo Hukkinen from the errors of his ways, Doctor Sheridan? You will regret that."

Doctor Julie Sheridan swore at the screen. She had been updating the schedule for her team of surgeons in the cardiac unit of the hospital when a white mask appeared on the monitor. The voice was metallic, not at all human.

"That was clever, Doctor Sheridan, replacing his pacemaker with one that didn't have any communication facilities."

"Who the hell are you?" Sheridan said. "Get off my system."

"Not until you've heard what your action is going to cost," continued the voice. "You may have saved Paavo, but in exchange, five of your patients will be dead within the hour. Think carefully about what you plan to do with the remaining implants, doctor."

The mask vanished.

Five people died in the next hour in towns around England. All collapsed without warning and were dead within seconds. All had received pacemakers at the hands of Doctor Julie Sheridan within the last year.

Cheshire Countryside, UK, February, 2024

The tiny screen on Lloyd's telephone indicated that his wife's uncle was calling. These calls were rare, but never failed to make a spasm of worry surge through Lloyd whenever he saw one coming. Anxiety spread through him, but he knew he could not ignore the call.

"Good morning, Uncle," he said after picking up the handset.

"William, I have a commission for you," said the voice at the other end. There was no greeting, no polite preliminary.

"Yes, Uncle, how can I help you?"

"This comes from the Italian side of the family," said Giorgio Grassano. "They want your associates to do something major for them."

"And what is that?" Lloyd sensed that this was going to be serious and the anxiety spread.

"Not over the phone, William. Anna-Maria will give you all the details."

"I understand," said Lloyd.

The handset at the other end was replaced without a further word. Lloyd swore aloud at the contemptuous way Grassano treated him, but he knew there was nothing he could do about it. Within seconds, the door to his study opened and his wife came in.

"Uncle Giorgio has called you?" she said.

"Just now," Lloyd said.

"This is from my father," she said. She took a seat across from Lloyd's armchair. "He wants one of the two boys to kill off somebody who has been a serious threat to the family for years."

Lloyd took a deep breath. There had been no direct interference from Anna-Maria's family before now. This new development represented a severe increase in pressure and it frightened Lloyd. What else might the family demand of him? And what if he was unable to fulfil the requirements?

"Tell me what they want," he said.

"It's a man called Giovanni Molino. He's a leading prosecutor in the Italian National Anti-Mafia Department and he's been a real problem for us in recent years. My father wants him gone. We discovered that he had a pacemaker installed last year and we know which hospital did it. Here are the details."

She handed over a single sheet of paper. Lloyd took it reluctantly.

"There's a good incentive for this," Anna-Maria continued. "We'll pay a million US dollars into the boys' bank account with no contribution back, so it's a huge deal. But it must be done within a month before this bastard opens a new enquiry into the family."

She stood up and moved to the door. "As soon as possible, William," she said and walked out.

It took Lloyd half an hour before he felt able to contact Chang by the secure internet path that Chang had set up.

"A commission for you, Peter," said Lloyd when Chang's face appeared on the monitor.

"A commission? What do you mean, a commission?" Chang looked irritated.

"Our controllers want you to do something special."

"I don't understand. Since when has anyone told us what to do? I thought we just did our thing, paid the proceeds into their bank account, and then they paid our commission to our personal account. What's changed?"

"They want a major service. Now, before you get all steamed up, let me tell you that they'll pay you a million US dollars with no commission charged back. It's a clear profit for you and quite simple. You've already done some similar stuff."

"Okay, give me the details."

"Note this down," said Lloyd. "His name is Giovanni Molino. His pacemaker was installed in April last year at the San Donato hospital in Milan."

"Italy? We haven't tackled anyone in Europe before and I don't speak Italian."

"You don't have to. Just wipe him out, there's no need to warn him, threaten him or any other communication. And do it quickly. It's got to be done before the end of the month."

"Okay, no problem." Chang showed no emotion. "Who is he and what's he done?"

"You don't need to know any of that," said Lloyd. "Just do it and as soon as we see it's done, the money goes into your account."

"Consider it done," said Chang and disconnected the call.

Lloyd went to his cupboard and poured himself a stiff drink. He was churning with a mixture of emotions. Ordering the murder of somebody he didn't know was both frightening and exhilarating with the sense of power it gave him. He swallowed the drink in one gulp.

What the hell had he got himself into?

The Guardian, January, 2024

One of Italy's most effective mafia-hunters, Giovanni Molino (57) has died in Rome two days ago. Molino, a major player in the Italian Ministry of Justice's war on the Mafia was reported to have died of heart failure following a heart attack last year after which he was given a pacemaker. He had been under police protection for some years because of his success in finding and prosecuting key Mafia members and was believed to be in the final stages of bringing a prosecution against Massimo Grassano, believed to be the head of the Italian Mafia operation. Despite the constant threat of Mafia attacks to silence him, there appear to be no grounds for a suspicious death. Molino is survived by his wife Francesca and two sons.

Chapter 23

Chicago, Illinois, USA, February, 2024

Robyn Trigg was preparing her usual lunch of salad and a small piece of fish when the computer burbled with the indicator that a video call was incoming. This was not unusual, several of her friends called during the day to check up on her condition since she had returned from surgery.

She moved to her desk and pressed the key. "Hi," she said, but the response was unexpected.

A masked face appeared, one that she had seen before on newspaper articles, magazine discussions and similar, a white face with a huge smile, framed by a thin black beard and moustache. She could just make out eyes behind the gaps but couldn't say whether they were those of a man or a woman. "Good afternoon, Robyn," said an ugly, distorted voice, like the eyes, impossible to define as male or female.

"Who is this?" she replied, half thinking this was a prank from one of her friends or possibly her son who lived in Decatur.

"Nobody you know, Robyn," said the horrible voice. "But I'm calling to congratulate you on being one of the first people to get an insulin pump installed in your body to control the diabetes."

Robyn felt some panic. There was something seriously malignant in the voice. She didn't reply.

"It must be a huge relief," continued the voice. "No longer do you have to monitor the blood sugar, you just let that neat little device do it for you and inject the precise insulin quantity to keep you conscious and alive."

Robyn found her voice. "Who the hell are you and what do you want," she snapped, anxiety adding an edge to her voice.

"Ah, so now we get to the heart of the matter," said the metallic, artificial voice. "Who I am is not important. What I want is a hundred thousand dollars."

"What?"

"You heard me, Robyn. Now I know you're a very rich woman. You own that expensive apartment near the Chicago Cubs baseball field, your late husband left you eighteen million dollars when he died last year. Such a waste, I thought. Such a brilliant man. But it means you can well afford the money. So here's what I want you to do. Place the money in your account within ten days and I'll just take it when I see it there."

"You can't do that!" Robyn's fear was replaced by anger. "Nobody can break into a bank's computer system. You're a fucking idiot, whoever you are. Not get off my phone."

She disconnected the call, realising she was breathing hard. She started the exercises she had learnt from her Yoga classes, slowly getting her breathing under control and returned to slicing mushrooms for her salad.

The phone rang. She picked it up, expecting a normal call like the several she received every day from friends. But it wasn't.

"That was very foolish of you, Robyn," said the nightmarish voice. "Let me give you some information. Not only can I break into any bank account I wish, I can also hack into your brilliant new insulin pump. You do realise that the pump communicates remotely with the computers at the hospital, don't you? So that means I can take over control of your insulin delivery at any time I want. Do you now understand?"

"You're lying," she snapped. "That's impossible."

"So now I'm going to prove it to you," said the speaker. "I've just stopped the pump. In the next couple of hours, you're going to slip into a coma. You could die quickly, but I'm going to restart the insulin flow and you will recover."

"I don't believe you."

"You had better. Now here's the rest. If you go to the hospital, they'll find nothing wrong. They won't see that the pump had stopped for a while, despite the monitoring system, because I've got into their computer and ensured it doesn't record a problem. Now do you see why you are going to pay me my hundred grand?"

"I'm calling the police."

Even with the distortion, Robyn heard the laugh.

"Do that, Robyn. They won't be able to trace this call and they'll think you're trying to fool them. They won't like that. Now, what I suggest is that you go and lie down for the rest of the day and when you sense the blackness starting, you call the ambulance to take you to the emergency ward."

Robyn no longer had any doubts about what that terrible voice was saying. Just two hours later, she did feel the oncoming of a problem. Her vision was blurred and she felt the room was getting dark. She was just able to press the emergency button on the pendant she wore round her neck and she collapsed onto the floor.

As she slowly returned to awareness, she looked at her watch. She struggled to her feet, just as the apartment door opened and two uniformed medical officers entered.

"Robyn," one of them said. "You pressed your emergency call." He gently nudged her to an armchair, took her hands and began a careful examination.

"I did. My insulin pump acted up and I went into a coma."

"But you're okay now?"

"I am. It must have been a temporary glitch."

"Let's check that," he said and took a small device from his bag. "I need you to open your shirt at your waist, so I can apply this." He waited while she lifted her shirt from the waist of her jeans then gently pressed the device on her stomach, where the pump was installed. He studied the screen carefully, then shook his head.

"No sign of a stoppage," he said. "Maybe we should take you to the hospital for a full check-up."

"No," she replied. "I just reacted badly. The pump was only installed a few days ago. I think I panicked."

"Well, you certainly seem okay now," the medic said and began packing away his monitor. "If you're sure you're okay…"

"I am," she said. "Thanks for coming so quickly."

When the two had left, Robyn realised she was completely under the control of the frightening caller and knew what she had to do. Then the phone rang. She picked it up, fully expecting what she would hear.

"So now do you believe me, Robyn?"

"I do," she said.

"And do you also believe that if you go to the police, I will kill you?"

"I do."

"Good. Make sure that money is in your account as soon as possible."

The call was disconnected. Robyn put down the handset and sat back, trembling over her whole body.

Each day, she checked her account. On the fifth day, the hundred thousand appeared after she had liquidated several assets and paid the receipts in. Three hours later, the money disappeared. Soon after that, the phone rang. Feeling panic, she lifted the handset. But the speaker was a normal male voice.

"Mrs Trigg, this is James Maloney, the bank manager. I've seen the big transfer in and out of a hundred thousand dollars. I need to be sure this is legitimate, as I'm required by law to advise the authorities of any transfer over ten thousand. Can you explain this transaction?"

"No problem, Mr Maloney. I'm just investing in a new building I plan to acquire."

"Can you give me more details? This seems very strange. I can't identify where the money went."

Robyn began to feel panic. "Please, Mr Maloney, there's nothing suspicious." She replaced the phone, feeling massive panic. If the manager reported this, would the caller know about it? Was she about to die?

Later that day, the doorbell to her apartment rang. When Robyn opened the door, a young girl stood there. She didn't speak but held up a card. On it were printed the words, *"Don't speak. Read this note. Nod if you understand."*

Not sure if this was part of the blackmail process, Robyn nodded. The girl handed over a single sheet of paper. The message was short and to the point.

"I am Lieutenant Jim Carstairs of the Chicago police. I know that you are being blackmailed. We need to talk. Don't say anything, don't let this paper near the computer. Come to the Old St Louis blues bar on Fullerton at seven. I'll see you and we can talk. We are on this case in other countries, you are not alone."

Later that day, Robyn took a seat at a table in the bar. The music hadn't started yet, and the noise level was quite low as the customers talked and drank. A heavy-set, African man drinking alone at a table across the room stood up and came to her.

"Robyn?" he asked. "Lieutenant Jim Carstairs." He briefly displayed a police identification card. She nodded and he sat down across from her.

"Up till now, we know of several cases where people with pacemakers have been attacked in the way you have. The demands have mostly been for money, but a couple have been for information that the subject has because of their position in government. This is the first time an insulin pump has been hacked, but this is relatively new technology, so it's a shock."

"My god," said Robyn. "Who the hell is doing this and can it be stopped?"

"We don't know yet, but it's happened here, in the UK and in Australia. The security forces of all three countries are working on it and some breaks have occurred. Did you get a demand?"

"I did. The voice was horribly distorted, I've got no idea whether it was a man or a woman and the first call on the computer had a horrible white mask. But it wanted a hundred thousand dollars."

"Can you pay such an amount?"

"I've already done it. Somehow, this bastard knew I'm a rich woman. How the hell could he know that?"

"Robyn, it seems he hacked into the hospital computer and identified you as the recipient of the insulin pump. It was probably easy then to find out more about you. This hacker is brilliant, there's no doubt."

"Is there any way you can protect me? He said he could kill me and it's obvious that he can."

Carstairs nodded. "Yes, Robyn, there's a way, but you may not like it. What has been done with a couple of pacemaker patients was replace the device with one without communication facilities. We could have the hospital take out the pump and you go back to the original way of injecting yourself with insulin when you need it. Meanwhile, what I want you to do is record the next internet call. There are ways of bringing back the original voice and that will help us identify him. When we break this open, maybe we can get the money back."

"That's not very comforting, Lieutenant. My medical bill was enormous for that new operation already, even with insurance. Who's going to pay for this?"

"That will be taken care of, I promise."

"How can he break into bank computers? I thought they were totally secure."

"Like I said, he's brilliant. But we do have the help of a guy who is probably just as brilliant, possibly even more so. He's working on identifying this bastard."

"Then I hope to god he finds him. You're sure that the medical bills will be handled?"

"That's the promise I've been given. And when this is all over, the same with replacing the pump."

"Okay, Lieutenant, will you see to it?"

He got to his feet. "I will, Robyn. And the computer record will show somebody with a different name and procedure, just in case he's still following you. Do you need a ride home?"

"No, I like this place. I think I'll stay and listen to the music and try and forget this is all happening."

The detective nodded and walked out of the bar.

Two days later, the computer signalled another video call. Seated at her desk, Robyn simultaneously pressed keys to answer the call and start the recording.

"Thank you for the money, Robyn," said the inhuman, distorted voice. "I can assure you, it has gone to a good cause."

Robyn said nothing.

"So I would just like to reassure you," continued the voice from behind the mask. "I won't make any further demands of you, not this year, anyway."

Robin continued her silence.

"Nothing to say to me, Robyn? Aren't you grateful that you're safe for at least a few months?"

"Yes, I've got something to say. I'm pretty sure you're doing this to lots of people. And it's a safe bet that you've killed at least one of them. So my forecast is that you'll get more and more confident of what you're doing and at some stage you'll make a mistake. And that's when they'll get you and you'll get the death sentence. You probably know that in America, we don't do executions very well, it takes a long time and causes a lot of pain. That's in your future."

Even behind the mask, Robyn saw the fear in the eyes. The call was terminated a second later.

"Gotcha," muttered Robyn. She felt she'd won that round.

* * *

For the second time, Robyn met the detective in the blues bar.

"Well done," said Lieutenant Carstairs. "We were able to restore the voice and it was a man, most likely British, we reckon middle-aged. We sent it to the security people in Australia and the UK where they have local knowledge and they said it was a man, probably in his forties, English from a specific region of England. They know rather more than that, but they're keeping it close to their chests."

"That's got to help," said Robyn.

"It does, a lot. And you were right, some deaths have resulted. And it's not just us working on this, the police and the security forces in Britain and Australia are all on it. We'll get them eventually."

"Them?"

"There's more than one, but that's as much as I can tell you. Enjoy the music."

The huge man rose from his seat and walked out.

Chapter 24

Mid-North Coast, NSW, Australia, February, 2024

Alex Weyland walked into Melanie Carter's office, brandishing several sheets of paper and a wide smile. Melanie looked up suspiciously.

"You're looking very smug, Senior Constable Weyland. Does this mean you've performed another feat of extraordinary genius?"

"We'd better get out of here, Ma'am."

Twenty minutes later, they were seated in a small coffee shop seven kilometres from the police station.

"Why this place, Alex?" Melanie asked.

"It's one of several I've found with no security camera and no wi-fi set-up. I think we're secure here, even if Miller's new firewall is working. Anyway, no need to talk, Ma'am. Just look at this."

A few minutes later, she looked up from the papers and stared at him.

"Holy shit, Alex. Now all we need is some help from Allen and we might have this broken wide open. Start working on your sergeant's exams, you've earned significant brownie points here. Tell me how you did this."

"Actually, not difficult, Ma'am. Just your standard police hard grind."

* * *

A Week Earlier

Alex took a desk in one of the university's library study carrels with its own computer. He was certain this would be safe from any hacker who could be watching him, which is why he told his wife he planned to be out much of the day. She was initially annoyed, but when he wrote the reasons on a sheet of paper, writing also that he could not risk his home computer being hacked and the conversation overheard, she nodded her understanding.

On this Saturday morning, the library was almost empty, and the rows of carrels had only a handful of other people working quietly.

The first phase, assuming that the linguistics professor had been correct in her analysis of the three voices they had heard, that one of the hackers had studied in Manchester and was of Hong Kong Chinese origin, was to find out the universities in that city. Ruth Blackston had named two, but there could be more.

He started the search with a query of the universities in the whole county of Lancashire. That list was far too long and he almost lost heart. Then he reviewed the information Ruth had given. If the hacker's family was wealthy enough to have sent the boy to school in England and the boy was of the intellectual abilities required to have the computer skills needed, it was likely that he went to the major city and the best university. The revised search showed five main universities in Manchester.

"Better," Alex muttered to himself. "How many of them offer degrees in computer technology?"

Only four of them did, including the two Ruth had named, Manchester and Salford. Reviewing the course contents of all of them, Alex felt that one of them was too business oriented and one, while only a small university had the degree awarded by Lancaster University which was an old, established institution.

"Let's hope I get lucky," he mumbled aloud. "Let's go with the big one."

It was time consuming, but eventually Alex had a list of graduates starting from ten years earlier, the point he had decided was the earliest date the hacker would have been a student. The data wasn't protected, he simply accessed the yearbook. Computer technology graduates were not separate, but each graduate was named with the degree earned, there was a small picture alongside their name and some brief comments about the graduate's interests and experience. Also listed was the name and location of their previous school. Slowly, Alex began to work his way through the long file. After twenty-three minutes, he sat back with a sense of a small victory. A young, Oriental face looked out of the computer screen. Alex wrote down the name and any details that looked relevant.

"One down," he said. He took a screen shot of the details and saved it to the flash drive he had inserted in the computer.

It took another ninety-seven minutes to complete the ten-year old list, with two more Chinese faces and names showing up. Alex closed the file and accessed the yearbook for nine years ago. The time was eight minutes past eleven in the morning.

At one-thirty, Alex turned off the computer, eased his stiff limbs from the cubicle and located the university refectory. A meat pie and a mug of coffee quickly consumed, he returned to the library, took a different carrel and started on the yearbook from three years ago. His list contained twenty-six names and faces. Three hours later, the list had grown to forty-one. Nine of those referenced Manchester schools attended before university. Alex took a deep breath, checked his watch, and saw it was five o'clock. He did one more thing and numbered each of the entries.

"Home, I think," he said softly, "or there could be a divorce in my future." Smiling at the idea, knowing how strong his marriage was, he left the university and drove home to his wife and baby daughter.

Sunday morning saw Alex back in the carrels by ten. By four that afternoon, he had twenty-three more names of potential prey from the second university.

* * *

Monday morning, Alex called Melanie at her home at just after seven.

"I need to take some time today, Ma'am. I want to take Cathie Lyn to the doctor."

"Understood," said Melanie. She really had understood. Using his daughter's two names was their agreed signal that Alex was working on a case away from the office. No chances were taken that the hackers would be listening in on their telephone conversations.

Alex returned to the university library.

"Great work, Alex," said Melanie, folding the eight sheets into her handbag. "Now it's up to Allen to check the remaining facts. That ability is outside our skill sets, I think."

"Yes, Ma'am," said Alex. "You can pay for the coffee and muffins."

"Not a problem," said Melanie. "Now I have a call to make."

She returned to her office, then spoke one word. "Allen?"

It was a few moments before Miller's face appeared.

"Yes, Melanie."

"I have some seriously useful information for you," she said. "Record these images. There are eight of them."

One at a time, she held the pages in front of the screen for a few moments.

"Interesting," said Miller after the last page had been folded away. "I'll get back to you."

* * *

Two days later, Miller appeared on Melanie's computer monitor.

"Four of them," said Miller. He recited four numbers. "These four all live in Hong Kong, all from wealthy families. There's no guarantee that any of them is the one we want, but it's a start. I've got into their computers, it was easy with three of them, but one has set up a first-class firewall and it's going to take me a while to break through that. That makes him number one suspect."

"Noted," said Melanie and discontinued the call.

Chapter 25

New York, USA, February, 2024

"Thank you for seeing me, Ms Faversham."

The short, thick-set young man placed his briefcase by his seat and sat down across from the desk of the thin-faced woman. He nodded at the two other men seated behind her, but they made no acknowledgement of the gesture. The woman had not offered to shake the hand of the newcomer.

"When the CIA tells me to meet somebody from the National Security Agency, I can hardly refuse," said Faversham. Her hostility was almost like steam rising from a wet body in the sun.

"I imagine so," said the visitor. "My name is Cory Wainright and, as you know, I'm from the NSA. Perhaps you could introduce me to your colleagues?"

"They are my legal counsel and my director of technology," said Faversham, but no names were announced.

"Then let me get right to the matter," said Wainwright. He seemed to be hiding some internal amusement. "Let me also tell you that similar meetings are taking place over the next few hours with your opposite numbers, the heads of the companies that produce pacemakers in the UK, Ireland and Belgium, as well as the other American company. The Chinese organisation did not return our request for a meeting."

The woman said nothing.

"You will recall, that when Vice President Cheney was elected back in 2001, considerable concern was expressed that his pacemaker might be susceptible to hacking," said Wainright. He looked around the room but none of the three faces before him showed any reaction.

"So what they did was equip him with a device that had no communication facilities at all," continued Wainright. "The main concern was not so much the sort of hacking we have experienced where some unknown party has literally stopped the actions of the device, but more a worry that somebody might be able to listen in to the Vice-President's conversations with critical personnel."

"This we knew, Mr Wainright," said Faversham. "Please get to the point."

"The point, Ms Faversham, is that the NSA took it upon itself to do something about the danger presented by the communication facilities of implanted medical devices such as pacemakers, insulin pumps and other devices still to be developed. We anticipated the possibilities of direct hacking into the devices and causing the sorts of problems that have been experienced in the last few months. We assigned some of the best medical and communications scientists to the task."

"We have done the same, Mr Wainright. And I have no doubt our people are closing in on the problem."

Wainwright smiled. "I have no doubt either, Ms Faversham. But this is the NSA. The security of communications technology is what we do best. And we solved the problem a long time ago. We were ready to offer it to the manufacturers at the time, but the administration of the day considered that socialism and stopped it. But the recent breakout of criminal hacking has made it critical that you adopt it."

The other three looked unmoved.

"And that's why I'm here," said Wainright. "We will provide the encryption technique and the design of the tiny electronic device that must be added to the circuitry of the pacemaker at no charge. The same offer is being made to all your competitors."

The woman folded her arms across her chest in a classically defensive posture. "And what if we decline your offer?" she said.

"Legislation goes before the House this week that will make it illegal to sell any implanted medical device without this technology," said Wainright. "You will surely develop the same solution some time, but meanwhile, your sales will be stopped until your devices conform to this new standard. I very much doubt that your competitors overseas will refuse our offer, it will save them huge sums in research and development and if you do not follow suit, frankly, they'll eat you alive."

He lifted up his briefcase from the side of his seat, opened it and extracted an envelope and a small box.

"In the box is the new addition to your circuitry," he said. "The papers in the envelope are the encryption coding you will need, plus the blueprints for the device. The coding can be transferred to the existing pacemakers during the standard tests the hospitals perform when the reader is placed over the device and the data transferred for the surgeons to review. The vast majority of people with pacemakers don't need the full security technical addition, so it's likely only a few critical personnel should get the updated devices. That's not a decision for your organisation to make."

He closed his briefcase and stood up.

"Ms Faversham, gentlemen, good day to you," he said and left the room.

Chapter 26

Canberra, Australia, February, 2024

The mood in the secure room was sombre.

"We saved the lives of two of the targets," said Gordon Porter. "But at a hell of a cost. Five people were murdered in the USA, five in the UK and and five here, all by the same method, stopping the heart by hacking the pacemaker."

"Any connection between them?" asked one of the agents.

Porter nodded. "In each country, all five were operated on at the same hospital and by the same surgeon. You can imagine how they feel."

"Holy shit," murmured the agent.

"Indeed," said Porter. "There's no way we can protect any other victim by using a safe pacemaker. As it is, we complicated the lives of those two already. They can't have their devices monitored remotely, so they have to visit the hospital at least twice a week to have them checked there. Until the manufacturers come up with a way of insulating their things, or we get the bastards doing it, they'll have to live with the inconvenience."

Porter picked up a single sheet of paper he had brought in with him. "However," he continued, "we may have a small breakthrough, courtesy of Melanie Carter and her team. She has a young detective working with her, Senior Constable Alex Weyland. Melanie has told me he has an impressive ability to hunt down data that helps the cases and he may have done it again. Following Ruth Watson's speech analysis, Weyland did some solid hunting by computer and identified a number of Chinese students who have graduated from Manchester's major universities in Information Technology. The list went to Allen Miller, who used his remarkable, if illegal skills to examine each of them and found that four of them lived in Hong Kong. One of them has installed a unique and so far impenetrable firewall which Miller is now trying to break, and that makes him suspect number one."

He paused as a murmur of interest ran round the room.

"This doesn't guarantee a successful search," said Porter. "There may be more possibles at the universities that Weyland has not yet investigated, but his work has shown a way of looking for our perpetrators. If and when Miller breaks into this man's computer, we may find more."

"Bright young man, there," said another of the agents, a woman in her twenties wearing a dress in autumnal colours.

"That's what Melanie said," agreed Porter. "He was a patrol officer in Melanie's original station, but he displayed some extraordinary talents and she had him moved to Criminal Investigation. Apparently, he's a first-class chess player and that may have helped. Okay, and now for something even more interesting."

The room went silent. Porter's tones indicated something critical.

"I got the information this morning from our Embassy in Beijing," he said. "They were able to learn that the Chinese government was deeply disturbed and angry at Australia's plans to install missiles near Darwin that could reach the sea bases China is building in the Pacific."

"But we're not planning to install such missile bases," said an agent. "Where did they get that from?"

Porter displayed a rare grin. "From the faked documents we gave to James Falwell of the Prime Minister's department."

A murmur of amusement ran round the conference table.

"So now we know who Chappie's client is, one of them at least," said the young woman agent. "Isn't it great when a plan works? It's going to be funny when the Chinese government registers a protest with ours. Much hilarity will ensue."

"Probably," said Porter. "But the implications are serious. If our pals in the UK and USA adopt this on a wider scale, we could generate considerable tensions between countries. It might be wise for us all to restrict false data to internal matters and not something that could get a major foreign power upset. I'll send them a note to that effect."

"Well at least we seem to be on a track that might lead somewhere," said the young woman agent.

"True," said Porter. "But we're not really any nearer identifying the culprits. Let's hope that Miller is able to get into that computer in Hong Kong and finds some pointers to the associates. Okay, that's it for now, all of you keep scouting out possible blackmail victims and I don't have to remind you, keep absolutely silent about this. Meanwhile, Melanie and her team will focus on criminal aspects of this event, our responsibility is the national security aspect, though our findings will probably be helpful to both of us."

He paused and the room went silent, recognising that something new was to be told to them.

"There's a new dimension and a worrying one," Porter said. "I heard from our American colleagues that a woman in Chicago is being threatened in the same way as those with pacemakers have been. She doesn't have a pacemaker, she has a relatively new piece of technology, an insulin pump to combat diabetes. In the same way as the pacemakers, these pumps are monitored through the internet by the hospitals and so can be hacked. This woman received the same distorted call, demanding a hundred thousand dollars and was sent into a coma when the pump was briefly stopped and then restarted. Medics arrived as she was able to press her emergency button, but they found no record of the pump malfunctioning. It's obviously the same operating people and it's a dangerous expansion. We must expect a similar event here and in the UK."

The meeting broke up, all the agents seemingly deep in thought.

Chapter 27

Mid North Coast, Australia, February, 2024

Melanie's screen flickered and Miller's face appeared.

"Yes," she said.

"Some information," said Allen Miller. "No identification yet, but this may be useful. I've broken into the systems the hackers did and had a look at how they would have done it. Something you may not know, but a hacker leaves indicators in the system they hack. It's not deliberate, it's just a pointer to the techniques used. I looked at the hospital computers in Australia and the UK and the servers used by the others. There are two separate hackers, they are using identical code, though one looks a little more polished. I would say the latter one is the originator who has polished the code a little after giving it to the other hacker. I found no signs of a third."

"Any luck with identifying those other computers?"

"Not yet. I have to admit, that guy in Hong Kong has done a clever job of building a firewall. I can't break it yet."

Even over the phone, Melanie heard the irritation in Miller's voice and couldn't help smiling.

"Keep at it," she said. "We're counting on you."

"I know."

The call was terminated. Yet again, Melanie wondered what part of the world Miller was using as a residence, then she made another call.

"Meeting in thirty minutes," she said when Jack answered.

"I'll get the noise level up," he said.

Melanie replaced the handset and returned to the office.

* * *

"I have some thoughts on this," said Jack.

Around them, the racket of several engines running at high speed made hearing difficult, but ensured nobody could overhear them, regardless of the technology available. Despite Miller's assurance, she still preferred to hold some meetings well away from the office, not knowing if she was being watched.

"I think we have a sort of Charles Dickens story going on," Jack continued. "All the indications are that the two hackers are young, brilliant but not especially worldly. The sort of things they have demanded from security agents and politicians would not be the sort of things they would think of themselves, they'd be far more likely to want money, as they have done with the first victims."

"They're doing that on orders or advice from somebody else?" said Alex.

"Exactly," said Jack. "And the stuff they asked for is not anything they could use on their own initiative. They probably sold the material to somebody else, like the Chinese government, or somebody with large sums of money to invest in likely profitable areas, like the fake municipal developments in the British Midlands."

"You think there's some Fagin-like character driving this?" Melanie was almost amused at the concept. Charles Dickens was one of her favourite authors in her teens and she had studied 'Oliver Twist' at school.

"I do. Notice that he hasn't done any of the high-tech stuff, though he has used the voice distortion software to make the demands. The voice analysis indicated an older person. This is somebody already involved in organised crime and somehow he found these two brilliant kids and recognised their potential."

"I wonder how he did that," said Melanie. "We know that the two hackers spent some years in the Manchester area and Ruth detected that accent in both their voices. But the other one was from the Birmingham region, with just a tiny trace of Manchester in his accent."

"I called her about that," said Jack. "She said the Birmingham regional accents are very strong, very much like Scottish accents or those from the North-east of England, what is known as Geordie. A speaker with those tones will probably never absorb an obvious Manchester accent, even after some years. This man may have been working in Manchester for a relatively short time, or maybe a regular visitor there, like a commercial traveller or contract consultant."

"And we sent Ruth the recording you made of the woman, said Melanie. "That provided some interesting additions to the profiles. Ruth said that the accent was predominantly Lancashire and some Cheshire, indicating a woman who had spent most of her childhood growing up in that region, but there was a tiny trace of southern European, probably Italian. Ruth thinks the woman's parents were from southern Europe."

"So perhaps the man's wife," suggested Jack.

"This certainly helps us build up a profile of the

likely crooks," said Melanie. "But still no identification. But I do see one possibility. As you said, the two hackers are young, brilliant but unworldly. As we all know, most criminals are found through some silly mistake they have made. I'd say the chances are high USAthat one or both of them will do something careless or even downright stupid that will open the doors."

"Very likely," said Jack. "I just hope they don't kill anyone else before then."

The discussion was over. Jack went round the various machines and switched off the engines. Melanie and Alex returned to their office, saying little but both of them deep in thought. On her return to her office, Melanie wrote a note to send to Porter, outlining the latest developments.

Canberra, Australia, March, 2024

"We're getting some interesting results from our false trails," said Porter. "I don't know how long this will continue before the hackers find out they've been scammed and it's a massive worry that they might take it out on innocent people again. But for now, this is what we've learnt from our own results and from those of MI6."

The agents in the secure room stirred with interest.

"As forecast, the Chinese government reacted badly to being informed that we are planning major defensive actions against their South Pacific bases. Our Prime Minister and Foreign Minister were both astonished to hear this complaint and their protestations that this was completely untrue met with strongly worded disbelief from the Chinese."

"Does this mean we'll have to inform the government of what's going on?" asked one of the agents.

"It's a dilemma," said Porter. "There's no way of knowing if our chappie has hacked into government computers and if he'd overhear ministers discussing the situation. That would blow our false trail gambit wide open and put people at risk. I've discussed this with our Director-General and he agreed that it was too big a risk. For now, we'll keep quiet, let the Chinese protest and our people deny it all. At least, that way, chappie will not know he's being scammed."

A murmur of amusement ran around the conference table.

"Our friends in the UK have had some fascinating results," continued Porter. "They provided the Cabinet Minister with some stuff to feed our suspect to avoid some falsified pornographic material being broadcast, which would have destroyed his career and his life. He fed this to chappie. One of them stated that the British were about to buy several Littoral ships for coastal operations against drug and people smugglers. The funny thing is that these ships are built here in Australia. Within days of the Minister providing this totally false information, shares in the company in Adelaide have risen by thirty percent after heavy buying on the stock exchange. The company is delighted, of course, but there's no indication of who's buying. They've tried to track the buyer, but this has only led to dead ends. But somebody has obviously bought the information from chappie and hidden the trail very well."

"Somebody is going to be seriously shat off when they discover the truth," said the young woman agent, trying to hide her mirth.

"Indeed," said Porter. "And that will put the hackers in serious difficulties with the buyers. But again, the worry is how they will react. They've shown they are quite ruthless."

"Was there something else the minister was given?" asked another agent.

"The second item was that a massive development of a new satellite town was to be built in the British Midlands," said Porter. "There has been some discussion on these lines in recent years, so a specific area had been suggested. As of a few days ago, several real estate agents have been getting inquiries about purchasing land in those regions. The inquirers were not identified and the agents were puzzled, as they had no knowledge of anything to cause the interest. However, what this proves is that the hackers appear to have clients willing to buy valuable information, regardless of how it was acquired. MI6 are working at identifying these people and we've assigned specialists to find out the buyers of the shipping company shares."

"It's a dangerous game," said one of the agents.

"Damn right," said Porter. "Horrible as it is to think it, we may be the cause of some innocents dying or being destroyed. I hope to god this doesn't happen." He looked round the room. All his agents looked sombre. "However," he continued, "I can report some very positive results from one case of attempted blackmail for military secrets."

The agents stirred, seemingly re-energised by this.

"I haven't reported this to you before, because this is the biggest example of potential damage to international peace, but now I can. Some weeks ago, a Group Captain in the Royal Air Force Command operations in High Wycombe received one of those calls. It was the same sort as had been received by the British Cabinet Minister, accompanied by a pornographic film apparently showing the officer engaged in a variety of sexual escapades. What is interesting is that the movie had several errors in it, chiefly obvious mistakes in the body of the man claimed to be Group Captain. It indicates some immaturity in the perpetrators. They were quite shoddy in this job, probably reflecting their belief in their own brilliance and so becoming careless. This may open up opportunities. The demand was for RAF plans in the event of an attack on what was termed, "a certain Middle-East country." This was assumed to be Israel. The officer recorded the call, as is standard operating procedure for calls from outside the station and our colleagues in MI6 applied the corrective software. They identified the caller as the British man from the Midlands of England."

A buzz of interest ran round the room.

"This presented an enormous opportunity for counter-terrorism," continued Porter. "But it also presented risks. While MI6 could create a false document as they did before, the issue was whether indicating that the UK would respond to an attack on

Israel with massive force, probably supported by the USA, would persuade the attackers to go to war immediately, or to back away from such actions. On the other hand, if the fake report indicated no support from the UK, would this encourage the attackers or delay any such actions for a few more years while they built up their own forces?

"So MI6 decided they needed to consult with their government and met with the Secretary of Defence and their Military top people. The decision was to indicate massive force would be sent to Israel. I won't give you the details, but what I can tell you is that a week after giving these fake details to the hacker, our agent in Tehran reported agitation in the Iranian government and top military officials.

"So now we know one of the clients of these hackers and this means we can apply some diplomatic pressures when needed. But it means these people are deadly serious in what they are doing. As they appear to be very young and also naïve, it suggests they are getting some high-level support from a foreign power, most likely China, North Korea, Russia or Iran. Keep this under your hats and we'll see what happens next."

The meeting broke up in sombre mood.

Phase Four

End Game

Chapter 28

Mid-North Coast, NSW, Australia, April, 2024

"Ma'am, I have an idea, but it would need Miller's involvement." Alex looked unsure of himself as he sat across from Melanie's desk.

"That's unusual," replied Melanie. "You've never asked for that before. Let's hear it."

"Can we get Miller on the line, save explaining it twice?" said Alex.

Melanie looked thoughtfully at the young constable, then tapped her computer screen. "Allen, you there?" she asked.

"As always, Melanie," came the immediate response. Miller's image appeared on the screen. A slight smile was evident. "Your faithful servant." The laugh in his tones was obvious.

"Alex would like a word with you," she said. "Alex?"

"Good morning, Allen," said Alex. "Or afternoon, or evening, wherever you are."

"Any will do. How can I help you?"

"As you know, I tracked down the likely Chinese Hong Kong hacker by just going through the year books of the top Manchester universities."

"I do, and very impressive work it was, young man."

"Thank you. And so it seems to me we could find the mystery man in Birmingham in much the same way. The year books were online, but this information won't be, but it might be identifiable by going through the university files to find somebody teaching in the top Manchester schools who was at school in the Midlands and also perhaps at university there. But I can't access those files. I bet you can."

This time, the laugh was obvious. "Thank you for that vote of confidence, Alex. This must be the first time a cop has asked me to do something illegal!"

"But can you do it?" asked Alex.

"Do bears crap in the woods? Of *course* I can do it. I'll get back to you."

The screen went blank before either Melanie or Alex could say anything more.

"Of course, he has a point," said Melanie. "You've just asked a known criminal to break the law to assist us."

"Technically, I didn't," replied Alex. "I just said he could do it."

"A very fine point that probably wouldn't save us if any police ethics review took place. But I doubt that will happen and I bet Miller has deleted the record of this communication already. So, off the record, a good idea, Alex. Let's see what he comes up with."

"Yes, Ma'am."

* * *

"Good morning, Melanie," said Miller on the monitor four days later.

"Yes, Allen?"

"His name is William Lloyd," said Miller. "As you all suspected, schooled in Birmingham, then did an honours degree in History at the University of Manchester, a teacher's certificate at a local college then became a teacher at the same school in Manchester where our Chinese buddy attended. He retired from that a year ago. Now comes the interesting part. The school's file didn't give his present address. I suspect he or one of his boys wiped that and nobody has noticed yet. I can't get into his personal computer, either. I located it, but surprise, surprise, it has the same impenetrable firewall around it as has that of the Hong Kong hacker."

"Very useful," said Melanie. "I've no doubt we could locate him, but I want him unsuspecting while we track down his associates. Well done, Allen."

"One more thing. In his final year at university, he married one Anna-Maria Grassano, the niece of Giorgio Grassano, believed to be the regional Mafia boss, reporting to his brother in Sicily."

"Now that does add another dimension," said Melanie. "And it seems to confirm the voice analyses that Ruth conducted. I'm sure the boys will be fascinated by that."

"Undoubtedly," said Miller and the connection was broken without another word.

"That's fascinating," said Alex. "That hunch paid off well."

"Indeed," said Melanie. "Something useful for us to take down to Canberra next week."

"Canberra again?" Jack Savage looked interested.

"We've got information to give them," said Melanie.

* * *

Melanie looked round the room and thought she detected a different attitude in the anti-terrorist group round the table. As always, she had been the focus of every eye as she entered, but instead of the obvious ogling, this time she sensed some professional respect.

"Welcome back, Chief Inspector Carter, Professor Savage," said Chief Superintendent Harvey. "I understand you have new information for us."

"Yes, sir, we do," said Melanie. "The solid, detailed grind work of our Detective Senior Constable Alex Welland was what first narrowed the hunt for the hackers. He brought the scope down to just a handful of likely suspects and it was then Allen Miller who pin-pointed the likely hacker as a resident of Hong Kong called Peter Chang. However, this Chang is a computer expert who may challenge Allen as the best hacker in the world and so far, Allen has been unable to break through the firewall that Chang has created. And it must be said, the only evidence so far pointing to Chang is that he has an impenetrable firewall in his system. We have no absolute concrete evidence that he is the hacker."

"So why hasn't this man been arrested?" demanded another speaker. He looked older than most at the table, a full head of hair that was almost white, with large, overgrown eyebrows. "Chief Inspector Griff Jackson," he added.

"A common situation, Chief Inspector," said Melanie with a pleasant smile to acknowledge his introduction. "As I said just now, we are confident that this is the man, but we have no evidence that could lead to a prosecutable case. Until we can break into his system and also examine the equipment he is using to hack into pacemakers and internal insulin pumps, we have no case. And when we can do this, it will have to be the Hong Kong authorities that arrest him and bring him to trial. We might be able to extradite him to Australia or the UK, or maybe the USA, all of us have a good claim to this man, but so far, the Chinese authorities have been less than helpful on the subject of pacemaker hacking."

"Do we know anything else about this Chang or his associates in Australia and the UK?" The speaker was possibly the youngest at the table, a man in his twenties with bright red hair and what looked like a three-day growth of beard. He didn't give his name.

"Let me answer that," said Jack. "We don't have an identification, but we know a bit about him, and I've developed a working hypothesis also. He's young, early twenties, graduated only three years ago from a university in England. The fact that between them this group has killed more than seventeen people in the UK, Australia and the US qualifies them as serial killers and the profiles of such people are well-established.

"I am certain that when we fully identify the two young ones, we will find that they are single children, with remote, distant parents who never gave them a secure childhood. Those parents may well be wealthy people with their own concerns and little affection for their offspring, even if they did give them excellent educations at considerable cost. But that is more likely to satisfy their own egos, rather than concern for the kids.

"However, just in the last two days, we have identified the character we have thought of as "Fagin," the one who precipitated this life of crime. He is William Lloyd, a resident in the Manchester region in the British north-west. An address will be found any day."

"And will the Poms then arrest him?" The young redhead looked enthusiastic.

Jack shook his head. "Same problem as with Chang. We are sure he's the man, he even has the same firewall around his computer, but we have no evidence that ties him to the case. When they do locate him, be sure the local cops will interview him and record his voice so that they can compare it to the voice that was recovered from the distorted version that has blackmailed some of the victims. At the same time, they will be able to search the house and examine the equipment. Once Miller has broken through the firewall, the computer will give up all its secrets and then maybe we can get Chang and the Australian third member."

"Do you have any idea of who that Australian might be?" asked French, who had earlier questioned Melanie's role and value but now seemed to accept her.

Melanie shook her head. "Not yet. Again, something may break, quite possibly a mistake by one of the group that will provide clues."

"But in the meanwhile, they might kill a few other innocents," said Harvey.

"That is a horrible fact," said Jack. "But let me add something hopeful. Our suspected hacker Chang is clearly a narcissistic case, loves to play power games with people. He's also young and naïve. I believe he will continue to play this game and he will be unable to boast about his accomplishments, even skating close to revealing them to gain the spotlight. He is almost certain to make a fatal mistake soon."

"There is one other thing," added Melanie. "This we only just found out about, courtesy of Allen Miller. Lloyd is married to the niece of the local regional Mafia boss, one Giorgio Grassano. Now that we know that the British cops will be listening to their every word and tapping every computer device if they can break through the protection Lloyd has on them. We may crack this thing quite soon."

"Meanwhile," said Harvey, "As I said at our first meeting, we have an unusual situation. By all protocols, we in the Law Enforcement side of things would concentrate only on the criminal aspects of these blackmailing operations and leave the international security investigations to ASIO. And of course, they are heavily involved. But as it seems clear that all the blackmailing is being performed by the same group, we have to keep each other informed and support everything being done to end this. Chief Inspector Carter, by default, you are the single connection between us and ASIO. I trust you will continue to keep this line open at all times?"

"Of course," said Melanie.

"A question," said the young, redheaded officer. "What do we do if the media get hold of this?"

Harvey made an expression of dismay, like a man encountering a dog turd in his driveway. "That's a real problem," he said. "In the old days, we could slap a Schedule D on all the media and keep them quiet. We can't do that anymore and the obvious worry is the degree of panic that might ensue if people find out that they could get killed by something that is supposed to save their lives. If this does happen, all we can do is try and talk to the various news agencies and just ask them nicely to try and keep it subdued."

"Lots of luck," said the redhead. "A story like that. They'll be having orgasms all over the bloody place, making it out as something like the Black Death."

"Some will, that's for sure," agreed Harvey. "We just have to try and keep it as quiet as possible. If you do encounter journalists, treat them civilly, politely and honestly."

A subdued round of murmurs ran round the room.

"Thank you, all," said Harvey. "Chief Inspector Carter, Professor Savage, this has been invaluable."

"It has," said Melanie. "But we must still be aware that Chang is able to break through some of the most protected systems in the world, even the communications between ASIO, MI6 and the CIA. We will have to follow the clumsy, slow communications protocols we have been following with ASIO."

Harvey nodded and the meeting broke up.

Chapter 29

Mid North Coast, Australia, April, 2024

Melanie sat at her desk, reading the latest report from Gordon Porter at ASIO about the developments with the hacking into an insulin pump in a Chicago diabetes sufferer. Jack Savage sat across from her, reading the same report. As they had done since this all began, her computer was switched off and turned to face the wall. Even with that precaution, their conversation was careful not to reveal anything that might be heard by the hackers.

Melanie finished reading first, put down the sheet and scrawled a note on her pad, handing it over to Jack. It read, "Not a good development."

IIe nodded when he had read it. "Agreed," he said. "Do they all know? I wonder if Miller knows?"

Before she could reply, a voice came from her computer.

"Hello, Inspector Carter." The voice was distorted, the same voice that they had heard in the recordings of demands made to blackmail victims.

Jack and Melanie looked at each other in surprise. The computer had been switched off. Melanie turned the monitor round. Looking out at them was a masked face. It was white, the smile was an exaggerated sneer, with wide lips and a thin black beard and moustache. Eyes were barely visible behind the ugly face.

"Melanie, how lovely to see you," said the electronically distorted voice. "My, what a lovely woman you are. And you must be Jack Savage? What an honour to meet you, Jack."

Neither Jack nor Melanie responded.

"Cat got your tongues?" continued the awful voice. "Not surprising, it must be a shock to finally hear from me. How's the hunt going? No luck, eh? That's not a surprise at all. You must be going nuts trying to find me."

Ignoring the taunting voice, Melanie looked past the mask at the wall behind it. There was something hanging on it, a picture, something in a frame. She and Jack continued their silence. It seemed the caller was irritated by this.

"So you're not going to speak, eh? So tell me, Melanie and Jack, what are you going to do when I keep killing people? Have you any idea how much money I've taken from those suckers with pacemakers? And have you heard about my latest venture? I'm sure you have. Just wait until people start dying of diabetic comas."

Melanie finally broke the silence. "How's the weather in Hong Kong?" she asked.

Abruptly, the connection was broken, and the screen went blank.

"That got to him," said Jack. "Interesting, the classic behaviour of the narcissist, the need to boast about his triumphs. It will bring him down at some stage. And it clearly got to him that we already know he's in Hong Kong. He's probably been certain that we have nothing at all on him. That shook his ego."

"I wish I'd recorded it," said Melanie. "There was something on the wall behind him, it might have given a clue. Damn."

"Ah, but I did," said a voice from the screen.

"Allen, you listened in?" Melanie felt curiously relieved.

"Like I said before, when my name is mentioned, I break in automatically. I have to admit, I failed you there. That little bastard broke through my firewall."

"No worries, Allen. This time, I think I'm pleased," said Melanie. "What about that voice?"

"Already decoded," said Miller. "It's the Hong Kong guy, but he confirmed that by the way he broke off."

"You recorded the whole thing?" asked Jack. "Audio as well as visual?"

"Both, Jack."

"Would you send us that recording?" asked Melanie.

"Right away."

Almost immediately, the conversation with the Hong Kong hacker began playing. When it was completed, Melanie copied the recording to a flash drive. The screen had gone blank, Miller had clearly ended the call. Melanie stood up, extracted the drive from her computer and began to leave.

"To the laboratory," she mouthed silently. Back in the corridor, she murmured softly, "I want to see what's on the wall. They've got the equipment."

"Do that," said Jack. "But I have to admit, I'm badly shaken. I thought Miller's firewall was secure, but that little bastard got through. It seems Allen's not the best hacker in the world any more."

"It's a shock," agreed Melanie. "We'll have to go back to our old approach, only discuss things in a safe place."

"Or we can turn this to our advantage," said Jack. "Let's pretend we haven't noticed Allen's failure and use this to feed Chang with false information that might get him disturbed, just like we did by revealing we know he's in Hong Kong. We might be able to upset him enough to make a mistake."

"He just did," said Melanie. "Let me get this picture to the techie geniuses."

Melanie studied the page handed to her by the computer technician.

"The School of Medical Sciences, Manchester University," she read. "The degree of Doctor of Medicine is awarded to Michael Chang Wu Li. Presumably his father, given the date of the diploma."

"Well, well, well," said Jack, a broad grin on his face. "I think we've got the bastard."

"I need to call Gordon Porter," she said.

Chapter 30

Mid North Coast, NSW, Australia, April, 2024

The stress was getting to Melanie. After the years of being a detective, she recognised the symptoms that seemed to return every few months. She sat in her lounge room with a glass of red wine and mused back on the years and experiences that had led to this state.

Always being so beautiful, while it may have seemed such a huge gift to a woman, Melanie had found it almost a curse. Parents and associates had inevitably been so eager to tell her to become a model or a movie actress and she had lost count of the times model agencies had approached her to offer such a career. But this had never appealed, she wanted to be valued for something other than a beautiful body and face. The same problem arose with men. They seemed unable to get past that beauty, never saw the intellect, almost always pushing their physical desires and despite the First Class Honours in Psychology gained at university, job interviews always ended with the same result, rejection, as she saw the suspicion from potential employers that she would be a disruptive influence on their organisations.

Then came the one man who was different. In their final year at University, their relationship grew into a close, loving affair, the first time a man had accepted her as a total package of great intelligence as well as the looks. She could never forget the evening they went to a pub in Sydney's Kings Cross to celebrate their graduation.

A man approached them as they left the pub. Without warning or provocation, he swung a punch at her fiancé's face, knocked him to the ground where his head struck the concrete and blood ran along the sidewalk as onlookers screamed. He was dead within minutes.

Melanie wiped tears from her face and refilled her glass. She was well aware of the mental confusion this had caused her, an inability to get emotionally close to a man again, the fear that if she did, he'd die. She had talked it over with Jack Savage, but while he understood, he was unable to help her develop a normal attitude with men.

But she knew she still had needs, and this was where the beauty helped. When her stress levels climbed as they had now, she had developed a standard approach. She flew to one of the major cities, booked into a hotel, dressed to maximise her advantages and went to a club. There was little time before she had a selection of men and she simply chose the one who seemed most physically attractive and went to his home, never the hotel. The nights were usually satisfactory, and she repeated the process on two nights before returning home, reasonably satisfied, never staying beyond the morning with the selected man.

The last time had been different. Rob in Adelaide had proved attractive beyond the merely physical, and she had stayed the weekend with him. She had been down to Adelaide twice since then and the weekends had all been similarly enjoyable and therapeutic. She knew she was becoming increasingly attached to Rob.

She picked up the phone.

* * *

Cheshire Countryside, England, April, 2024

William Lloyd was enjoying a glass of beer while watching a British cop show on television when his computer buzzed to indicate a video call. He hit the mute button on the television controller and went to his desk to respond. There was no face displayed on the monitor.

"Yes," he said, irritated by the interruption.

"We've had a few problems."

William now recognised the clipped, perfect intonation of the speaker.

"What the hell are you doing, calling me?" he said, anger raising the pitch of his voice a note. "We agreed, it's far too risky."

"Not at all," said the perfect English accent. "Nobody could break through the firewall I built around my computer and that you have, not even Allen Miller, or whatever he's calling himself these days."

"Alright, make it quick. I'm not as confident as you are."

"The spooks have caught on to what we're doing."

Lloyd exploded. "What the hell do you mean, the spooks have caught on?"

"The Finnish mark and the Australian both had their pacemakers replaced with non-communication devices. They're immune."

"How the fuck did that happen?"

"I can only assume they somehow told the cops without going through phones or emails."

"How?"

"Who knows? Maybe they wrote a letter, or something. Anyway, I made them realise the error of their ways, I killed off a few others, just to make my point."

"You did what? Holy shit, how many did you kill? Do you realise what that means? It means the cops and the spooks are going to go balls to the wall to find us."

"I killed five in England and in the US and our Aussie friend did the same there."

"Jesus Christ, man, you're insane!"

"Not in the slightest," said the perfect English voice. "If the dumb spooks realise we've caused that, they'll be very careful about what they do next. Anyway, we've still got a few marks on the hook."

"Okay, what have you got so far?"

"Quite a bit. We got the million dollars from the Finn in London and the same from the guy in Virginia. Then we got some really good stuff from the British Cabinet Minister. Your boss sold the information to two of our clients, one of them will make a killing on the stock market with the news that the British are buying several coastal ships for drug interdiction and people smuggling and the other is buying up land where the government is going to build a new hi-tech satellite town, actually in your part of the world."

"I haven't heard anything about that," said Lloyd.

"Of course not, it's still in the planning stages for the next budget."

"Okay. But go quiet for a while, no point in rushing this. But it's still a worry that the spooks know about it. It means they know in Australia and the US as well, you can bet your life they're cooperating on this."

"How can they? They haven't caught on to the fact that we can listen in on their international conference calls and there's no way they can talk to each other any other way. And they'll never identify who we are, that distortion system works beautifully."

"You'd better hope so. And you'd better hope that Miller is not trying to track you down. There's nothing I would put beyond that bloke's ability."

"That's the other problem. I found something very interesting. A couple of days ago I broke into a telephone conference between several police officers who are on a task force investigating our efforts. It's amazing how stupid these people could be, because one of them said they shouldn't be talking like this in an unsecured location."

"And what did you hear?"

"They mentioned the cop on the mid-North Coast of Australia who is a key figure on the case. Would you believe she's working with Allen Miller?"

"Miller? Holy shit, Peter, how the hell did he get involved? You said he was old and past it."

"He is," said Chang. Lloyd could sense the irritation in the young man's voice. "But he's still the best hacker they have ever known, he's world-renowned in all the major security forces, it's not really a surprise that he became involved."

"And who's the cop on the case? How did he get the job?"

"It's not a he, it's a she. It's a Detective Inspector Melanie Carter. Apparently, she knew Miller from a previous case in that part of the world. The others all seem to have a very high opinion of her. I suggest she needs to be scared off, maybe even got rid of."

"Getting rid of her would be stupid," said Lloyd. "That would warn the others we know about her and the investigation. It would only make things worse."

"Well, okay, if you say so. But we need to do something about her. Maybe this will help. I did some more work and found she's booked a flight to Adelaide in a few days. Maybe she's meeting somebody."

"Leave it with me," said Lloyd. He got up and went to talk to his wife.

"Phil, I have a small job for you."

Murray had expressed surprise when the video call from Lloyd in England came through, but he was not worried about the security. He had every faith in the firewall protection that Peter Chang had created. But surprise was quickly replaced by anxiety. What did this Pommie want?

"You may have to take a few days off," continued Lloyd.

"Okay."

"Peter has discovered the identity of the cop handling the Australian side of the investigation. The big concern is that she's working with Allen Miller."

"Allen Miller? Oh shit, how did he get involved? He's still the greatest hacker in the world."

Murray's panic reverberated through the network.

"Peter doesn't agree with you," said Lloyd. "Anyway, this is what you have to do. Peter tapped into her phone and heard her make a reservation to fly to Adelaide next week. He can't find a hotel reservation, so she's probably staying with somebody, probably a boyfriend. I need you to get on that same flight and see who meets her in Adelaide. If nobody does, then there's no way you can follow her, but if some bloke does meet her, follow them as carefully as you can, see if they go to a car in the parking area and get the registration number. Peter will do the rest."

"You mean I've just become an errand boy for you two?" Murray's irritation was audible over the network.

"You're not an errand boy, this is something essential to keep us safe." Lloyd's own tension was causing a similar irritation in him. Anna-Maria's recommendation, which always had the feeling of a direct order, had caused the same sense of helplessness in him that Murray was feeling.

"And will you then tell me to kill her, or something? I'm not up to directly killing somebody face to face," said Murray. The frustration was still evident.

"You won't have to kill anybody," said Lloyd as soothingly as he could. "We just need to know what her movements are and who she meets."

"Okay," said Murray. "Just as long as I don't have to do any bloody stuff."

"Why are you so worried?" asked Lloyd. "You and Chang have already killed a few people. Why are you bothered by this?"

"That's different," said Murray. "I do that by pressing a key, I don't know where the person is, usually I have no idea of what they look like or anything about them."

Lloyd took a deep breath. "But you will do this? I guarantee, it's really critical."

"Okay, I'll do it," said Murray.

"Good. Now here are the flight details. Make sure you get on. If you can't, get an earlier flight and watch for her to arrive."

"Will do."

"Make sure you do."

Lloyd recited the details and hung up without another word.

Melanie didn't notice the young man with the untidy haircut, dressed in ordinary jeans and sweater during the flight. Nor did she notice him as she disembarked at Adelaide, by now feeling excited and some anticipation at the thought of the weekend with Rob. Not in all of her sexual adventures over the years had she ever wanted to meet up again with a man with whom she had spent the night, but now she was eager to do so. He had touched her mind and emotions in a way that had never happened since her fiancé years before at university and whose ugly, violent death had closed her off from any similar relationship.

He was there! Waiting for her was the one man who had affected her capacity for love since that long-ago death.

"Hi!" he said and opened his arms.

"Hello, you," she replied, her words muffled into the side of his neck.

She didn't notice the young man watching them from the shelter of the crowds greeting the arrivals, nor did she notice as he followed her as she and Rob walked hand in hand to the parking area. She was almost bursting with anticipation of the weekend ahead.

"I tell you what," said Murray as Lloyd answered the video call on his computer. "That is one drop-dead gorgeous woman. I'd hate to think she's going to be hurt."

"It's not her who's going to be hurt," said Lloyd. "Was she met by somebody?"

"Yeah, some bloke and it was obviously a big deal for both. Kisses at the gate, hand in hand to the parking area, all that stuff."

"And did you get the rego of his car?"

"Sure did." Murray recited the registration numbers, waited while Lloyd read them back, confirmed they were correct and hung up without further words. He didn't want to think about what was going to happen.

Chapter 31

Cheshire Countryside, UK, April, 2024

Lloyd had never got over a frisson of fear when he got a call from Giorgio Grassano, head of the British operations of the Mafia. This call fully justified the fear.

"William, you are disappointing us," said Grassano when Lloyd picked up the telephone.

Lloyd gulped and tasted the acid in his throat.

"I'm sorry to hear that, Uncle," he said. "Can you tell me why? Then I can work on improving my performance."

"It seems that the British and Australian security forces have discovered what we are doing with your internet experts."

"How could that be, Uncle?" Panic began rising in Lloyd. "Nobody could have worked out that we were hacking into pacemakers."

"You are naïve, William. Two of our projects were disrupted when our targets failed to succumb to the work of our young man in Hong Kong. We have assumed that the authorities learnt of the project and replaced the pacemakers with devices that were not susceptible to internet communications."

Lloyd felt shattered. "I know nothing of this development," he said, his voice cracking with tension.

"And far worse," continued Grassano, "some of the information gained from threats to political or defence figures proved to be invalid. The family invested large sums with the assumption that the information was correct, and we have lost some millions because the information was fake. We have to assume that the security forces realised what was happening and fed false information to the victims."

Lloyd's panic grew further. "I didn't know, Uncle," he whispered.

"For now, you must cease this approach until we have worked out an alternative," said Grassano. "There must be no more of the pacemaker attacks. If the authorities know of it, we can be certain that they will develop some form of security against it. This was a useful and potentially big business line, but it has come to an end."

"Can we continue the use of deep fake videos as we have used successfully on a few occasions?" asked Lloyd.

There was a pause at the other end.

"Yes," came the reply eventually. "That is still functioning in certain cases. But be very careful. Any more failures that cause problems for the family will be dealt with."

Grassano terminated the call without a further word, leaving Lloyd in a cold sweat. He had never felt so frightened in his life before.

Chapter 32

Mid North Coast, NSW, Australia, April, 2024

Melanie returned home in a happy haze, thoroughly satisfied by the weekend. Lunches at delightful local restaurants, a drive into the Barossa Valley and some tastings of wonderful wines, and evenings and night spent making up for the months of celibacy. While she had experienced many nights of wild sexual activity with a variety of men over the years, nothing had been as emotionally satisfying as the time spent in Rob's bed. She knew that it would not be long before he proposed to her, and she had no doubts that she would accept.

She changed flights at Sydney for the local hop home, found her car in the secure area in which she had left it and drove home. She slept soundly that night.

Adelaide, South Australia

Robert Cranshaw left his Adelaide town house at his usual hour of 7:30am to head to his office. He felt happier than he had in years. Not that there was anything wrong with his life. High income, many friends, a varied social life, rarely short of female company, and the memories of a brief, bad marriage five years before had faded. But the arrival of Melanie in his life had been miraculous. He thought about buying a ring, but decided she was the sort of woman who would want to make the choice together. But a proposal... he knew that would not be far ahead. After this past weekend, he could not imagine life without her.

He didn't see the anonymous grey Subaru Forester pull out behind him as he drove away from his house. He didn't notice it staying two cars behind him as he navigated his way into the city. He drove into the parking lot of his company and only then saw the Forester park alongside him. He looked up in astonishment as a shadow appeared at the car door, barely had time to feel terror as a gun was pointed at his head. The bullet smashed through the side window and hit him above his right temple, scattering blood and brains over the interior of his car.

He never saw the killer's car leave and so was unable to see that the number plates front and back had been smeared with mud and unreadable.

* * *

Mid North Coast, NSW, Australia

Melanie's phone rang soon after her arrival in the office.

"Detective Inspector Melanie Carter," she said.

"Detective Inspector?" A man's voice indicated shock. "I didn't know you were a police officer."

"Who is this?" Melanie was irritated.

"This is Detective Inspector Ralph Owens, Adelaide police."

Melanie felt a growing cloud of dread coming over her. There was something terribly wrong about to happen.

"Inspector, you must know Robert Cranshaw in Adelaide," said Owens.

"I do, why are you asking?" The sense of dread grew stronger.

"Inspector Carter, we found Robert Cranshaw's body in his car an hour ago. Your name and phone number were in his telephone. We're contacting those names as part of our inquiries."

Melanie felt as if she had been punched hard in the stomach. Gasping for breath, she managed to speak.

"You found his body?"

"He'd been shot by somebody standing by the driver's side window. Can I ask when you last saw Mr Cranshaw?"

Melanie began to tremble. Terrible memories flew into her mind, of standing by the body of her fiancé in Sydney after he had fallen, knocked down by a single punch to the head by a thug, his blood running down the pavement to the gutter.

"I was with him all weekend," she managed to say through the trembles in her throat.

She knew she couldn't last much longer. Despite the voice continuing to speak in the phone, she replaced it as the tears rose in her eyes and she collapsed, face down in a storm of weeping.

"Melanie! Melanie!"

Slowly, painfully and unwillingly, Melanie began to leave the black pit of nightmares that had swallowed her. She was dimly aware of Jack's voice by her ear, realised that she was lying on the floor, curled up tight, sobbing her heart out. Somebody, she assumed Jack, had placed a pillow under her head.

"What's happened, Melanie? The last time I saw you like this, your car had been blown to pieces."

She struggled to control her breathing. *This is no way for a police officer to be seen,* flashed through her mind and it helped her begin to regain control. She took a deep, shaky breath.

"They killed him," she whispered.

"Who? Your bloke in Adelaide?"

"Yes." Slowly, she sat up, her hands over her face, realising that Jack was kneeling by her side.

"Let's get you into your seat," said Jack and helped her get to her feet and back into the seat behind the desk. He turned her round and pulled a second chair to sit next to her. He said nothing but waited for her to get back a reasonable level of control.

"A cop in Adelaide just called," she began. "They found Rob in his car, shot through the head by somebody standing by the door. They didn't know who I was, they were just calling the people in his mobile."

Jack picked up the telephone on the desk. When the front desk answered, he said, "Get the doctor here. Melanie's had a severe shock, she needs a sedative. And tell the Superintendent I'm going to take her home and she'll be off for a couple of days." He replaced the phone without waiting for an answer.

"Somehow, they found out about him," Melanie continued. "That bastard must have hacked into a computer or a phone and heard something that referenced me as being involved in the case. This was to scare me off."

"Almost certainly," said Jack.

"Jack, why am I cursed like this?" Melanie felt like a small child, pleading for help. "I've only fallen in love twice and each time, he gets murdered."

"You're not cursed," he said. "The first time was just horrible luck. This one is because of your job and you're damned good at it."

She shook her head violently. "I tell you what, Jack, I'm not going to get involved again. I'd be handing a death sentence to any bloke." A storm of tears overwhelmed her again and she sobbed into her hands. A few moments passed before it eased. "I must look a sight," she whispered. Jack said nothing. Finally, she looked up at him. "Was that a silly female sort of comment?" she said, her voice stronger.

"You're entitled," he said, just as the door opened and the doctor entered.

"A close friend of Melanie has been murdered," said Jack. "Can you give her a sedative?"

The doctor didn't question him. He took a quick look at Melanie, opened his bag and extracted a small jar, taking two pills from it. Jack understood the quick glance he got and went to the washroom, returning with a glass of water. Melanie downed the tablets without question.

"I'm taking you home," said Jack and helped her up, escorted her from the station in front of a few curious looks from other officers and drove her home.

Chapter 33 – The Journalist

Coogee Beach, NSW, Australia, April, 2024

Annette James had a strict routine. Up at six in the morning, thirty minutes of exercise on the indoor bike and with weights, then a shower and a light breakfast.

The next hour was spent at the computer, reviewing the news from around the country and around the world. This routine generally found her ready for the first meeting of the day at the newsroom of the television studios, rarely surprised by events from around the world introduced by her boss, Gregory Clairmont, the head of the news division.

Something caught her eye almost immediately she sat down at the computer. In the local paper for the town of Coffs Harbour, a few hours north of her home in the Eastern Suburbs of Sydney, she saw a short report.

> *"William Gaines, aged 65, a well-known landscape gardener in our region died suddenly while sitting on a bench near the jetty. No reason has been given for his sad death. Mr Gaines was well-liked in the area. He leaves behind his wife of forty years, Enid and two sons, Eric and Andrew. The funeral will be on Friday at 10:00am."*

There was nothing major in that report, but sudden, unexplained deaths tended to interest Annette and had done since her school days when she had decided that she would become a journalist. Her degree in journalism, high intelligence and classical good looks had made a path to television relatively easy, and she had taken on the newsreader role just a year ago. She made a note of the report and continued browsing the country's local newspapers. The second one caused her interest levels to spark a little more. The paper was from Collaroy on the Northern Beaches of Sydney.

"The death is reported of Garry Lewis, aged 69, a local builder who has built several houses in the Collaroy region. Mr Lewis was apparently crossing the road in the shopping area when he collapsed. Two cars nearly hit him and passers-by lifted him to the pavement where one person attempted to give him the kiss of life, without success. He was pronounced dead on arrival at the hospital. Mr Lewis leaves behind two daughters and a son, all living in Sydney. His wife, Angela died only last year."

"This is a good start to the day," muttered Annette and took a sip of coffee. She noted the details of the report and continued browsing. The third report made her sit up. "What the hell is going on?" she said aloud. The newspaper was from Wauchope, a small town, like Coffs Harbour, a few hours north of Sydney.

"Lesley Freeman, well known as a solicitor in Wauchope, died unexpectedly while in the high street. She was just about to enter her favourite coffee shop for her regular morning brew when she collapsed. Witnesses called an ambulance, but she was pronounced dead on arrival at the hospital. Ms Freeman was 75 and considered to be in good health. No reason for the tragedy has been given by the hospital. Ms Freeman had no family."

"Curiouser and curiouser," murmured Annette. "Two sudden, unexplained deaths is a coincidence. Three is bloody careless. What the hell's going on?"

243

She took a break to refill her coffee mug and resumed her computer research, which had suddenly become intensely interesting. And it continued that way.

The next report was from much further away, in Broken Hill on the western side of the state.

> *"Raymond Potter, a retired electrician who had worked in the mines until last year, died suddenly yesterday morning. Mr Potter, aged 67 had taken a casual job at the Pro Hart Museum and was sweeping the floors before the day's opening when he suddenly collapsed. He was taken to the hospital by ambulance but pronounced dead on arrival. No cause was given for the tragedy. Raymond had moved to Broken Hill five years ago but was a regular visitor to Newcastle where his two sons and their families lived."*

"Okay, not even bloody carelessness," said Annette aloud "This is outright conspiracy. There couldn't be any more, surely?" But there was. The Newcastle paper gave some additional information.

> *"A major accident was narrowly averted yesterday when a car driven by Angela Maynard lost control as she was about to turn into her driveway. Ms Maynard, 66, had been shopping and was almost home when the car seemed to lose control, narrowly missed an oncoming vehicle and crashed into the wall of her apartment block. Eyewitnesses said the impact didn't seem severe, but Ms Maynard*

was unresponsive when her door was opened. An ambulance was called but Ms Maynard was pronounced dead at the scene. A neighbour of the dead woman was severely upset. She reported that Angela was in excellent health, having had a pacemaker installed after some heart difficulties a year ago."

Annette smelled a major story. Failures in medical equipment were nothing new and she remembered a study done a few years earlier when a researcher with a British documentary-maker had investigated failures in hip and knee replacements in the UK and Australia. But this number of sudden deaths, all almost at the same time smelled fishy. She checked the time, just after seven-thirty and decided to get to work first and make the phone calls then. She dressed rapidly in casual clothes with a minimum of make-up, knowing that she would put on the formal gear and subject herself to the make-up girls at the studios before going before the cameras for the evening news.

Seated at her desk, she opened her manual file and checked the numbers of the associate reporters in the regions covered by the morning's research. Coffs Harbour was first.

"Jason," she said, when the phone was picked up. "Annette James, how are you doing?"

"All the better for talking to you, you gorgeous creature," said the man in Coffs Harbour.

"Yeah, yeah," she replied. "Cut the lustful drooling and pay attention. Something interesting is happening." She had known Jason Lewis since university days. A brief but intense affair had ended amicably, and she considered him a close friend.

"Okay, what?" Jason was all business now.

"Your local rag reports this morning that some bloke called William Gaines died suddenly while sitting on a bench near the jetty. He was only sixty-nine and this doesn't seem right. It wouldn't be a problem, but I found five people around the state who have just died without any rational reason, all around the same time. Can you go and see what you can find? Particularly see if you can find anyone who knew him well. Five sudden deaths is just not kosher."

"Will do. Are you coming up here at all in the near future?"

"Not that I can think off, Jason."

"Well, when you do, make sure you wear your shortest skirt and lowest neckline."

"Fuck off, Jason." Annette couldn't quite hide the laugh. She heard the echoing one from him and both hung up their phones.

She looked up the next number.

* * *

The emails started coming the following morning.

"Garry Lewis died quite unexpectedly," said the email from Jennifer Cole in Collaroy. *"I talked to his family and a couple of friends and they reported that he'd had a triple bypass four years ago at St John's hospital in Newcastle. They'd said then that he might*

need a new heart valve at some time and last year this was done at the same hospital, but they decided to install a pacemaker at the same time. The operation was successful and he was told his health was excellent. Nobody could get any information from the hospital or his GP on what had gone wrong."

"William Gaines had received a pacemaker last year, following some heart difficulties," said Jason in Coffs Harbour. *"His health had been perfect since then. The operation was done at St John's Hospital in Newcastle."*

"Lesley Freeman had a pacemaker installed at St John's Hospital in Newcastle two years ago," said Connor Brough in Wauchope.

"Angela Maynard had a pacemaker installed at St John's Hospital eighteen months ago," said Marylin Smith in Newcastle.

"Raymond Potter had a pacemaker installed at St John's Hospital just thirteen months ago," said Jeff Carpenter in Broken Hill. *"He had been visiting family in Newcastle when he had a heart attack and was rushed to St John's Hospital where a pacemaker was installed."*

"Well, well, bloody well," said Colleen. "I think Stage Two is in order here."

She switched her system to the corporate search engine that could trace newsworthy events and began searching for sudden deaths of healthy individuals anywhere in Australia. Several came up, most of them the results of accidents, but one caught her attention.

"The death is reported of Colonel William Henderson (Retd) in Forster, NSW. Colonel Henderson had a distinguished career with the Australian Special Air Services Regiment and after retirement, joined the Australian civil service in an advisory role. Colonel Henderson died suddenly while outdoors near the beach."

"Oopsie," muttered Annette. "The stink is rising to Heaven."

Sydney Television Studios, April, 2024

"I'm heading up to Newcastle," said Annette.

"Are you now?" replied her boss. "Any specific reason?" Gregory Clairmont was a short man of immense energy and a philosophy of management that let his subordinates do what they wanted but would let them know rapidly if the results were less than successful. Annette thought the world of him.

"Something about pacemakers implanted at St John's Hospital is a touch smelly," she said.

"Then why are you still sitting there?" said Clairmont.

"Me? Sitting? No, I left ten minutes ago," said Annette, rising to her feet.

"I'll have Jessie take your place for the evening news," said Clairmont and picked up his phone.

* * *

St John's Hospital, Newcastle, NSW, Australia

"I'm Brooke Kettering," said the tall, elegant woman in a white coat seated in an armchair in her office. "I head up the pacemaker implant unit in the Cardiology Department. I'm curious why you have expended so much energy to come and talk to us."

Annette laughed. "I did my usual bashing away until I got the result," she said. "I'm grateful that everybody was so nice about trying to block me."

Kettering smiled. "You weren't as obnoxious as others have been," she said. "So how can we help?"

"I found five items in local newspapers around the Mid-North Coast and one from Broken Hill that reported elderly people in otherwise good health, but who had received pacemakers, all installed at this hospital and who had died on the same day. There seems to be no logical or medical reasons why this had happened. I also found a report of a Colonel William Henderson who had died in similar fashion in Forster. Did Colonel Henderson also get a pacemaker implanted here?"

"You know I can't reveal such information," said Kettering. The smile had vanished.

"I understand," said Annette. "However, we have confirmed that these five people most certainly did get pacemakers implanted here within the last two years." She read out the names of the people who had been reported as dying in the local papers. "Our reporters talked to friends and family this morning, and all confirmed that fact. Can you comment on this?"

Kettering shifted in her seat and stared at her hands for a moment before resuming her direct stare at Annette.

"You put me in a very difficult situation," she said. "I know I can't stop you reporting on these events, but

I have to tell you that you could be on the verge of causing a huge problem."

"Is there a defect in the pacemakers?" asked Annette. Her curiosity was aroused by Kettering's reaction.

"Not exactly."

"Not exactly? What does that mean?"

"Here's where I get into difficulties," said Kettering. "I must tell you that we have already had serious discussions with the legal people, knowing that somebody like you would be along eventually and we couldn't hide the full facts."

Annette decided she could be onto the story of a lifetime. She felt huge sympathy for Kettering, whom she could see was seriously tormented by the situation, but her professional training drove her to get the information.

"So what can you tell me without revealing confidential medical information?" she asked.

"Here's what my people have suggested I say to you," said Kettering. "I'll tell you now, that you could cause quite severe international panic in several countries, and we have to ask you to moderate your reports if humanely possible."

"My god, it's that serious?" Annette was quite shaken.

"It's that serious and more," said Kettering. "First thing to assure you, there is absolutely nothing wrong with any of the brands of pacemakers implanted in millions of people, all over the world."

Annette said nothing. She felt her heart rate increase with excitement.

"Once pacemakers and other devices such as insulin pumps implanted in the body became linked to the hospital computers by communications technology, and patients were given a home device that monitored their pacemakers constantly and reported results back to the hospitals, the medical world began to worry that somebody might one day find out how to hack into the pacemakers. Until now, we thought it most unlikely unless within a metre or two of the patients."

Kettering paused and took a deep breath as if about to dive off a high board. "But now it's been done, and somebody is blackmailing people and killing some of them."

For a moment, Annette was too shaken to speak. She could do nothing but stare at the woman opposite.

"Do you know who?" she asked after a short silence.

Kettering shook her head. "We don't. But others might. Remember a few years ago, somebody hacked into the Medibank systems and stole massive amounts of personal data? They demanded money and placed much of that data on the dark web when Medibank refused to pay up."

"That was thought to be Russian hackers, as I recall?" said Annette.

"It was. But the interesting thing was that the police forces combined with the Australian Signals Directorate and ASIO to trace the hackers. The same has been done here."

"And they're not telling you everything they've found so far?" said Annette.

"They won't," said Brooke. "But if you broadcast this story, they may be in touch with you. But here's something I can tell you. It's not just happening here in Australia. It's international. There have been similar cases in the UK and in the USA."

"Holy shit," said Annette.

Chapter 34

Mid-North Coast, Australia, April, 2024

After two days, Melanie felt strong enough to return to the office. Jack had called in a favour from friends in the medical profession and a nurse had stayed those two days, proving a huge help with making meals and providing an empathic ear to Melanie's grief. Soon after arriving at her desk, a familiar face had appeared on her computer monitor.

"Melanie, would you like some good news?"

"That would be a pleasant change." She turned to face the monitor completely.

"My god, Melanie, what's happened? You look a mess."

"Thank you, Allen. Just the sort of comforting comment a girl needs."

"Melanie, I'm sorry, but you really do look ill."

"Not ill, just shattered." Briefly, she related the events of the last few days.

"I'm truly sorry," said Miller. "But in that case, what I'm about to tell you pleases me even more."

"Go ahead. What's happened?"

"I've been working hard on the firewall around the computer of this bloke, William Lloyd. I finally broke in and found something wonderful."

"What, all his connections in Australia and Hong Kong?"

"Not yet, but even more damaging. I found the Mafia bank account in the UK."

"Go on."

"I took twelve million pounds out of it, leaving just a few hundred. I'd already returned the million pounds to Hukkinen before and I'm working on finding the others who paid the mob. But I've also sent a few million to charities, like the RSPCA, various children's protection groups, Doctors Without Borders and a few other like that."

Despite the heaviness in her mind, Melanie smiled. "That'll stir the shit mightily," she said.

"Massively," said Miller. "So now I'll see if I can break into Chang's computer and find out who the Australian member is. But I suspect it might be interesting to see if the Mob in the UK or anywhere else respond to my little bit of larceny."

"Thank you, Allen. I'm sure this will help the case."

Miller disappeared from the monitor.

* * *

"You look crabby, Alex," said Melanie as the young detective entered her office. She had a lot of faith in the officer whom she had discovered as a patrolman and found his excellent investigative skills to enhance the work of her department.

"Can you come outside for a moment, Ma'am?"

Realising he had something not to be heard by illegal listeners on her system, Melanie joined the young officer in the corridor and walked down to the front entrance.

"Did you see the news on the television last night, Ma'am?" asked Weyland.

"Did I miss something?"

"Annette James on the seven o'clock news. She had a story about people dying in significant numbers from pacemaker issues. She said at least five died on the same day last week and somebody has learnt how to hack into them."

"Oh good grief! That's going to cause some panic. How did she find this out?"

"She just said her investigations revealed this, and also that the same was happening in Britain and the United States."

"This is not going to help our case," said Melanie. "But I suppose somebody was going to find out some time. Annette James has done some good work in the past, so I'm not surprised it's her. The problem will be if other news services pick it up and get a bit hysterical."

"That's the worry, Ma'am. I hope they don't find out that we're the lead detectives on the case. We could take some flying crap if they do."

"You have a nice turn of phrase, Senior Detective Constable Weyland," said Melanie, trying without success to hide a smile. "But remember a few years back when Russian hackers broke into the Medibank website and demanded money to refrain from broadcasting personal details on the dark web? That didn't cause quite the global panic the police and spooks expected."

"I'll keep my fingers crossed," said Alex.

"And toes," said Melanie. "Call Jack and see if he saw the broadcast. Then we'll just keep on looking and hope we don't get shown up."

"Will do, Ma'am," said Alex and they returned to their respective offices.

* * *

Less than an hour later, her screen became alive again, this time with the appalling white mask.

"So, Melanie, do you now understand how serious we are? I didn't want to kill your lover, but you needed a warning."

Melanie felt vomit rise in her throat and she swallowed firmly. She would not reveal her feelings to this mass-murderer. She said nothing and stared hard at the eyes behind the mask but could not identify anything obvious, and the voice told her nothing

"Here's your second and final warning," said the mask. "Back off. Stop looking for us. You'll never find us. If you keep going, believe me, we'll kill a lot of people. Do you want that on your conscience?"

Melanie maintained her silent stare and she sensed that whoever was behind the mask was feeling some discomfort. She looked behind the speaker and didn't see anything on the far wall. This was not Chang, she decided. She thought it was most likely the Australian member of this murderous group.

"And it's unfortunate for you that the media have got hold of it," said the face on the screen. "You'd better pray this doesn't get the whole world looking for us, because you'll pay for it if this happens."

Melanie refused to be drawn into the conversation.

"Be warned, Melanie," said the distorted voice again. "Back off or be responsible for hundreds of deaths."

The face disappeared.

Chapter 35

Australia, April, 2024

Within two days, the media had become a circus.

"International hackers killing pacemaker recipients," bellowed the headlines of one major newspaper, followed by similar headlines all over Australia.

All the television news channels reported similar stories, most of them having followed Annette James' example and tracked down the series of deaths in New South Wales on a single day

Hospitals which had implanted pacemakers were deluged with frantic calls from patients asking how to protect themselves from these attacks and few seemed reassured by the hospitals' statements that safety precautions were being taken and all devices would soon be reprogrammed with security software.

When a mob of some thousand attacked one of the American manufacturers' companies, many of the attackers armed with automatic rifles which were fired at the building, the National Guard was called in to enforce the peace, but this took some hours and lives were lost on both sides.

The manufacturers called a video conference.

"Thank you for coming," said the British company's Chief Executive Officer, looking at the multiple faces on the big screen before him. "This has become critical, and we need to talk about it."

"How many of us have been offered the systems from NSA?" asked Arnold Peterson, one of the two Americans.

All of them signified that they had been offered the technology.

"And what are you doing about it?" asked Peterson.

"We're modifying our devices with that," said Monique Thielemans of the Belgian company.

"So are we," said Michelle Curran of Ireland.

"We've been making the changes from the very first," said Williams.

"As have we," said Sunil Anand of India.

"Us too," said Peterson. "Caitlin, what about you?"

"I decided this was nonsense," said Caitlin Faversham, the CEO of the other American company. "The cost is massive, the number of people being killed was tiny and anyway, the whole thing would blow over when they find the pricks doing this. We decided it was cheaper just to pay some compensation to any victims and wait for the storm to pass. Congress tried to pass a bill making it compulsory to make these changes, but it failed. So we ignored it"

"You mean you'll do what Ford did all those years ago when it was shown that the Ford Pinto would burst into flames if hit from the back?" said Peterson. "That didn't do Ford any good. You really are a silly bitch if that's your decision, Caitlin. I assure you, I'll make certain all the hospitals know you're not changing your devices and you can imagine what that will do to your sales, never mind having the licence removed from them."

A ripple of scorn ran round the faces on the screen.

"Well, I hope you'll do that," said Williams, a broad smile on his face. "All the better for us."

Abruptly, the American woman's face disappeared.

"I think she got the message," said Peterson. "So everybody else is making the changes?"

Nods all around were evident on the monitor.

"I see that the Chinese organisation is not here," said Michelle Curran. "I know they claimed to have security in place when we met in London, but the fact that several deaths resulted soon after that meeting indicated that whoever is doing this wanted to prove a point. They've been manufacturing their own models for a few years now, does anyone know their situation?"

"We've all lost sales to China since they began making their own," said Williams "And they're not subject to the same market rules as we are, so it would not surprise me if they decided not to install safe systems. Maybe we can ask our respective security agencies if they have any updated information?"

"Sounds good," said Anand. "So now, what do we do about the current crisis?"

"I suggest a press release issued jointly with the police and spooks in each of our countries," said Curran. "Let's say that we are only manufacturing new pacemakers with revised security systems that prevent hacking and that the police all over the world are looking for the hackers as a first priority and the situation is expected to be resolved soon. Meanwhile, we have modified the standard testing procedures to allow enhanced software to be installed and the hospitals will be able to offer it."

"Won't that cause a rush on hospitals by patients with pacemakers?" asked Anand.

"Sure," said Curran. "But the hospitals have said they will set up outpatient units and conduct a lot of updates each day."

"I suppose that's partly true," said Williams. "All except for the early resolution. I hope to god that's true."

"Amen," said Thielemans and the meeting ended with nods of agreement all round.

Chapter 36

Sydney Television Studios, April, 2024

Annette James picked up the phone while continuing to read the draft of that evening's news bulletin. The call was from the reception desk, she noted.

"Yes," she said.

"Annette, you have a visitor. His name is Gordon Porter and I think you'd better see him."

Something in the receptionist's tone alerted her. "Send him up," she said.

A few moments later, a security man appeared at her open office door. He stood aside and another man entered, closing the door behind him.

"Gordon Porter," he said and displayed a card. Annette read it with interest.

"ASIO?" she said. "Why does Australia's Security Intelligence Organisation want to talk to me?"

"Miss James," he began.

"Call me Annette," she interrupted. "This might be a difficult enough conversation as it is. Let's make it easier, if possible."

Porter laughed. "Okay, Annette. You've stumbled on something that has serious security issues and I need to talk to you about it."

"The pacemaker story? Are you going to slap a gag order on me? If so, why?"

Porter shook his head. "No, we can't do that anymore. I'm going to make you an offer I think you'll like and in return you may consider moderating the story a little."

"Okay, you have my interest."

"You're the one that uncovered the story and that required some good work. So far, your one broadcast was fairly conservative, didn't get hysterical like most of your competitors and you didn't indulge in wild fantasies. We appreciate that, so here's my offer."

Annette leaned forward in her seat and folded her arms on the desk.

"I'll tell you quite a lot more about what is going on," said Porter. "And I promise I'll give you the complete scoop when it's all over. In return, I want you to tell your audience the facts that I give you, as these may well cause a panic in the perpetrators, and they'll start to make mistakes. I assure you, you will be well ahead of your competition with what I'm going to give you."

"How can a girl resist an offer like that?" said Annette.

Porter smiled. "Okay, pin your ears back and take whatever notes you want. Here's the good stuff."

* * *

The seven o'clock news that evening was rated one of the highest audience numbers of the year and the news was repeated in several newspapers around the country the following day.

"Good evening, I'm Annette James with the evening news. Our lead story is the outbreak of deaths among pacemaker recipients which we broke two days ago and on which we have now obtained significant new facts.

"The first point to make is that similar deaths have occurred in the United Kingdom and the USA. On the same day that five deaths occurred in New South Wales, five similar deaths occurred in England and in areas around the USA. The deaths in England occurred with five patients who had received pacemakers at the same hospital in London and those in the USA had received theirs at two hospitals in Chicago and Washington.

"But these were not the start, nor were they the result of malfunctions in the devices. We have learnt that a number of people in all three countries had been subjected to blackmail by a group of hackers who had learnt how to hack into the hospital systems and then the devices. This had been considered as a possibility in earlier years but so far considered only possible when within a few metres of the patient.

"Second, what we have also learnt is that the first cases of blackmail were with wealthy people who could afford to pay significant sums to be left unhurt. But a later development was to threaten people in the military, government and security forces to gain information that could prove invaluable to hostile agencies.

"Here's what we discovered from various sources quite recently. First, all the manufacturers of these devices have been coordinating intensive research to make them impervious to electronic hacking and the first revised models are now being produced. A number of people in sensitive positions have already been refitted with the new models and are now safe.

"As with the case a few years ago, when Russian hackers broke into the Medibank systems and sold personal data on the dark web, the Federal Police joined forces with the Australian security forces in a task force that applied huge efforts to finding out the people behind these crimes. What we have learnt is significant.

"One, the hackers are part of organised crime syndicates operating in the UK and Australia, using the internet to attack victims around the world. There is also an operator in Hong Kong. The police and security forces believe they are closing in on them.

"Two, in a case of the poacher becoming the game-keeper, the Australian police have been working with a man who is considered the best computer hacker in the world and who is now working to locate the criminals conducting these attacks.

"We will continue to update you with information as we uncover it.

"In other news..."

Chapter 37

Cheshire, UK, April, 2024

"Anna-Maria, we have serious matters to discuss."

"Yes, Uncle Giorgio, how can I help you?"

"It has become completely obvious that William has failed us." The slight Italian accent in Grassano's voice, not noticeable in face-to-face speech was exaggerated by the telephone connection and the anxiety in the speaker. "He cannot be of use to us any longer."

"Uncle, he has done excellent work over the years, finding suitable marks for us."

"That is true, but that was the limit of his ability. When he tried take matters beyond that, the limitations began to show."

"In what way, Uncle?"

"Trying to gain government and defence information that we could use was a terrible mistake. It seems the security forces in England and Australia realised what was going on and provided information that was false and cost us several millions. That alone was intolerable. Then having the man in Adelaide killed as an attempt to frighten off the female detective was an even worse error. It has only increased their efforts to identify us. And somehow, a journalist in

Australia has now revealed too much of the facts behind our operation, including the news that the operators are in Australia, England and Hong Kong. It also seems the manufacturers of pacemakers have been working on producing safeguards against what we have been doing. This whole operation must close down, immediately."

"I am truly sorry, Uncle."

"So am I, Anna-Maria. And now we have been hit with a massive blow. Nearly all the money, some twelve million pounds has been taken from our account."

"Oh my god, Uncle, all of it?"

"Nearly all. Our leader in Sicily is almost ready to kill both of us, even though we are the same blood. We are very fortunate that I had transferred much of the money to Sicily before this happened."

Anna-Maria's voice was shaky. "You think one of the boys took it? Or maybe William?"

"I doubt they would be so stupid. No, the opinion of many is that somehow Allen Miller has become involved, and this is his doing."

"Allen...? My god, this is worse than I thought."

"It is, and it's William who started this whole story and that's how Miller became involved. You must then understand what has to be done."

"Uncle Giorgio, he's my husband." The horror in her made her shout into the phone.

"But he's not our blood. And you know which is more important to us. You must do what must be done."

"Yes, Uncle." Her face white, Anna-Maria replaced the phone with a trembling hand.

"William, let's take a drive."

Anna-Maria's suggestion was a surprise to Lloyd. The marriage had been growing increasingly distant in recent months and any conversation at all was rare. The idea of a social drive was even more unusual.

"Why and where to?" he asked.

"There's a property in the country I saw recently and it's for sale. I thought we might buy it and perhaps build a little get-away cottage."

"A get-away? Anna-Maria, what brought this on? We don't spend much time together anymore, why would we want a get-away cottage?"

"William, please, go with me on this one. I'm trying to get things back to normal."

That comment also surprised Lloyd. He had sensed her withdrawal in recent months, but any attempt to discuss the subject had been met with a cold refusal. The marriage had been declining in the last few years, partly as a result of her inability to have children, something Lloyd had wanted.

"Well, okay," he said, though he knew he really didn't want this. It had been a while since he had felt relaxed in her company.

"I'll drive," she said and picked up the car keys from the hook by the front door.

Nothing more was said while they entered the car and she drove out on the road south. It was twenty minutes before he spoke.

"Where are we heading?" he asked.

"Another couple of miles," she replied and accelerated.

"Do we need to go this fast?" he said, feeling tensions rising.

She didn't answer. Lloyd stared ahead, increasing worry running through him. *What was this really all about? She's not relaxed any more than I am.*

A few minutes later, she slowed and turned off into a narrow lane that led into woodlands.

"What's all this?" Lloyd said, tension making his throat tight. "There's no land sales in this area."

"We're not buying," she said and pulled off the lane into a clearing surrounded by trees. "William, we've come to the end."

"What the hell do you mean?"

"Why do you think I married you?"

He stared at her. "Why do people get married at all? I thought you loved me."

"I did it because Uncle Giorgio said you'd be useful to us."

"What?" Lloyd felt coldness run through him. "You told me you loved me and wanted to have our children. I thought the recent difficulties were because you couldn't have kids."

"It was a useful story. Fact is William, I never went off the pill. I didn't want your kids, any kids at all. This was all just a business matter for the family."

Lloyd went limp in shock. "The family? The Mafia family?"

"Just that, William. Nothing matters more than the family. *Nothing.* I did what was needed. And for a time, it worked. You gave us good, useful contacts and they paid off."

"So what's changed?"

"Those two kids you recruited. They sounded good and they certainly paid their way with some of the initial blackmails. But then it all dried up. And when they tried going for state secrets, the whole thing fell apart. The security forces found out what was happening and they started feeding fake information. The family lost millions and it caused a lot of stress with major clients."

"I couldn't help that. But it was your uncle who ordered that and he provided the names of people to be attacked. I always thought they should have stayed with just demanding money from wealthy people."

"But your decision to kill the cop's boyfriend, that confirmed it. It has caused even more worries."

"But Anna-Maria, you organised that." Lloyd's panic was increasing.

"I thought it had been authorised by my uncle."

"I was just trying to keep things under control. I can't help what the cop would do."

"Somebody has to take responsibility, William. Uncle Giorgio called me yesterday and told me to wrap this up."

"What do you mean, wrap this up? Anna-Maria, what the hell is happening?" Lloyd's fear broke into full scale panic.

"I'm sorry, William. Like I said, the family is everything and you failed us."

"Christ, have you brought me here to kill me? Anna-Maria, for God's sake, what are you doing?"

"You know the rules, William. We just don't tolerate failure. And you failed."

"Jesus Christ, you're my wife! How can you kill me? Please Anna-Maria, stop this. Let's go home and I'll see how to improve the situation. Please, you can't kill me."

"Sorry William. Uncle Giorgio ordered it."

She opened her door and slipped out. Two shadows appeared at the side of the car as two men moved in. Neither wore any face coverings, They opened Lloyd's door and pulled him out. He screamed, struggled hard but could not break the iron grasp on his arms. He was forced down to a kneeling position, his arms held behind him, his head almost on the grass.

A single bullet smashed into the back of his head and tore most of his face away, spattering blood and brain material over the grass.

The two men walked to where Anna-Maria was standing, some twenty metres away. She showed no emotions.

"All done," said one.

She nodded, returned to the car and drove back in the direction she had come.

* * *

"Looks like your standard gangland killing, Ma'am." Detective Sergeant Wallace, acting as Scene of Crime Officer, stood looking down at the body on the grass. Around him, three other officers in full protective clothing combed through the ground looking for any clues that could be found.

"Who called it in, Nick?" Detective Inspector Emily Goodwin was a full head shorter than her lanky sergeant and tended to avoid looking him in the eye to avoid a cricked neck.

"Couple of kids rode here on their bikes for an early morning bit of slap and tickle before school." Wallace suppressed his laugh.

"They're still here?"

"No, Ma'am, we've taken their statements, told them not to be late for school. Reckon they're about fifteen."

"Kids, eh?" Emily Goodwin sighed. "So what have you got?"

"Looks like a big calibre, probably a .45 in the back of the head, totally obliterated the face, no chance of a dental identification. Definitely a gangland-style execution. You can see where his knees were forced down on the grass, probably his arms held upright behind him."

"Anything more positive?"

"Actually, Ma'am, you can almost read the event like a story." Wallace pointed to his left. "There are tracks of one car over there, not good ones, the tread is badly worn, but it looks like your standard small car size. But over there," he pointed behind him, "there are excellent tracks. A bigger vehicle and the tyres are obviously very new, they've left a perfect trail."

"You've photographed them and taken casts?"

"We have. One of the blokes reckons those are the top-end Michelins, especially for SUVs and such."

"You'll start the hunt with all the local tyre distributors for any sales in, say, the last three months? There can't be too many sales of those things."

"Of course, Ma'am."

"Good. Nick, I'll leave you to it." Emily Goodwin returned to her car.

"Bloody hell, you silly bitch," muttered Wallace. "I bet I've done more of these than you've had hot sex. Anyone would think I don't know how to run these things."

* * *

"Five dealers within fifty kilometres reported selling a full set of Michelin Latitude Sport 3 tyres, which is what these were, within the last three months." Detective Sergeant Wallace slid the single sheet of paper across the desk to Goodwin. "Expensive tyres for very expensive vehicles."

DI Goodwin read through the list. "Great, Nick. Names, addresses and serial numbers of each tyre shown. Do we know any of these people?"

Wallace shook his head. "No, Ma'am."

"Okay, Nick, you know what to do."

"I believe so, Ma'am."

* * *

The police patrol car rolled up to the front door of the sizeable mansion in the Lancashire countryside. The driveway was at least fifty metres long.

"How the other half lives, eh, Nick?" said the constable driving the car.

"Indeed. Let's see if they're gang members and killers."

The door was already open when the two officers reached it. A tall, extremely thin man stood there, a pleasant smile on his face.

"Good morning, officers, what have I done?"

"Just a routine check, sir. I believe your Mercedes was fitted with a set of new Michelin tyres in recent weeks?"

The smile was replaced by a puzzled look. "That is so. Is that a problem?"

"Probably not, sir, but would you allow us to check those tyres?"

"Certainly officer." The tall man leaned inside and took a bunch of keys from a hook. He pressed a button on one of them and the doors to the garage at the side of the house swung open. "Feel free," he said.

"Thank you, sir."

The two officers walked into the garage to find a black Mercedes SUV.

"Nice," said the patrol car driver, pulled out a flashlight and bent to the nearest tyre. Wallace did the same and it only took a few moments to complete the examination.

"All of them on that list?" said Nick. His colleague nodded. They returned to the house. The departure was courteous.

"One down," said Nick.

The second house was similar, long driveway, impressive door, a puzzled but courteous woman with an impressive display of pearls round her neck. She watched as the two officers checked the serial numbers on all four tyres of the Hybrid Range Rover parked next to the house. Again, the serial numbers of the tyres matched those on the list they had.

By the end of the shift, with one more residence to check, Nick and his driver were weary.

"Nothing suspicious at any of those," said Nick. "But I don't suppose we were expecting some obvious Sicilian Mafia boss to come out and get ugly with us."

"That would make a change," said Constable Derek Rollings, the driver. "These rich nobs, they're all too bloody polite!"

"Let's see how this one goes," said Nick as they arrived at the pleasant house, somewhat smaller than the others they had visited and without the lengthy driveway. Another Mercedes SUV was parked by the front door.

The door was opened by an attractive woman dressed in a black pantsuit.

"Good afternoon, Madam," said Nick and displayed his warrant card. "Mrs Lloyd, is it? Just a routine check. May we examine your vehicle?"

"Just why would you do that?" The woman seemed hostile.

"Like I said, Mrs Lloyd, just routine. We're following up on some reported sales of pirated tyres in this region and we'd like to check the serial numbers of the ones on your vehicle."

The woman seemed less tense. "Go ahead," she said.

"Who normally drives this car, Mrs Lloyd?"

"My husband, but he's away on business, so I use it then."

"Thank you. We'll be done quickly."

The woman closed the door as the officers began their examination.

"Hey, Nick," said Rollings. "There's fresh grass on the inside of the bumper."

"Interesting. Bag it, Derek."

"Done. My two tyres are on the list."

"Mine too. Let's get out of here."

The front door being closed, the two officers returned to the car and back to the police station.

"Nothing suspicious, Nick?" Emily Goodwin waved Nick to a seat across from her desk.

"Not with the first four. But the last one made us think. We found some grass on the front bumper of the vehicle. I sent it to the laboratory with the sample we took from the crime scene."

"Good work. And while you were out, we checked up on those five residences. The first four are all normal, wealthy people of long-established residences and known in the community. That last one, this William Lloyd is different. He's a teacher at a grammar school."

"A teacher?" Nick sat upright. "I doubt a teacher could afford a place like that, never mind a massively expensive vehicle that he has."

"That's what we thought. Okay Nick, we've been asked to coordinate with the Australian Federal Police on something going on. Copy that list and give me both copies. Our instructions are to communicate with the Aussies in a strange way. We have to send any information by King's Messenger, would you believe."

"King's...? Holy cow, Ma'am, this is high level stuff."

"Damn right. I hope we get to hear the whole story some day."

* * *

Anna-Maria walked shakily to her lounge, poured a large gin and tonic and sat down, trembling. Having to kill her husband had been a distressing enough business, even though she had not loved him for the last few years, but there had been some emotional connection in the beginning. Even so, having to drive William to his execution and watch it happen had ripped her apart.

And now it looked like the police had some suspicions about her. Just the fact that they had shown up on some pretence of looking at her vehicle had hit her like a mule's kick in the guts. The whole blackmail through pacemaker attacks had proved hugely profitable until they had over-reached themselves by trying to obtain valuable government information and discovered that they had been played by the security forces with false information.

The final blow of losing millions of pounds in their bank account was too much. Anna-Maria burst into hysterical sobs and remained helpless for over half an hour before she recovered some self-control.

Damn that Australian detective! William had told her about this Melanie Carter and she had endorsed his plan to dissuade her from further investigations by killing her boyfriend. Anna-Maria finished her drink and poured a second one, working out how to make this Carter woman pay for her opposition that had caused this total collapse of their plans.

She went to her computer, found the addresses of major newspapers in Sydney and the television stations and began to compose a letter.

Chapter 38

Mid North Coast, NSW, Australia, May, 2024

Phillip Murray was severely worried. He had twice tried to call William Lloyd in England, but nobody had responded to his internet call. He had tried to call Chang to see if his friend in Hong Kong had any news, and had got nothing but "Please try again later" messages on the screen. He entered Lloyd's video address once more and this time a face appeared on his monitor. But it wasn't Lloyd. The woman's face was unfamiliar.

"You must be Phillip Murray," said the woman. Her smile and pleasant tone did nothing to ease Murray's anxiety.

"Who are you?" he asked.

"We've never met," replied the woman. "I'm Anna-Maria, I'm William's wife, or should I say, I *was* William's wife."

"Was? What the hell do you mean, was?"

The woman smiled again. "Sadly, I must tell you, William has departed from us."

"What, he's dead? What happened?"

"Let's just say he made too many mistakes. Our rules are very clear, if somebody starts to threaten our security, they get removed."

"You killed him? Jesus Christ, who *are* you people?" Murray began to feel sick with fear from what she was telling him.

"I'm sure you know who we are, Phillip. We've been providing you with connections for your brilliant abilities to make large sums of money for a long time now. But please don't worry, nothing is changing. It's just that I've taken over my husband's duties and we'll keep this working relationship as long as we need to. You and Peter Chang have done very well out of this arrangement, there's no need for it to end."

Murray struggled for self-control. This woman said she was Lloyd's wife but displayed no regrets about his murder. *Had she done it herself?* he wondered.

"However," Anna-Maria continued, "I must caution you against trying to change our arrangements."

"I'm sorry, what?" Murray was confused.

"Don't try going out on your own, Phillip," she said. "Don't do any operations without advising me of what the return will be and please don't try hiding the returns from me and putting the money in a private bank account."

Murray felt his guts freeze. He had done exactly that for fifteen thousand dollars he had taken from a blackmail victim just a month ago and quite a few thousand had been directed the same way over the time he had been operating.

"Okay, Mrs Lloyd," he said. "I understand. I'll wait for future instructions from you."

"Good man," she said with a pleasant smile. "We'll be in touch."

The connection was broken.

Murray got to work. With the skills he had acquired over the last few years, he had opened up three fake bank accounts in Sydney and into those, he had fed several thousand dollars from small-scale blackmail routines of wealthy people in the country as well as more sums simply removed from corporate bank accounts. At the same time, he had opened up a personal account in the Caymans. One other action had resulted from the study of several processes in the dark web, and he had successfully procured himself a new passport under another name.

His first step was to access the Cayman Islands account into which he and Chang had paid the proceeds of their numerous blackmails around the world. Over the next thirty minutes, he accessed that and found there was still over six hundred thousand dollars in there. Clearly, the Mafia had not yet been paid their proceeds from recent activities. With a few keystrokes, he transferred that amount to his personal account in another Caymans bank, leaving no track of where the money had gone.

He packed a small travel bag, took out his legal passport and his second, false one and left his apartment. He took the bus into Sydney, visited each of his banks in turn and withdrew six thousand dollars in cash, not enough to cause suspicion. The balances he would transfer to the Caymans account later. Then he headed to the airport.

Chapter 39

Mid North Coast, May, 2024

Melanie heard the beep on her computer and turned to it, not surprised to see Miller's face.

"Yes, Allen," she said. "You have news?"

"Send Alex to Hong Kong," said Miller.

"What? Why?"

Miller's face showed no expression, but Melanie could hear the amusement in his voice.

"I sent them a message," he said. "They're expecting one of you, but I'd say you're busy there. He'll be met at the airport, they'll tell you all about it."

"They haven't been too cooperative in the past. What's changed?"

"They've suffered at the hands of this group, even if they haven't admitted it. They'll welcome the information you'll give them. Send the recording of Chang's call with Alex."

"So why didn't you send them that already?" Melanie was intrigued by whatever game Miller was playing."

"You'll work it out, young lady."

"Maybe. Allen, you can be bloody infuriating sometimes, you know that?"

"It's all part of my hobby, Melanie. But then I do nice things for people, as you know. Maybe I have a split personality."

"Definitely something."

"And now here's your bonus, Melanie. After Alex had done such sterling work in finding Peter Chang, I decided to do some follow-up work myself."

"And what was that?" Melanie felt her senses sharpen. Allen was about to give her some useful information, she knew.

"I went back to the university yearbook that Alex had accessed and saw that Chang had been at a grammar school in Manchester since he was fifteen, before he went to University, also in Manchester. I suspect he was given a place because his eminent surgeon father had also been at school there and considerable sums of money were donated. Anyway, I got to work and finally accessed the computer files of that school and looked up Chang's record, which was pretty spectacular, I can tell you."

"That doesn't surprise me, but what of it?"

"So I looked at the records of the students who were there in Chang's year and I found one interesting name, a boy who had also been granted a place from an Australian family."

Melanie sat forward. "Yes, Allen, that is interesting. Who was it?"

"His name is Phillip Murray. His home address is in Bondi, near Sydney. It's on your screen now."

Melanie watched as an address appeared on her monitor. She noted it down.

"Was that the only Australian you found at that school?"

"No, there were three others, but they were not there in Chang's time."

"Allen, you can be as infuriating as you want when you provide help like that. I wish we could celebrate this with a drink."

"Not a chance, Melanie."

The call was disconnected. Melanie began to think that she had already worked out Allen's game. But first things first, she decided, and picked up the phone to call the police in Bondi.

Chapter 40

Chek Lap Kok International Airport, Hong Kong, May, 2024

Whatever weariness Alex Weyland was experiencing from the nine-hour flight from Sydney vanished as soon as he stepped out of the Cathay Pacific airliner. This was his first venture out of Australia, and he felt as if he had been hit by the energy and excitement of this airport. Masses of people were waiting to be processed in the arrival area and Alex felt overwhelmed. *What the hell do I do now?"* he thought.

"Senior Detective Constable Alex Weyland?" the voice came from a petite, attractive young woman dressed in a tailored suit in dark blue. The voice was clear, well-spoken and the tones reminded Alex of the almost too-perfect intonation of Chang.

He turned to the woman. "That's me," he said.

She left the throng and walked up to him.

"Sik Ling Wong," she said and displayed a formal-looking identification card. "But you can call me Kathleen. Ministry of Public Security. Please follow me."

Somewhat shaken by all this, together with the fatigue and excitement of his first overseas trip, Alex walked alongside her to the outdoors where a black sedan was waiting by the kerbside. They had not gone through any customs or immigration procedures. The officer opened the door nearest to her and climbed in, leaving Alex to walk round and climb in the other side. In the front, a uniformed police officer sat at the wheel. He said nothing but moved off as soon as Alex closed the door.

"Better look at my card again," she said, a slight smile on her lips. "I don't like to show it too widely in public."

Alex studied the card she handed him. The picture was certainly of her, he decided. "Senior Constable?" he asked.

"Again, keep it fairly quiet."

"And Kathleen? Not a Chinese name."

"It's common among Chinese people who interact with Westerners. It all started when British missionaries ran our schools, they gave us Western names to avoid confusion. The habit stuck. It's not my legal name, but I use it with visiting Westerners."

Alex began to feel more comfortable. She didn't seem to represent a repressive police society as he had expected.

The ride into the city took just over half an hour and it passed easily as Alex admired the view over water and the entry into the city. Kathleen chatted like a tourist guide, obviously trying to put Alex at his ease.

"Many years ago, before this new airport was opened, the arrival into Kai Tak airport could terrify some people. The final approach was right over houses and at the last bit, you could actually look into people's top floor apartments. I used to love it."

But eventually, the car pulled into the underground parking area of a high-rise tower and Kathleen led Alex to a floor near the top and to an office. Three men sat at a conference table. All had the appearance of senior military or police officers, despite their conventional business suits. Alex felt he could have placed them as such at any time. Kathleen pointed to a seat at the table then took a seat against the wall.

"Welcome, Detective Senior Constable Weyland," said the man at the head of the table. He did not introduce himself. "We received a message on my computer a few days ago from a man named Allen Miller. We have encountered this man before, not to our advantage, and for a time we believed that he was responsible for the computer hacking, blackmail and deaths from interference into pacemaker devices. He assured us that he was not guilty of these crimes and advised us to contact your senior officer to gain information about the real culprit. We decided to go along with this because although our government did not admit to any such problems here and in China, there have been deaths of senior government personnel. So, Constable, what do you have for us?"

Alex took the flash drive from his pocket and passed it down the table. The man at the head waved to Kathleen who came and took it. She went to a computer by the wall and inserted it. A moment later, the call from Chang was displayed on the opposite wall. It was watched in silence.

"And what does that give us?" asked the officer.

"On the wall behind the caller is a frame containing a picture," said Alex. "Our technicians were able to expand that and develop the details. Here is the result." He took the picture of the certificate from his case, Kathleen took it and carried it to the senior officer. He studied it, said nothing but passed it to his two colleagues.

"Miller has already confirmed that the caller is in Hong Kong," said Alex. "It seems obvious that the caller is the son of the Doctor Chang in that certificate. Let me give you some further information."

Alex outlined the analyses done of the voices in the blackmailing calls, the evidence of the accents from Manchester and the education that Peter Chang had received at school and university in that city. He was heard in silence. When he had finished, the officer nodded at Kathleen. She left the room and returned twenty minutes later. In that time, Alex was not questioned further, and he sat in tense silence. Kathleen handed a note to the officer. He read it, handed it to his colleagues and nodded at her. She looked at Alex and beckoned him to follow her. With relief, he left the room.

"Now we go and get him," she said.

* * *

The apartment building looked impressive from the outside as three police cars stopped at the front. Alex followed Kathleen and a new officer, briefly introduced as Inspector Law, a name which Alex privately thought was most appropriate. Six armed police officers followed him. The lobby was even more impressive than the front, black and white tiled floor and high walls with a number of pictures hanging on them. There was a desk with a security guard behind it, but he seemed almost to shrink away as the group of police walked in. He made no move to prevent their entry.

The Lieutenant, Kathleen and Alex took one lift, the others took a second one. At the eighteenth floor, all of them gathered outside one apartment as the officer banged on the door. After a few moments, a male voice inside spoke something which Alex assumed to be in Cantonese, the officer barked out an order in the same dialect and the door opened. A very frightened youth stood there, an elderly woman behind him. A short conversation occurred, and the police party left with the young man escorted by a large officer on either side of him, each holding an arm. Alex stared at him. Was this the serial killer and genius hacker they had been seeking for so long?

* * *

"You are being given an amazing professional courtesy," said Kathleen. She and Alex sat comfortably in a small office in front of a large computer screen. The picture showed two officers in uniform on one side of a table, Peter Chang sat on the other side. His hands were handcuffed and the cuffs were locked into a clamp on the table. He looked completely defeated. Seated in one corner facing the prisoner, was another man in a smart business suit.

"Your name is Peter Chang?" said one of the officers.

Alex looked at Kathleen. "In English?" he asked.

She smiled, the first time he had seen that. "That's the amazing courtesy," she said. "Not only are you being permitted to watch the interrogation, but it's also being conducted in English for your benefit. I suspect this is not only a courtesy, they are also sending a message to the countries who have been affected by this man and his group."

"Holy cow," said Alex and turned back to watch the proceedings. He hadn't heard Chang's response to the first question.

"And you were at school in Manchester, England and then gained a first-class honours degree in Computer Sciences, also in Manchester?"

"Yes," said Chang.

"We have found the system you use to distort your voice when calling your victims," said the interrogator.

"That's commonly available," said Chang. A small spark of defiance showed in the way he sat up from his slumped position, lifted his head and stared directly at the officer. "That's not evidence."

"But are you aware that the suppliers of such systems create a key to restore the original voice and they supply it only to law-enforcement organisations?"

That hit Chang. He fell back against his chair in defeat.

"And we have clearly identified the voice as yours," continued the officer. "We recorded you as you were booked in and checked that recording against the one we have of your call to Detective-Inspector Melanie Carter in Australia."

That clearly shook Chang. He stared down at his hands and said nothing.

"So even if we disregard the crimes of murder and blackmail committed against citizens of the UK, Australia and the United States, you remain guilty of the crime of murder of two members of the Chinese National government," continued the officer. "That brings the death sentence. We don't follow those soft, weakling systems in the west, we are practical. As of now, I pronounce you guilty of murder. I can have you taken from here to the special area we have in the basement where you will be shot. Do you have anything to say?"

Chang looked like he was choking. His mouth opened and closed convulsively, and his face was deathly white.

The officer turned to the man in the corner. "Mr Tsiu," he said. "Do you wish to add anything?"

The man named Tsiu stood up.

"Mr Chang," he said. "I am from the Ministry of State Security."

His English was as immaculate as that of everybody else Alex had met so far. He hid a smile and concentrated on what this new speaker was saying.

"We do have an alternative path for you, if you are interested," said Tsiu.

"Ah, now I see the real purpose of allowing you to witness this," murmured Kathleen.

"As the Officer of the Ministry of Public Security has told you, they could execute you now for the crimes you have committed," continued the new speaker. "However, we in the Ministry of State Security have a wider perspective. You can save yourself and serve your nation if you come and work for us. We have need of such talents as you possess."

"Now, I understand," said Alex. "They want us to know that we will have no secrets from you after this."

"At least as long as it takes to develop even higher security to your systems," said Kathleen. "Your medical equipment companies will have to find a block to hacking into their equipment and all the banks, hospitals and security forces will need to develop even tighter firewalls."

"I suppose you could consider they have done the world a favour," said Alex. "And when they have all that, young Chang's life will be worth nothing."

"Can't say I have sympathy for him," said Kathleen. "And now this is over, I suspect you'd like to see your hotel and clean up. Then I'll show you around my city and take you to eat at one of the greatest restaurants in the whole place."

"Sounds good," said Alex.

Chapter 41

Mid North Coast, Australia, May, 2024

The storm hit Melanie as she dressed to go to work soon after six-thirty in the morning. The television was on in the background and she was half-listening. But the sound of her name shook her from the semi-attention to full alertness.

"This news department has learnt that the leading agency in the hunt for the pacemaker killers was a detective force on the mid-North Coast of New South

Wales," said the young man on the screen. "This was because the lead detective, Inspector Melanie Carter had previously led a case in which the notorious internationally-sought computer hacker, Allen Miller had been involved and it appears he had offered his assistance to Inspector Carter.

"The disturbing aspect of this arrangement is just why Miller was working with the Australian law enforcement agencies. One explanation is this picture of the detective."

On the screen came a picture of Melanie. She recognised it as her graduation picture taken some years ago at university.

"It's clear that this woman, who resembles a Victoria's Secret model or a famous movie star rather than a police detective would cause any man to want to be involved with her. Carter is awfully young to be a Detective Inspector and it's impossible not to wonder just what she has traded for her unusually rapid promotion.

"So we in the newsroom must ask just why has this investigation taken so long? Months have passed while innocent people have been blackmailed and many killed through the work of a few computer hackers. Is this deliberate delaying tactics or simply incompetence? News at Breakfast will continue to investigate."

Melanie sat on her bed, stunned. *Where had this come from? Who had given this information to a television station? Had this been sent to other such organisations.*

She soon found out just how terrible was the storm. As she drove into the office, the news on the car radio echoed the story on television.

"Why is this extraordinarily beautiful young woman working closely with an internationally-renowned computer criminal? Is there some unknown relationship and arrangement that has delayed the resolution of the series of murders and blackmails around the world? Is it deliberate or is it merely astonishing incompetence? Does this indicate a possible collusion between the law enforcement agencies and organised crime?"

At the traffic lights, she stopped on the red light, opposite the newsagent where she normally bought her occasional magazine. Already, the boards at the front held headlines.

"Local police involvement suspected with organised crime," said one board.

"Possible police corruption in cover-ups of serial killers," said another.

Melanie drove on through the lights, turned round the block and returned home. She could not face her colleagues at work, and she knew her entire world was collapsing.

Almost like a robot, she parked the car, entered her apartment and locked the door behind her. She felt icy cold and completely numb, unable to think of anything but the obvious fact that her entire career had hit a wall and she could never recover from the calamity. She sat in an armchair, staring at the wall, frozen into immobility. She didn't hear the knocking on her door or the calls from unknown people with questions. The phone rang continuously but she was unable to answer it.

Time meant nothing. She had no idea of how long she sat in her frozen state. She'd missed breakfast, with the shock of the television news, and the idea of food did not occur to her. Slowly, one simple thought grew in her mind until it blocked out every other thought. There was nothing left. She had lost her first big love just as she graduated. The second love in her life had been deliberately murdered as a way of attacking her. Now her career had been destroyed.

There was only one path open to her.

Finally, she got to her feet, went to the bathroom and opened the cabinet. There was a small jar of a substance she had confiscated from a killer some years ago. She knew the effects of the little red seeds inside and she could see no alternative.

* * *

"No answer?" Jack's anxiety showed in his face.

Alex shook his head. "Just the usual recording."

"Christ, it's been four hours," said Jack. "I can't imagine what she's going through."

"Who the hell sent that crap to the media?" said Alex. "Every newspaper and television channel is pouring out accusations of corruption against her." His face showed severe pain. Jack was well aware of the almost hero-worship with which Alex regarded Melanie.

"I suspect it's one of our hackers," said Jack. "It's typical of the mindset."

"Whoever it was should get eternity in hell," said Alex. "Jack, let's get round there, maybe we can help."

"I've got a key," said Jack. "Let's go."

"Her car's there," said Alex. "She must be home."

Jack opened his side door, and he and Alex approached the apartment building. As they reached the second floor, they saw two men standing by Melanie's door.

"Media?" asked Jack.

"Do you know this officer?" asked one.

Alex took out his warrant card. "Police," he said. "We'll take it from here. Go."

Unwillingly, the two reporters moved away from the door, but stayed hovering by the stairwell. Jack opened the door and they walked in. There was no sign of any living being, and Jack walked into the bedroom.

Melanie was lying motionless.

"Jesus Christ," exclaimed Jack and moved to her, placing a finger at the side of her neck and stayed silently for a few seconds. Alex had stopped by the doorway.

"Maybe," said Jack. "Get an ambulance."

Alex pulled out his phone.

* * *

"Touch and go," said the surgeon. The sadness in his eyes was obvious. "We're still working. We can't identify the poison. It's nothing we've encountered before."

"Probably *Abrus Precatorius*," said Jack.

The surgeon's eyes widened. "The Rosary Seed? Shit, that's rare. No wonder..." Without another word, he raced back to the operating theatre.

"The Rosary Seed?" said Alex. "Isn't that what...?"

"Yes, your first case with us," said Jack. "That awful woman, Nona, killed a few people with it and then Allen Miller fed it to her as his last act before disappearing."[6]

"Melanie must have taken a jar of the stuff from Nona's place," said Alex.

"I wish she hadn't," replied Jack and both men settled down for a long vigil.

Chapter 42

Mid-North Coast, May, 2024

"I wish you hadn't brought me back."

Melanie's face was almost as white as the pillows supporting her head and shoulders.

"Don't be daft," said Jack. He sat by the bedside, holding her hand, which felt cold and lifeless. "For a start, Alex and I need you around. You make the job worthwhile."

A ghost of a smile showed briefly on her colourless lips.

"Maybe," she whispered. "But my career's done. Rob's dead. My life's a shambles. I can't carry on like this."

"Let me update you on the first part," he said. "We had an interesting meeting with the management

---

[6] See "The Ninth of the Month Murders" by Michael Davies

executives of the tv stations that broadcast that crap about you."

"We came to this meeting because your lawyer threatened us with a multi-million libel suit," said the chief executive of one of the three station present in the room. "Haven't you bozos heard about freedom of speech for the media?"

"Oddly enough, we have," said Jack. "And my lawyer here, Bill Fleming also has heard of it. But there's a difference between raising questions and making statements that destroy somebody's career and life."

"We acted on the information we received," said another of the executives.

"Ah, but I believe that news organisations require something called substantiation of the facts," said Jack. "That usually means you have several sources of verification. Not blind acceptance of what is sent to you."

"The facts seemed obvious," said the first executive. "That letter we received laid out some clear details."

"Let me tell you about that letter," said Jack. "Who sent it?"

"Somebody called Anne Grisham. She said she was a lawyer."

"Whereas in fact we examined the letter," said the lawyer, Bill Fleming. "And the email address which the sender had so conveniently left open was traced back to the computer owned by a man called William Lloyd. He had been killed a few days earlier, the killing suspected to be arranged by Anna-Maria Grassano, the wife of said William Lloyd. She is the daughter of a man named Grassano, known to be the head of a Mafia family in Italy and the niece of Giorgio Grassano, his brother and the head of the UK operation."

The television executives were silent, but the dismay on all their faces was obvious.

Jack picked up the theme.

"And it gets worse," he said. "William Lloyd was the sort of "Fagin" character who recruited two young men to run operations for the Mafia. One of them is called Peter Chang, a remarkably brilliant computer hacker who worked out how to hack into hospital systems and then to pacemakers. He now lives in Hong Kong and we have identified him. The other is an Australian man, a close associate of Chang, named Phillip Murray. He learnt the routines from Chang and performed many of the blackmailing operations and also murders, as did Lloyd."

One of the executives murmured, "Oh my god," and folded his arms across his chest in a standard defensive position.

"Indeed," said Jack. "Now let me tell you about the police officer whose life and career you have destroyed. Chief Inspector Melanie Carter has a first-class honours degree in Psychology and has had a successful career with the New South Wales police force. I have worked with her on two cases where she identified a serial killer responsible for numerous murders."

He looked round the table and stared briefly into the eyes of all three executives. None of them maintained the contact for more than a second or two.

"After your organisations threw their evil shit out into the airwaves, Melanie Carter tried to commit suicide. She very nearly succeeded."

Jack sat back in his seat. There was silence in the room. The lawyer took control of the meeting.

"And so to damages," he said. "To begin with, you will all issue detailed public apologies to Melanie Carter. You will lay out the origins of the letter which precipitated your outbursts and make it very plain that Chief Inspector Carter behaved professionally throughout, supported by a task force of the Australian Federal Police and the Australian Security Intelligence Organisation. Is that clear so far?"

All the executives nodded their heads. All looked to be in deep shock.

"You will make these broadcasts on the morning show news breaks, midday news, the prime-time news and the late evening news for three consecutive days," continued Fleming. "All of them will be monitored, and if we judge that you have not been completely clear in your messages, we will make formal complaints to the authorities and request severe penalties. Are we still clear?"

More nods from around the table. Fleming passed a sheet of paper to each of the executives.

"Finally," he said, "here is a list of charities known to be supported by Melanie Carter. Each of you will donate twenty million dollars in total to any or all of those charities and you will announce those donations in your broadcasts, explaining that they are made because police officers cannot receive such money."

He waited a moment while the three men studied the list.

"Good," he said. "A similar meeting to this will be held with the executives of the newspapers which published similar defamatory articles. Do you have any questions? No? Then I wish you all a good day."

Jack and Fleming watched as the three men left, all looking badly shaken.

"Well, at least some good may come out of this," said Jack. "Now I'm going back to the hospital."

Another tiny smile appeared on Melanie's lips.

"So I may be able to go back to work some day?" she said. "But don't the rules say anyone who has tried to commit suicide cannot return to the police force? I'm far too young to be retired on mental health grounds."

"That's another thing," said Jack. "Normally, that would be the case. But the review committee has decided that the pressure you took from this media onslaught were more than anyone could be expected to take rationally. And your record makes you a highly valued member of the force. When you've recovered, you can return to duties after a medical examination."

"That's a relief," she said.

"And with the confirmed rank of Chief Inspector," said Jack.

"That's nice, too," she whispered.

"And one funny thing," said Jack. "Allen Miller called me. He said to tell you that if you don't want to go back to the police, he thought you and he would make a great team tracking down some of the worst criminals around the world."

"That's silly," said Melanie. Her eyes began closing.

"And one last thing before you drop off," said Jack. "Gordon Porter said if you didn't want to go back to the police, there was a position for you with ASIO. He'd love to have you on his team."

But Melanie was asleep.

Chapter 43

Bondi, NSW, Australia, May, 2024

The patrol car stopped by the nondescript house two blocks from Bondi Beach. The officers walked up the short pathway and banged on the door. It was opened by a middle-aged woman wearing a tracksuit, her hair bound up in a hairband. Behind her, a similarly-dressed man stood. Both showed surprise at the sight of the police.

"Mrs Murray?" asked the leading officer.

"Yes. What on earth are you asking for?" the woman replied.

"I'm Senior Constable Adams. This is Senior Constable Nowell. We have a warrant for the arrest of Phillip Murray. I assume he's your son?"

Her puzzlement changed into shock.

"Yes, he is. Arrest? Why are you arresting him?"

The man finally spoke. "Arrest Phillip? What the hell are you talking about?"

"He's under suspicion of blackmail, larceny and possibly murder, Mr Murray. Now, we need to see him immediately."

"Murder? I don't believe it," said Murray. "This is rubbish."

"Is he here, Mr Murray?" said the officer

"No, he doesn't live here anymore. Why are you arresting him? What's he done?"

"As I said, we need to talk with him about a series of crimes. Now, can you give us his current address? This is urgent."

The woman was showing severe agitation, her hands held before her mouth and her eyes wide open. Her husband looked furious. But she stammered out an address in a high-rise block of apartments overlooking the beach.

"Please," she said as the officers walked back to their patrol car. "He could never have done those things."

"We'll be in touch soon, Mrs Murray," said Adams. "Everything will be explained then."

She stared at them until the patrol car had driven out of her sight.

"No answer," said Adams after ringing the doorbell and waiting a minute or two. "Let's go to Plan B." He located the janitor's name on the board and buzzed that. When a male voice answered, he replied. "New South Wales Police, sir. We're trying to contact Phillip Murray. Can you let us in? We have a warrant to search his place."

"Good god," said the voice, but the door buzzed and opened. Ten minutes later, the janitor opened the door to Murray's apartment and followed the two officers inside. Adams went straight to the bathroom and came out a short time after.

"He's done a runner," he said to his partner. "Shaving gear, toothbrush and paste all gone. Laptop gone but you can see where he left all the cables."

"And no underwear or socks in his drawers," replied Nowell. "He's done a runner alright."

"Let's get back to the nick," said Adams.

Phase Five

End Game

Chapter 44

Mid North Coast, NSW, Australia, June, 2024

"I just couldn't stand being in hospital any longer when there's a job to be done."

Melanie had checked herself out of hospital within days of her near death, insisting that she had to return to work, despite the protestations of the hospital staff. She still showed the effects of the trauma, her face pale, despite the make-up and a loss of weight, but nothing could stop her.

"I hope you didn't return just to try and prove you're still needed and shouldn't be retired on health grounds?" asked Chief Superintendent James Willoughby. "Because Jack has already told you, there's no question of that."

"I suppose there was an element of that," replied Melanie. "But really, sir, I just needed to get back to the job. We have to find Murray now that Chang has been swallowed up by the Chinese security."

"Okay, your choice," said Willoughby. "I know Jack has been working with you the whole time and I trust his judgement that you're fit to work. But if he says you have to take a break, I want your assurance that you'll follow his advice."

"I promise," she replied.

Soon after, she was sitting in her office with Jack and Alex with Miller's face in her computer monitor.

"Passport control reported that he flew out of Sydney two months ago to Singapore," she said. "He went through Immigration there, giving his temporary address as the Westin Hotel, but there's no record of any stay there. He flew out of Singapore the following day, still travelling on his Australian passport on a flight to Bahrain, but there's no record of any arrival in Bahrain."

"Obviously used an illegal, fake passport to arrive," said Alex. "And there's no way of knowing what name he used or how many fake passports he's managed to acquire."

"You're quite right," said Miller. "We had this problem before, when our quarry vanished and used several identities to travel the world, but for that one, we had a face to search for. We don't have a face for Murray."[7]

"We don't," said Melanie. "The two cops who entered his apartment saw no pictures of anyone there. They went back to his parents' house and asked them for a recent photo but got nothing. Doesn't indicate a close family unit."

"That fits the psychological profile," said Jack. "We may have difficulties tracking him."

---

[7] See "The Death Gambit" by Michael Davies

"Maybe," said Melanie. "But Jack, let's put your psychiatric talents to work. See if this works. If Murray has fled because he no longer felt safe, where would he go that feels safer to him?"

"Interesting," said Jack. "I suspect you've been thinking along this line already, so you tell us, what do you think?"

"I have. I believe he felt at his best when he was working closely with Peter Chang conducting their first blackmailing exercises. And it was when he was nowhere near his parents' influence, so felt he was more in control of himself and his destiny."

"And that is...?" Jack prompted.

"Manchester," said Melanie.

Jack laughed. "Your near-death experience hasn't blunted your intellect, Melanie. I agree, he's most likely headed to Manchester."

"And I've been thinking about travelling on a different passport," said Alex. "Murray may have opened up a small possibility here."

"Explain, young Detective Constable," said Melanie.

"The issue is that with international travel, especially by air, the passport is checked on departure and again on arrival at the destination," said Alex. "Now I know that the two could be different and there's probably no comparison check. I know that, because a friend of mine is a dual national, Australian and Canadian. He shows his Australian passport on departure and Canadian one when he arrives in Canada and has no problem."

"I think that's true," said Melanie. "So what are you thinking?"

"This is probably a long shot, but if we could get the immigration people in Singapore and Bahrain to check their records and compare them by computer, they would surely find one less Australian passport arriving in Bahrain than left Singapore."

"Okay," said Melanie. "But that wouldn't identify our suspect. We know that would be Murray."

"True," said Alex. "But if we could run a similar check on all the remaining passengers, we would probably identify the one extra passport on arrival than left Singapore."

"Interesting," said Jack. "Very logical. Just to play Devil's Advocate for a moment, that might well work, but it would be a real problem to get the two immigration offices to play the game. And second, he's already left Bahrain, so tracing him after that would be possible, but he's probably arrived where he's going already."

"If we went through Interpol, they might play," said Melanie. "And they almost certainly take pictures of arrivals in Bahrain. If we could relate the excess passport holder to the picture, we might have a fighting chance."

"I think you're correct," said Jack. "So let's see if Interpol will help and we identify him, even though he's left there by now. What do you think he did then?"

"If I was doing a runner like him," said Alex, "I'd fly to somewhere in the European Community. He'd travel on his fake passport, but after that, he could move across borders with very little risk. Sure, his passport would be checked on crossing, but without any international alert, he's unlikely to have a problem. And again, if that was me, I'd cross to England, and I'm sure you're right, Ma'am, that's where he's gone, not by air, but by a more casual method, maybe the cross-channel ferry or the rail tunnel."

Melanie and Jack looked at each other.

"Damn, I think the kid's right," said Jack.

"One of my better promotions," said Melanie, straight-faced. "Alex, well done. I'll request assistance from Interpol."

"And talk to the Manchester cops," said Jack. "But we still need a face for them if we don't get one from Bahrain immigration."

"I hate to think that yet again, we've solved the case but we don't get to make an arrest," said Melanie.

"At least, we've stopped the killings," said Alex. "That's a major plus for us."

"I have an idea," said Miller. "Leave it with me."

"Whatever you can come up with," replied Melanie. "Allen, it seems a pleasant evening there. You're obviously sitting outside, it's night in your part of the world and nicely warm."

"It's beautiful," agreed Miller. "A perfect cloudless night. Let me show you this gorgeous sky."

His hand appeared in the monitor, expanded to fill the screen as he took the camera from his own monitor and scanned the sky above him. It was truly beautiful, a massive canopy of stars. The camera was returned to its place and Miller reappeared on the screen.

"See what I mean?" said Miller.

"Truly beautiful," said Melanie. "Allen, we have to go, other duties call, get back to me if you get anything we can use."

"Will do," said Miller and his face disappeared.

Carefully, Melanie switched off her computer and disconnected the network cable.

"Allen just made an incredibly silly mistake," she said. "Either that, or he was giving us an interesting invitation. It's just as well I have always recorded his conversations. Gentlemen, I think I have to go."

Ignoring the querying looks from Jack and Alex, she extracted the flash drive from her computer and left.

* * *

"British high schools don't produce yearbooks the way American schools do," said Allen Miller. It was three days since the last conversation. "But I got into the school computers, hunted around a bit and found that Phillip Murray had played hockey for the school in his final year. I found a picture of the team after their last match. The names are underneath, so you'll see which one is Murray. Here's the picture."

Miller's face was replaced by a standard team picture of eleven young men in two rows, all dressed in white shorts and dark blue shirts with a crest on the breast pocket, one standing behind the seated row and an older man in blazer and flannels, presumably the coach standing at the end. Underneath, two lines of names identified the players. Melanie followed the names and found Murray, two from the end where the coach was standing.

"So that's what you look like," murmured Melanie. "Gotcha, you bastard."

She printed the picture and took an electronic copy for the technical wizards to get a larger, clear image of the face. "Thanks, Allen, you've done wonders for me, yet again."

"My pleasure," said Miller and the call was disconnected.

"Shall we tell him what really happened?" asked Alex, sitting in the corner out of view of Miller.

"Let's not," said Melanie with a smile. "That would only upset him and make him think he's getting old."

"It may be the truth," said Alex. "How could he not have thought of getting a passport photo from the government? He could probably have broken into their systems quicker than he did finding Murray's picture in the school archives."

"Possibly," said Melanie. "But we were lucky, having the link to ASIO. Without that, it could have taken days to get the picture which Porter said we'll have tomorrow. But anyway, now we can set Interpol onto the task of locating him."

"Great," said Alex. "I'll set the wheels in motion." He got up and left the office.

Moments later, her phone rang.

"Melanie?" said a man's voice. "Professor Gareth Llewellyn. I think I have something for you."

"Department of Astronomy," said the sign above the blue door. Inside, a small area contained six cubicles and there were four office doors along one side of the room. She knocked on the one she had visited earlier and watched the familiar scene of a young man, his eyes opening wide at the sight of her and a small shortness of breath as he greeted her.

"Lovely to see you again, Melanie," he said and waved her to a seat across from his desk.

"My pleasure," she replied with her best smile and watched his face melt. *Oh, Rob, I wish it could be you in front of me, not this brilliant, shallow young man.* "You said you have something for me?"

"I do." Llewellyn touched a key on his computer and a projection of a map appeared on the wall to Melanie's left. She shifted her chair to watch.

"We analysed the sky map you gave us, checked it against the time you noted to the minute, and we found that this was the area. It's the north of Italy. In fact, a short distance east of the French border in a small town called Ventimiglia. I must admit, I've never heard of the place before."

"Nor have I," replied Melanie, her excitement rising. "Gareth, this is wonderful, you've been a huge help."

"Have I helped you discover an international crime boss?" he said, a small smile showing.

"Actually, Gareth, that's exactly what you have done. Somewhere in that region is a man hunted by the police forces of several nations."

"Good god, I was joking," he exclaimed.

"I wasn't," she said. "You really have performed a huge service to police forces everywhere." She stood up, repeated her best man-melting smile and left him looking dazed.

It didn't take her long. Some research was needed to locate the police department in the little town of Ventimiglia, a video call that connected her to a young man in uniform who displayed the usual reaction to her appearance. Fortunately, he spoke adequate English and was happy to meet the request for information on any Americans in the area.

"There are three, Inspector Carter," said the young officer. "One old couple in their seventies who have lived here for twenty years and a middle-aged man in his fifties who came here about two years ago. None of them have been any trouble, quite the reverse. Mr Peter Black, the single man has taught some computer classes in our local school and he's very popular."

"That's the one," she said and melted him with her best smile.

* * *

The report on Melanie's computer lifted her spirits enormously. It came from the Manchester police force.

"Phillip Murray was arrested by the Greater Manchester Police two days ago. He was identified by face recognition software in a department store. His face had been slightly modified by an early growth of a beard and moustache, but he had not had enough time to grow a full covering. He is now in custody, awaiting an extradition order from Australia, but will also face charges relating to blackmail and fraud offences stemming from his time as a student here."

* * *

Anna-Maria walked confidently into the police station.

"I'm here to see my client, Harold Brown," she said to the front desk sergeant.

He took the identity card she flourished at him and studied it suspiciously. "Jennifer Michaelson? We haven't seen you here before, Ms Michaelson."

"No, I'm new," said Anna-Maria. "Just moved here from Birmingham. Now, can I see my client?"

The sergeant grinned. "Sure, but he's not called Harold Brown. We arrested him when Interpol sent us a picture of who he really is, he's an Aussie called Phillip Murray. The passport is bloody good, we have to admit that. It fooled the immigration people at Dover."

"Nonetheless, I want to see him. He needs a lawyer."

"Them's the rules, alright," said the sergeant. He waved at a police constable sitting at a table in the front office. "Larry, take Ms Michaelson to the cell where we parked that Australian guy."

"This way, Ma'am," said the young constable and led Anna-Maria to the holding pens. He showed her in, locked the door again and stood outside.

Phillip Murray stared at the new arrival.

"Mrs Lloyd? What the hell are you doing here?"

"Be quiet," she said in a cold tone. "Who the hell said you could try and run away from us? You took the money from that account and somehow got a new passport. You really think you could get away like that?"

Murray shrank back in his seat, his face white and said nothing.

"And how the hell did you find the family account?" she continued. "You took over twelve million from that."

Bewildered, Murray shook his head. "I didn't," he managed to say, his voice harsh with fear. "I never touched that, I didn't know about it."

She stared hard at him. "No, I think you're right about that, you don't have the talent to get into that account. It must be Chang, if we can ever find him. We'll deal with him then. Now, what are we going to do with you, Phillip?" she continued.

Murray stayed silent, fear written all over his face.

Anna-Maria stood and held out her hand. "Don't worry, Phillip," she said. "It will all be over soon."

Automatically, Murray took her hand. He barely felt the tiny prick in his palm. Anna-Maria tapped on the cell door, the officer opened it and closed it again after her. She walked up to the front desk, waved, and continued towards the front door.

A lightly-built young woman walking past the office stopped and stared, but Anna-Maria didn't notice as she left.

"Good morning, Ma'am," said the sergeant to the new arrival.

"Detective Inspector Goodwin," said the woman, displaying her warrant card. "I have a meeting with the Superintendent."

"Yes, Ma'am," said the sergeant. "You're from the Chester nick, I believe."

"Who was that woman just leaving?" asked Goodwin.

The sergeant consulted the card. "Ms Jennifer Michaelson from the legal aid people," he said.

"Like hell she is," said Goodwin. "That's Anna-Maria Grassano, she's the niece of the Mafia Grassano bloke and we think she murdered her husband, William Lloyd."

The sergeant lost his casual attitude. He raced out of the door and found Anna-Maria about to get into her car. He grabbed the car door and held it firmly.

"Not so fast, Miss Grassano," he said and waited silently while two other officers joined him. "You're nicked," he said with satisfaction.

Chapter 45

Mid North Coast, NSW, Australia, June, 2024

The report on Melanie's computer was short and most satisfactory.

> "UK Immigration reported that the face submitted to us by Interpol is the face of a man called Harold Brown, a UK citizen carrying an apparently valid UK passport who entered the UK at Dover eight days ago. He is now known to be Phillip Murray, an Australian. He was traced through face recognition systems to a house in Manchester where the local police arrested him. While awaiting extradition, he was found dead in his cell. He had just been visited by a woman claiming to be legal aid, but was recognised as Anna-Maria Grassano, the niece of local Mafia principal, Giorgio Grassano. She was arrested by the local police.

An autopsy of Harold Brown, or Phillip Murray, as now identified showed traces of cyanide in his blood stream, apparently administered by a needle held by Ms Grassano. Murder charges are pending against her."

* * *

"We've just about wrapped up our end of things," said Melanie to Chief Superintendent James Willoughby. "I'm due some leave."

"No problems," said Willoughby. "Enjoy the break. You deserve it, that was great work."

* * *

The door to the smart townhouse in the north of Italy opened and a familiar face looked out cautiously.

"Hello, Allen," said Melanie. "Care to offer a girl a drink?"